SKY
IN
THE
DEEP

ADRIENNE YOUNG

WEDNESDAY BOOKS
NEW YORK

SKY IN THE DEEP. Copyright © 2018 by Adrienne Young. All rights reserved. Printed in the United States of America. For information, address St. Martin's Press, 175 Fifth Avenue, New York, N.Y. 10010.

www.wednesdaybooks.com
www.stmartins.com

Designed by Devan Norman

The Library of Congress Cataloging-in-Publication Data is available upon request.

ISBN 978-1-250-16845-0 (hardcover)
ISBN 978-1-250-29393-0 (signed edition)
ISBN 978-1-250-16847-4 (ebook)

Our books may be purchased in bulk for promotional, educational, or business use. Please contact your local bookseller or the Macmillan Corporate and Premium Sales Department at 1-800-221-7945, extension 5442, or by email at MacmillanSpecialMarkets@macmillan.com.

First Edition: April 2018

10 9 8 7 6 5

FOR JOEL,

WHO HAS NEVER TRIED TO TAME MY WILD HEART

SKY
IN
THE
DEEP

ONE

"They're coming."

I looked down the row of Aska hunched against each other, ducking behind the muddy hill. The fog sat on the field like a veil, but we could hear it. The blades of swords and axes brushing against armor vests. Quick footsteps in sucking mud. My heart beat almost in rhythm with the sounds, pulling one breath in and letting it touch another before I let it go.

My father's rasping whistle caught my ears from down the line and I searched the dirt-smeared faces until I found a pair of bright blue eyes fixed on me. His gray-streaked beard hung braided down his chest behind the axe clutched in his huge fist. He tipped his chin up at me and I whistled back— our way of telling each other to be careful. To try not to die.

Mýra's hand lifted the long braid over my shoulder and she nodded toward the field. "Together?"

"Always." I looked behind us where our clansmen stood

shoulder to shoulder in a sea of red leathers and bronze, all waiting for the call. Mýra and I had fought for our place at the front.

"Watch that left side." Her *kol*-rimmed eyes dropped down to the broken ribs behind my vest.

"They're fine." I glared at her, insulted. "If you're worried, fight with someone else."

She shook her head, dismissing me before she stood to check my armor one last time. I tried not to wince as she tightened the fastenings I'd intentionally left a bit loose. She pretended not to notice, but I caught the look in her eye.

"Stop worrying about me." I ran a hand over the right side of my head where my hair was shorn to the scalp under the length of the braids.

I pulled her hand toward me to secure the straps of her shield onto her arm by memory. We'd been fighting mates for the last five years and I knew every piece of her armor as well as she knew every badly mended bone in my body.

"I'm not worried," she smirked, "but I'll bet my supper that I kill more Riki than you today." She tossed my axe to me.

I pulled my sword from my scabbard with my right hand and caught the axe with my left. *"Vegr yfir fjor."*

She settled her arm all the way into her shield, lifting it up over her head in an arc to stretch her shoulder before she repeated it back to me. *"Vegr yfir fjor."*

Honor above life.

The first whistle cut into the air from our right, warning

us to get ready, and I closed my eyes, feeling the steadiness of the earth beneath my feet. The sounds of battle rushing toward us bled together as the deep-throated prayers of my clansmen rose up around me like smoke from a wildfire. I let the words march out under my breath, asking Sigr to guard me. To help me bring down his enemies.

"Go!"

I reared back and swung my axe, sending it deep into the earth, and launched myself up and over the hill, flying forward. My feet hit the dirt and I ran, punching holes into the soft ground with my boots, toward the wall of fog hovering over the field. I kept track of Mýra in the corner of my eye as we were swallowed up by it, the cold rushing past us like a spray of water until dark figures appeared in the hazy distance.

The Riki.

The enemies of our god ran toward us in a swarm of fur and iron. Hair tangled in the wind. Sun glinting off blades. I picked up speed at the sight of them, tightening my fingers around my sword as I pushed forward, ahead of the others.

I let the growl crawl up the inside of me, from that deep place that comes alive in battle. I screamed, my eyes settling on a short man with orange furs wrapped up around his shoulders at the front of their line. I whistled to Mýra and leaned into the wind, running straight for him. As we neared them, I turned to the side and counted my steps, plotting my path to the moment when the space between us was eaten up by the sound of heavy bodies crashing into each other.

3

I bit down hard as I reached him, my teeth bared. My sword came up behind me, my body lowering to the ground, and I swung it up as I passed, aiming for his gut.

His shield lifted just in time and he threw himself to the left, catching me with its edge. Black spots exploded into my vision as my lungs wheezed behind my sore ribs and the breath refused to return. I stumbled, trying to find my footing before I fell to the ground, and came back with my axe, ignoring the bloom of pain in my side. His sword caught the blade above his head, wrenching it back, but that's all I needed.

His side was wide open.

I sunk my sword into it, finding the seam of his armor vest. His head flew back, his mouth open as he screamed, and Mýra's sword came down on his neck in one smooth motion, slicing through the muscle and tendon. I yanked my blade free, pulling a spray of hot blood over my face with it. Mýra kicked the man over with the heel of her boot as another shadow appeared in the fog behind her.

"Down!" I shouted, letting my axe fly.

She dropped to the ground and the blade plunged into the chest of a Riki, sending him to his knees. His huge body fell onto her, pinning her to the dirt. The blood bubbling up from his mouth poured out, covering her pale skin in a stark shining red.

I ran to her, hooking my fingers into his armor vest from the other side of his body, and sunk down, pulling him with me. When she was free, she sprang to her feet, finding her sword and looking around us. I gripped the handle of my axe and pried it up, out of the bones in his chest.

The fog was beginning to clear, pushing back in the warmth of the morning light. From the hill, down to the river, the ground was covered with fighting clansmen, all pulling toward the water. Across the field, my father was driving his sword behind him, into the stomach of a Riki. I watched him fling it forward to catch another in the face, his eyes wide with fight and his chest full of thundering war cries.

"Come on!" I called back to Mýra as I ran, leaping over the fallen bodies and making my way toward the river's edge, where the fighting was more concentrated.

I caught the back of a Riki's knee with my sword, dropping him to the ground as I passed. And then another, leaving them both for someone else to finish.

"Eelyn!" She called my name just as I slammed into another body, and wide arms wrapped around me, squeezing so hard that the sword slipped from my fingers. I grunted, trying to kick free, but he was too strong. I bit into the flesh of the arm until I tasted blood and the hands shoved me to the ground. I hit hard, gasping for breath as I rolled onto my back and reached for my axe. But the Riki's sword was already coming down on me. I rolled again, finding the knife at my belt with my fingers as I came back up onto my feet and faced him, the breath puffing out before me in white gusts.

Behind me, Mýra was fighting in the fog. "Eelyn!"

He lunged for me, swinging his sword up, and I fell back

again. It cut through my sleeve and into the thick muscle of my arm. I threw the knife, handle over blade, and he dropped his head to the side. It narrowly missed him, grazing his ear, and when he looked back at me his eyes were on fire.

I scrambled backward, trying to get to my feet as he picked up his sword. My eyes fell to the spilled Aska blood covering his chest and arms as he stalked toward me. Behind him, my sword and my axe lay on the ground.

"Mýra!" I shouted, but she was completely out of sight now.

I looked around us, something churning up inside of me that I rarely felt in a fight—panic. I was nowhere near a weapon and there was no way I could take him down with my bare hands. He closed in, gritting his teeth, as he moved like a bear over the grass.

I thought of my father. His soil-stained hands. His deep, booming voice. And my home. The fire flickering in the dark. The frost on the glade in the mornings.

I stood, pressing my fingers into the hot wound at my arm and saying Sigr's name under my breath, asking him to accept me. To welcome me. To watch over my father. *"Vegr yfir fjor,"* I whispered.

He slowed, watching my lips move.

The furs beneath his armor vest blew in the damp breeze, pushing up around his angled jaw. He blinked, pressing his mouth into a straight line as he took the last steps toward me and I didn't run. I wasn't going to be brought down by a blade in my back.

The steel gleamed as he pulled the sword up over his head, ready to bring it back down, and I closed my eyes. I breathed. I could see the reflection of the gray sky on the fjord. The willow bloomed on the hillside. The wind wove through my hair. I listened to the sound of my clansmen raging. Fighting in the distance.

"Fiske!" A deep, strangled voice pierced through the fog, finding me, and my eyes popped open.

The Riki before me froze, his eyes darting to the side where the voice was coming toward us.

Fast.

"No!" A tangle of wild, fair hair barreled into him, knocking his sword to the ground. "Fiske, don't." He took hold of the man's armor vest, holding him in place. *"Don't."*

Something twisted in my mind, the blood in my veins slowing, my heart stopping.

"What are you doing?" The Riki wrenched free, picking his sword back up off the ground and driving past him, coming for me.

The man turned, throwing his arms around the Riki and swinging him back.

And that's when I saw it—his face.

And I was frozen. I was the ice on the river. The snow clinging onto the mountainside.

"Iri." It was the ghost of a word on my breath.

They stopped struggling, both looking up at me with wide eyes, and it dove deeper within me. What I was seeing. *Who* I was seeing.

7

"Iri?" My shaking hand clutched at my armor vest, tears coming up into my eyes. The storm in my stomach churned at the center of the chaos surrounding us.

The man with the sword looked at me, his eyes running over my face, working hard to put something together. But my eyes were on Iri. On the curve of his jaw. His hair—like straw in the sun. The blood smeared across his neck. Hands like my father's.

"What is this, Iri?" The Riki's grip tightened around the hilt of his sword, my blood still thick on its blade.

I could barely hear him. I could barely think, everything washed out in the flood of the vision before me.

Iri stepped toward me slowly, his eyes jumping back and forth on mine. I stopped breathing as his hands came up to my face and he leaned in so close that I could feel his breath on my forehead.

"Run, Eelyn."

He let me go, and my lungs writhed and pulled, begging for air. I turned, looking for Mýra in the mist, opening my mouth to call out for my father. But my breath wouldn't come.

He was gone, devoured by the fog, the Riki disappearing with him.

As if they were ghosts.

As if they were never there.

And they couldn't have been. Because it was *Iri,* and the last time I saw my brother was five years ago. Lying dead in the snow.

TWO

I BROKE THROUGH THE FOG AND RAN TOWARD THE RIVER
as fast as my feet would carry me with Mýra on my heels, her
sword swinging. My eyes were on the trees, in the direction
Iri had gone. They jumped from shadow to shadow, looking for a streak of flaxen hair in the darkened forest.

A woman leapt from the tree line, but her shriek was cut
off as Mýra came from the side, plowing into her with a knife.
She dragged it across the woman's throat and dropped her
where she stood, falling into step with me again as I ran.

The retreat whistle for the Riki sounded and the bodies,
still tangled in battle, parted to reveal the green field now
painted red with the death of clansmen. I took off, weaving
through the retreating Riki and grabbing hold of the fair-
haired men one by one, searching their faces.

"What are you *doing?*" Mýra wrenched me backward, her
sharp face pulled in confusion.

The last of them disappeared into the trees behind her and I turned, looking for the blue wool tunic my father was wearing beneath his armor. "Aghi!"

The heads of the Aska in the field turned toward me.

Mýra took hold of my arm, pressing the heel of her hand into the wound to stop the bleeding. "Eelyn." She pulled me to her. "What is it? What's wrong?"

I found my father's face across the field, where the fog was still pulling up from the land like a lifting cloud.

"Aghi!" His name was raw in my throat.

His chin lifted at the strangled sound and his eyes searched the body-littered expanse. When they found me, they transfigured from worry into fear. He dropped his shield and ran to me.

I sank to my knees, my head swimming. He fell beside me, hands running over my body and fingers sliding over blood and sweat-soaked skin. He looked me over carefully, dread pushing its way onto his face.

I took hold of his armor vest, pulling him to face me. "It's Iri." The words broke on a sob.

I could still see him. His pale eyes. His fingers touching my face.

My father's gaze went to Mýra before the breath that was caught in his chest let go of his panic. He took my face into his hands and looked at me. "What's happened?" His eyes caught sight of the blood still seeping from my arm. He let me go, pulling his knife free to cut at the tunic of the Riki lying dead beside us.

"I *saw* him. I saw Iri."

He wrapped the torn cloth around my arm, tying it tight. "What are you talking about?"

I pushed his hands from me, crying. "Listen to me! Iri was *here*! I saw him!"

His hands finally stilled, confusion lighting in his eyes.

"I was fighting a man. He was about to . . ." I shuddered, remembering how close to death I'd come—closer than I'd ever been. "Iri came out of the fog and saved me. He was with the Riki." I stood, taking his hand and pulling him toward the tree line. "We have to find him!"

But my father stood like a stone tucked into the earth. His face turned up toward the sky, his eyes blinking against the sunlight.

"Do you hear me? Iri's alive!" I shouted, holding my arm against my body to calm the violent throbbing around the gash.

His eyes landed on me again, tears gathered at the corners like little white flames. "Sigr. He sent Iri's soul to save you, Eelyn."

"What? No."

"Iri's made it to *Sólbjǫrg*." His words were frightening and delicate, betraying a tenderness my father never showed. He stepped forward, looking down into my eyes with a smile. "Sigr has favored you, Eelyn."

Mýra stood behind him, her green eyes wide beneath her unraveling auburn braids.

"But—" I choked. "I *saw* him."

"You did." A single tear rolled down my father's rough cheek and disappeared into his beard. He pulled me into him, wrapping his arms around me, and I closed my eyes, the pain in my arm so great now that I could hardly feel my hand.

I blinked, trying to understand. I had *seen* him. He was there.

"We will make a sacrifice tonight." He let me go before he pressed his hands to my face again. "I don't think I've ever heard you scream for me like that. You scared me, *sváss*." A laugh was buried deep in his chest.

"I'm sorry," I murmured. "I just . . . I thought . . ."

He waited for me to meet his eyes again. "His soul is at peace. Your brother saved your life today. Be happy." He clapped a hand against my good arm, nearly knocking me down.

I wiped at my wet cheeks with the palm of my hand, turning from the faces that were still watching me. There were very few times I'd cried in front of my clansmen. It made me feel small. Weak, like the early winter grass beneath our boots.

I sniffed back the tears, piecing my face back together as my father nodded in approval. It was what he had taught me—to be strong. To steel myself. He turned back to the field, getting to work, and I followed with Mýra, trying to smooth my ragged breath. To hush the waves crashing in my head. We walked toward our camp, collecting the weapons of fallen Aska warriors along the way. I watched my father from the corner of my eye, still unable to shake Iri's face from my mind.

My feet stopped at the edge of a puddle and I looked at my reflection. Dirt spattered across my angled face and neck. Blood dried in long, golden braids. Eyes a frozen blue, like Iri's. I sucked in a breath, looking up to the thin white clouds brushed across the sky to keep another tear from falling.

"Here," Mýra called to me from where she was crouched over an Aska woman. She was lying on her side, eyes open and arms extended like she was reaching for us.

I carefully unbuckled her belt and scabbard, piling them with the others before I started on the armor vest. "Did you know her?"

"A little." Mýra reached down to close the woman's eyes with her fingertips. She gently brushed the hair back from her face before she began, the words coming softly. "Aska, you have reached your journey's end."

In the next breath, I joined with her, saying the ritual words we knew by heart. "We ask Sigr to accept your soul into *Sólbjǫrg*, where the long line of our people hold torches on the shadowed path."

My voice faded, letting Mýra speak first. "Take my love to my father and my sister. Ask them to keep watch for me. Tell them my soul follows behind you."

I closed my eyes as the prayer found a familiar place on my tongue. "Take my love to my mother and my brother. Ask them to keep watch for me. Tell them my soul follows behind you."

I swallowed down the lump in my throat before I opened my eyes and looked down into the woman's peaceful face one more time. I hadn't been able to say the words over Iri's body the way I had when my mother died, but Sigr had taken him anyway.

"Have you ever seen something like that before?" I whispered. "Something that wasn't real?"

Mýra blinked. "It *was* real. Iri's soul is real."

"But he was older—a man. He spoke to me. He *touched* me, Mýra."

She stood, shifting an armful of axes up onto her shoulder. "I was there that day, Eelyn. Iri died. I saw it with my own eyes. *That* was real." It was the same battle that took Mýra's sister. We'd been friends before that day, but we hadn't really needed each other until then.

I remembered it so clearly—the picture of him like a reflection on ice. Iri's lifeless body at the bottom of the trench. Lying across the perfect white snow, blood seeping out around him in a melted pool. I could still see his blond hair fanned out around his head, his empty eyes wide open and staring into nothing.

"I know."

Mýra reached up, squeezing my shoulder. "Then you know it wasn't Iri—not his flesh."

I nodded, swallowing hard. I prayed for Iri's soul every day. If Sigr had sent him to protect me, he really was in *Sólbjǫrg*—our people's final sunset. "I knew he would make it." I breathed through the tightness in my throat.

"We all did." A small smile lifted on her lips.

I looked back down to the woman lying between us. We would leave her as she was—as she died—with honor. Like we did with all our fallen warriors.

Like we'd left Iri.

"Was he as handsome as he was before?" Mýra's smile turned wry as her eyes flickered back up to meet mine.

"He was beautiful," I whispered.

THREE

I BIT DOWN ON THE THICK LEATHER STRAP OF MY SCAB-bard as the healer worked, sewing the gash in my arm closed. It was deeper than I wanted to admit.

Whatever Kalda was thinking, her face didn't betray it. "I can still fight," I said. It wasn't a question. And she had treated me after battle enough times to know it.

Mýra sighed beside me, though it looked as if she was enjoying it a little. I shot my eyes to her before she could say a word.

"That's your decision." Kalda looked up at me through her dark eyelashes.

It wasn't the first time she had stitched me up and it wouldn't be the last. But the only time she'd ever told me I couldn't fight was when I broke two ribs. I'd waited five years to avenge Iri in my second fighting season and I spent a month of it sitting in the camp, cleaning weapons and seething with anger while my father and Mýra went out into battle without me.

"It won't stay closed if you're using your axe." Kalda dropped the needle into the bowl beside her before wiping her hands on her bloodstained apron.

I stared back at her. "I have to use my axe."

"Use a shield in that hand." Mýra glowered, flinging a hand toward me.

"I don't use a shield," I bit back at her. "I use a sword in my right and an axe in my left. You know that." Changing the way I fought would only get me killed.

Kalda sighed. "Then when you tear it open again you'll have to come back and let me restitch it."

"Fine." I stood, pulling my sleeve back down over my swollen arm and trying not to let the wince show on my face.

The Aska man waiting behind us sat down on the stool and Kalda got to work on the cut carved into his cheek. "I heard Sigr honored you today." He was a friend of my father's. Everyone was.

"He did," Mýra said through a traitorous smile. She loved to see me embarrassed.

I didn't know what to say.

He reached up with his fist, tapping me on my good shoulder with his big knuckles as I reached for his shoulder and did the same.

We ducked out of the foul smell of the tent and walked

through camp as the sky grew warm with the setting sun and my stomach growled at the smell of supper cooking over flames. My father was waiting for me in front of our fire.

"See you in the morning." Mýra squeezed my hand before she broke off from me.

"Maybe," I said, watching her walk to her tent. I wasn't convinced the Riki wouldn't be back before the sun rose.

My father stood with his arms folded over his chest, staring down into the fire. He had washed his hands and face, but I could still see the blood and dirt clinging to the rest of him.

"Taken care of?" His bushy eyebrows lifted up.

I nodded, raising my scabbard over my head. He unbuckled the axe sheath on my back and took my arm into his hands, inspecting it.

"It's fine," I said. He didn't worry about me often, but I could see it when he did.

He pushed the unruly hair back from my face. I was an Aska warrior, but I was still his daughter. "You look more like your mother every day. Are you ready?"

I gave him a tired smile. If my father believed Sigr sent Iri's soul to me, I could believe it too. I was too afraid of any other truth that lingered in the back of my thoughts. "Ready."

We walked side by side to the other end of the camp. I could feel the eyes on me, but my father paid our clansmen no attention, putting me at ease. The meeting tent that served as our ritual house sat at the end of our encampment with white smoke trailing up into the evening sky from its center. Espen stood like an enormous statue beneath its frame, the

Tala beside him. Our clan's leader was the greatest of our warriors, the oldest Aska leader in three generations. He lifted his chin, his fingers pulling at his long beard.

"Aghi." He called to my father from where he stood.

My father pulled three coins from his vest and handed them to me. He walked toward them, grasping Espen's shoulder in greeting, and Espen did the same before he spoke. I couldn't hear what he was saying, but his eyes found me over my father's shoulder, making me feel suddenly unsteady.

"Eelyn."

I jolted. Hemming was waiting at the gate of the pen.

I pressed the coins into his open hand and he dropped them into the heavy purse hanging from his belt.

He smiled up at me, one tooth missing from the front of his mouth where he was kicked by a horse two winters ago. "I heard what happened." He stepped over the wall of the pen and grabbed a pale gray goat by the horns. "This one okay?"

I crouched down, inspecting the animal carefully. "Turn him around." Hemming shifted, pulling the goat toward him, and I shook my head. "What about him?" I pointed to a large white goat in the corner.

"He's four *penningr*." Hemming struggled to keep his hold on the gray goat.

A heavy hand landed on my shoulder, and I looked up to see my father, peering over me into the pen. "What's this?"

Hemming let go of the animal, standing up straight under my father's gaze. "He's four *penningr*."

"Is he the best?"

"Yes, Aghi." Hemming nodded. "The best."

"Then four *penningr* it is." He pulled another coin free and tossed it to Hemming.

I climbed into the pen to help the boy wrangle the goat to the gate. My father took one horn and I took the other as we led him to the altar in the middle of the meeting tent. The fire was already burning strong, its flames licking up around the wood and warming me through my armor as the cold crept in from outside.

"May I join you?" Espen's voice came from behind us.

My father turned, his eyes widening a little before he nodded.

The Tala followed, looking at me. "You've brought honor to Sigr by destroying his enemies, Eelyn. He's honored you in return."

I nodded nervously, biting down hard on my bottom lip. The Tala had never spoken to me before. I'd been afraid of him as a child, hiding behind Iri in the ritual house during sacrifices and ceremonies. I didn't like the idea of a person who spoke the will of the gods. I was afraid of what he may see in me. What he may see in my future.

Espen found a place beside me and we led the animal forward to the large trough in front of the blazing fire. My father pulled out the small wooden idol of my mother he had tucked into his vest and handed it to me. I pulled the one I had of Iri from my own and set them beside one another on the stone before us. Sacrifices made me think of my mother.

She'd tell the story of the Riki god Thora, who erupted from the mountain in fire and the flames that had come down to the fjord. Sigr had risen up from the sea to protect his people and every five years, we went back to battle to defend his honor, bound by the blood feud between us.

There wasn't much about my mother that I remembered, but the night she died still hung clearly in my mind. I remembered the river of silent Herja that streamed into our village in the dead of night, their swords reflecting moonlight, their skin as pale as the dead against the thick furs they wore upon their shoulders. I remembered the way my mother looked, lying on the beach with the light leaving her eyes. My father, covered in her blood.

I sat, holding my mother's still-warm body as the Aska followed them into the winter sea, where they disappeared in the dark water like demons. We'd seen raids before, but never like that. They hadn't come to steal, they'd come only to kill. The ones they took, they sacrificed to their god. And no one knew where they came from or if they were even human. Espen had hung one of the bodies from a tree at the entrance to our village and the bones still hung there, knocking together in the wind. We hadn't seen the Herja since. Perhaps whatever god had sent them had quenched their anger. Still, our blood ran cold at the mention of their name.

Iri and I had wept over the sacrifice my father made the next morning, thanking Sigr for sparing his children's lives. Only a few years later, he made another—when Iri died.

"Draw your knife, Eelyn," my father instructed, taking both horns into his hands.

I stared at him, confused. I'd only ever stood behind my father as he performed a sacrifice.

"This is your sacrifice, *sváss*. Draw your knife."

The Tala nodded beside him.

I tugged my knife from my belt, watching the firelight against the letters of my name, forged into the smooth surface of the blade below the spine. It was the knife my father gave to me before my first fighting season five years ago. Since then, it had taken too many lives to count.

I came down beside the goat, taking its body into my arms, and found the pulsing artery at his neck with my fingers. I positioned my knife, taking a breath before I recited the words. "We honor you, Sigr, with this undefiled sacrifice." They were the words I'd heard my father and fellow clansmen say my whole life. "We thank you for your provision and your favor. We ask that you follow us, protect us, until the day we reach *Sólbjǫrg* in final rest."

I dragged the blade swiftly across the goat's soft flesh, tightening my grip on him with my other arm as he kicked. The stitches in my arm pulled, sending the sting of the wound down to my wrist. His hot blood poured out over my hands, into the trough, and I pressed my face into his white fur until he was still.

We stood in silence, listening to the blood drain into the trough, and my eyes lifted to the idols of my mother and my brother on the stone. They were lit up in the amber light, shadows dancing over their carved faces.

I'd felt the absence of my mother as soon as she stopped breathing. As if with that last breath, her soul had let go of her body. But with Iri, it had never been that way. I still felt him. Maybe I always would.

FOUR

WE WOKE TO THE WARNING WHISTLE IN THE MIDDLE OF the night. The horse's hooves stamped nervously outside our tent and my father was on his feet before my eyes were even open.

"Up, Eelyn." He was a blur in the dark. "You were right."

I pulled myself up, reaching for the sword beside my cot and breathing through the pain igniting sharp and angry in my arm. I fought with my boots and pulled my armor vest on, letting my father fasten it for me. He slid my scabbard over my head and across my chest, followed by my axe sheath, and then patted me on the back, letting me know I was ready. I took up the idol of my mother from where it sat beside his cot and quickly pressed it to my lips before I handed it to him. He tucked it into his vest and I tucked the one of Iri into mine.

We slipped out into the night, heading toward the end of the river that wrapped around one side of our camp. The starless sky melted into the night-cloaked land beyond the fires and I could feel them out there.

The Riki.

Thunder grumbled over us and the unmistakable smell of a storm rode on the wind. My father planted a kiss on the top of my head. *"Vegr yfir fjor."* He pushed me toward the other end of the line, where I would find Mýra.

She pulled me to her, lifting my axe from its sheath on my back and handing it to me. I tightened the bandage around my arm and shook the numbness out of my hand. She didn't say it this time, but I knew what she was thinking because I was thinking it too. My left side was almost useless now. I'd fought in the dark with my clan before, but never this injured. The thought made me uneasy.

"Stay close to me." She waited for me to nod in agreement before she led us to the front of the line.

The fighting erupted before we were even in place. To the left, down by the water, the shouting began, but this end of the line was still quiet. I said my prayers, my eyes searching for movement around us as raindrops began to fall. Beside me, Mýra's eyes closed, her lips moving around the ancient words.

The next whistle sounded like the soft call of a bird, and we lifted onto our feet, moving silently as one entity into the black. I put my hand on the back of the Aska in front of me and felt the hot hand of the warrior behind me, keeping us together. We stepped in rhythm, our boots breaking the thin frost on the grass. The sound of the river pulled in from the left and the muted quiet of the forest from the right as the familiar sound of battle grew between.

Straight ahead, the Riki moved toward us like fish under water.

We walked until I could hear them and Mýra's elbow pressed into me, letting me know she heard it too. I clicked my tongue, and the clansmen around me repeated the sound, spreading the message through the line. They were close. Mýra pulled up her shield and I tucked myself closer to her as we moved faster. Beneath my vest, my heart beat unevenly, sending my sore ribs into spasms.

A gurgling wail beside us signaled the Riki's arrival to our end of the line and as soon as I saw movement ahead of us, I swung, driving my sword forward and catching the hard surface of a shield. The form knocked Mýra to the ground and I lunged again, swinging my sword up and around me to let it cut down. This time, I heard the scrape of bone on my blade. I kicked at the lump, freeing my sword, and we pushed farther in. The rain fell harder as the sky opened up and the clouds pulled back just enough for a bit of moonlight to fall down on us.

I couldn't help it. My eyes were already combing through the Riki on the field. Searching.

Lightning washed across the night sky and the mass of warriors scrambled like insects, crawling over the land as it lit everything white and then flickered out again. The crack exploded around us, shaking the ground.

Mýra caught the thigh of a man with her knife, knocking him over with her shield, and I came down on him with my axe, grunting against the searing burn in my arm. Mýra caught me as I fell, yanking me up and throwing my weight forward. I gripped the handle of my axe as we jumped over the body and the silhouette of a screaming woman came at me from the left. I swung again, catching her in the side. She went down, splashing in the mud, and I doubled over to keep from losing my balance.

"Eelyn!" Mýra called for me, getting sucked into the fighting as I searched the ground for my axe.

I raked my fingers through the grass until I found the handle. "I'm here!" I ran toward her voice.

Lightning lit across the sky again, howling and hissing, and I found her standing over another body.

We headed toward the trees and my eyes trained on the figures before me. We cut them down one by one, reading each other's movements, until we had a clear path. Mýra pushed harder, trying to balance the deficiency of my arm and ribs. I bit down, gritting my teeth, and tightened my grip on my sword, trying to pull my body in line.

And then I saw it. From the corner of my eye—a pale flame moving in the trees.

I stopped short, sliding in the mud with my heart jumping up into my throat. "Iri."

I took off running, tracking him with my eyes and dodging Riki as I neared the tree line. He wielded his axe, sending it into an Aska and then rearing back and sending another one to the ground. Beside him, a Riki was swinging his sword, dropping my clansmen left and right. The Riki who'd almost taken my life.

I followed them as they moved together, weaving between the trees deeper into the forest. Behind me, Mýra's faint voice called my name.

I jumped over the bodies on the forest floor and ducked into the cover of the trees. I pushed my sword into my scabbard and sunk my weight as close to the ground as I could, running with my axe out before me. My stomach twisted, knowing I should stop. Go back to Mýra.

Instead, I followed the familiar form driving deeper into the darkness. The lightning multiplied and the sound of rain on the canopy beat above us. When a hand caught me in the dark, I snapped my arm back, swinging my axe. The fingers clamped down on me, digging into my wrist until I dropped it. I fell flat on my back and the hand grabbed ahold of my boot, dragging me in the other direction. I reached for the trees as they passed, searching for something to hold onto as I slid over the wet ground, my ribs screaming.

The shadow reached down and pulled me upright, slamming me into a tree.

The Riki who'd sunk his blade into my arm was staring down at me. The blue of his eyes glinted like fire-steel striking in the dark. The hair fell down around his face, unraveled from its knot, and his broad frame towered over me as his hands tightened on my armor vest to hold me in place.

"Stop following us." His voice rose above the sound of rain falling.

I felt for the knife in my belt. "Where is he?"

He shoved me before he let me go and turned, stalking off into the trees.

I ran after him.

He turned suddenly, lifting the handle of his axe to catch me in the shoulder. "Go back. Now," he growled.

"Where's Iri?" I shouted.

He shoved me again, sending me back into another tree. The bark grated against my vest as I slid down the trunk and landed on the ground.

I got back to my feet, following him. "Where is he?" I tried to even the shaking in my voice.

When he turned again, he snatched my injured arm up and dug his thumb into the fresh wound he'd made the day before. I screamed, falling to my knees as the stitches popped through the skin. Bursts of light ruptured before my eyes and my stomach turned on itself, making me feel like I was on the water.

He stood over me, his face hidden in the shadows. "You're going to get us killed. Stay away from Iri."

I opened my mouth to speak and he clamped his hand down harder until my eyes lost focus. I was going to faint. His voice echoed in my head as the Aska retreat whistle sounded far away.

"Fiske." Iri's voice came from somewhere behind us—a voice I knew in my bones.

He stood behind us, holding an axe in each hand. "Let's go." He nodded toward the tree line, avoiding my eyes.

"Wait!" I stumbled to my feet, but he was already walking away. "Iri!"

"Go back, Eelyn. Before someone sees you." The strain in his words was buried deep beneath the hardness that knit his face together.

His face.

My jaw dropped as I marveled at it. He was fair like me and our mother, but he looked like my father. There, in the eyes and the line of his wide shoulders. He wasn't a boy anymore, but it was him. It was my brother.

"You're real," I rasped, trying to catch my breath. I slid my axe into its sheath on my back, staring.

"Iri." A warning sounded in the Riki's voice.

"Go." Iri turned again, giving me his back. "Forget you saw me."

I leaned into the tree, pinching my eyes closed against the pain in my arm. Against the ache in my chest. Because Iri was alive. And if he was alive, it meant something terrible. Something far worse than losing him.

"Iri?" Another voice sounded in the forest and my feet slid out from under me in the mud.

Iri stopped mid-stride, turning slowly and searching around us.

Ahead, a large man stepped forward, into the slice of moonlight cutting through the trees. "Fiske?"

The three of them looked at each other for a moment and the air turned cold around me, my senses heightening. I pulled my knife free again and looked toward the river. I wasn't stronger, but even injured I was probably faster than all three of them.

I could make it.

Iri's jaw clenched, something working in his mind before he looked back to Fiske. He gave a slight nod before his eyes dropped and my breath caught.

Fiske was already reaching for me.

I pitched myself from the tree, propelling my weight forward, but he caught me, wrenching me back toward him. His fingers wound around my throat, his thumb pressing to the pulse at my neck. I kicked, trying to slide free, but his grip tightened until I couldn't pull the air into my lungs. I clawed at his hands as the black pushed in at the edges of my vision. Behind him, Iri's tight eyes were pinned on the ground.

Fiske's gaze locked on mine, his hands like iron. My heartbeat slowed, my body growing heavier with every missed breath. I blinked, my eyes turning up to where the stars glimmered through the treetops. The pounding of my heart thrummed in my ears. One beat. Two.

Then dark.

FIVE

I WOKE TO THE SOUND OF WOODEN WHEELS CRACKING over stones in the dirt and light passing like shadows over my closed eyelids. I tried to place the smell.

Winter. Pine and woodsmoke. My eyes opened to a stretch of empty blue sky overhead. The footfall of horses. The shifting of a cart.

I threw myself forward, sitting up, and struggled to get my feet beneath me before I fell back down. My hands were bound at the wrists, the wound on my arm bleeding fresh through my sleeve. A few Riki glanced up from where they rode on their horses around me, and my eyes widened, trying to focus.

We were in the eastern valley. Headed toward the mountain. Thora's mountain.

The Riki marched in a massive group stretching out before and behind me.

My heart rammed against my chest, my breath frantic, sending puffs of fog out before me in the cold air. I crouched back down, studying the edge of forest to my right.

He came into view as I fixed my hands on the side of the cart, ready to make a desperate leap for the ground, and I froze. Iri was riding a silver horse behind me, his eyes boring into me, strained. He gave the slightest shake of his head and glanced up ahead of me. I turned to see a line of archers riding side by side, bows slung over their backs with full quivers of speckled feather arrows at their knees.

I measured the distance between myself and the trees; I'd have five or six arrows in my back by the time I made it to cover. If one of them didn't run me down with their horse first.

I tried to think. The wound on my arm was still seeping and the swelling on the side of my face was pounding. I licked my lips and tasted dried blood. In the cart in front of me, two men lay on their backs, one missing a leg and the other with his face wrapped in bloody bandages. I sat back down, pulling my knees into my chest.

Iri was still watching me. The dark leather of his armor vest made his hair look like an icy waterfall of bloodstained braids. The scruff on his face sat below sharp cheekbones and round, blue eyes.

Eyes I'd known all my life.

I pressed the heels of my hands into my forehead, thinking about the last time I'd seen him. Five years ago. Fighting beside me in the snow-covered glade with an axe in each hand. Snowflakes in his hair. Blood on his hands. He was tangled in the fight with a young Riki before they fell over the edge of a deep crevice carved into the earth. I could still hear the sound of my own scream as I watched him disappear. I'd crawled on my hands and knees to the edge, where the ground almost gave beneath me. He was lying on his back, his insides spilling out from a gaping wound. His eyes were already empty, staring up into the sky. And beside him, the Riki boy was half-buried in the snow.

I looked up, and Iri's eyes fixed on mine for another wordless breath, as if he was remembering the same moment. And then he kicked his horse, cutting left into the group, and disappeared.

Ahead, the mountain rose up over the valley. Dark slate rock melting into green forest beneath strokes of snow-crested peaks. Away from the fjord. Away from home.

I didn't know where the Riki lived, but we had to be on our way to one of their villages. And there'd be no way back to the valley until after the thaw. If I could get free, I could make it back to the fjord.

The cart jolted, coming to a stop as I came onto my feet. The Riki were moving into the trees, where a river snaked into the dense forest. They were stopping to water the horses. I could pick out the back of Iri's head, weaving in and out of the others.

A Riki woman's angry eyes met mine as she passed, headed for the water. They hadn't killed me yet and I'd been fighting the Riki long enough to know why. There weren't many uses for an Aska prisoner. They would either make me a *dýr* or sell me to another clan who would. Either way, it would cost me *Sólbjǫrg*.

A hand slapped me hard in the back of the head and the man driving the cart grunted, spitting at me before going back to his horse. "Sit down or I'll tie your feet and drag you."

I obeyed, watching over the side of the cart. Iri stood with his horse in the shade of the forest. He wore two crossing axe sheaths on his back, missing the scabbard the others wore. Just like he did when we were children. His gaze was fixed down the tree line, on Fiske, before they drifted in my direction again. They landed on me for only a moment before he turned his attention to his horse, checking the riggings and running his hands over its spotted hide. In the cart in front of us, the man missing his leg was groaning.

The cart rocked as the driver climbed back up onto his horse and he called out as one of the archers came out of the forest. He walked across the clearing toward us with a water skin in his hand, his horse sauntering behind him. His long red hair matched his beard, braided into three haphazard strands.

He waved a hand at the driver as he came to his side, handing him the water. I clutched onto the railing with numb fingers, watching them talk as the horse walked alongside the cart. My heart kicked up, my eyes darting from the horse back to the archer. His quiver of arrows was still fixed to the saddle.

I sat up just enough to look back over the rail. Most of the Riki were off their horses.

I gathered up a handful of hay from beneath me and slipped my hand through the slats, holding it out to the horse. When he spotted it, he rocked his head and took a step toward me.

The men were still talking as I reached for the reins, closing my eyes and murmuring a prayer under my breath. I looked at Iri one last time and, and as if he felt my gaze, his eyes shot back to me. They went wide as I threw myself up and over the rail, landing on the saddle. I slid, my weight falling to one side, and caught myself as the animal reared up.

"Aska!" the driver roared.

I kicked the horse with the heel of my boot and stood in the stirrups, leaning forward to keep my body as low as possible, while chaos exploded around the clearing. From the right, Riki were already running in the distance, weapons drawn as they disappeared into the trees to head me off. It was the only way I could go. If I didn't get into the trees, the archers would have me.

I shouted, urging the horse faster.

Ahead, Iri's horse was running with no rider, spooked by the commotion. Iri stood with his hands dropped by his side, eyes bewildered. Behind him, Fiske jumped up onto his horse and took off in the same direction I was headed.

The shriek of an arrow flew past me, striking a tree, and the splinters flew into the air as I passed. I tried to get lower.

The Riki were like stones rolling across the overgrowth, coming at me with the same faces I saw on the battlefield the day before. Feet pounding into the ground. Weapons swinging.

I cleared the tree line, swallowed up by the cool of the forest, and looked back.

Fiske was already in my line of sight as I glanced back to the river. He rode in fast, lifting his bow from where it was tucked against his horse, and I cursed. He slowed, falling back as he yanked an arrow free from his saddle, and pulled back on the string. The shot was clear.

The wet pop in my left shoulder sounded in my ears and the forest went quiet around me as I looked down to see the head of an arrow pushing through the leather of my armor vest. The horse kicked up, tilting, and I fell back, landing on the ground so hard it knocked the air from my lungs.

I rolled onto my right side, trying to pull my feet under me, but I still couldn't breathe. The trees above me swayed, bending over each other in my vision as my stomach roiled. The shouting stopped and I pressed my face into the damp dirt, panting and coughing.

Fiske's boots hit the ground in front of my face as he dismounted and the sound of more footsteps filled my head.

He reached down, snatching up a handful of my hair, and pulled me to my feet. From the corner of my eye, I could see the others taking hold of the horse's reins. I moaned, the arrow wedged through my shoulder joint radiating a hot pain down into my arm, neck, and back. I tried to swallow it down as he pulled me, my braids tangled in his fist, back toward the clearing.

Where Iri was waiting.

SIX

I PULLED AT THE ROPES TYING MY HANDS AND FEET TO the cart with blistering fingers, trying to hold myself still on my right side as it rocked and swayed over the uneven ground. The arrow was still threaded between my bones, the pain so deep now that I could feel it spreading through my entire body.

Iri rode behind, watching me, and I gave up trying to read the look on his face so I could focus every ounce of strength I had left on keeping still. When darkness fell and the cart began to slow, I watched fires light through half-opened eyes and was asleep before the camp quieted.

Morning came a wheezing breath later. I swallowed against a raw throat and listened to the Riki come awake, putting out fires and readying their horses. I bit down so hard I thought my teeth might break when we started moving again, hooking my arms and legs into the rails of the cart to brace myself.

The white-hot heat in my shoulder ached all the way into my ears, making my head feel like it was going to crack open. I didn't look for Iri again. The only thing cutting deeper than the agony of the arrow was the knowledge that he was a traitor. That he was alive. All this time.

Hours passed in between waking and sleeping until I wasn't sure if I was dead or alive. The cart slowed again and the crunch of hooves on frozen ground replaced the sound of sliding rock. I curled up tighter as we started to go uphill and tried not to scream as my weight was pulled toward my feet.

We didn't stop until the air turned cold in the setting sun and the scent of snow met the smell of fire. Then there was cheering. The muffled sound of crying. Warriors coming home for the winter to wives and husbands and children. I knew that sound. I could see the fjord in my mind. The view of it from up on the ridge. Blues and greens jetting up out of the water and disappearing into the foggy sky. The black rock beach with whitewashed driftwood piled on the shore. My clansmen were probably already there, warming themselves before the fires in their wood-planked homes. Burrowed into their beds with full stomachs.

My father. Mýra.

It stung almost as much as the arrow punctured through my flesh.

The Riki left me lying there until voices pushed in at the

edges of my blurred thoughts and the cart shook again. I cringed.

"Where am I going to put her?" A rasping voice came from the darkness beside me.

Another body climbed up and I winced against the pain it sent running through my back. "I'll do it."

The ropes around me were cut and hands pulled at my legs, sliding me to the end of the cart. As I was lifted up, the arrow caught on something and I groaned. My insides churned in a violent sea and my eyes flew open to see Iri's face above me. I blinked, trying to bring him into focus before my eyes rolled back into my head.

When I pulled them open again, I was on the ground. Inside. The color of fire lit the dark room around me. A barn. Or maybe a storehouse.

A calloused hand pressed to my face. "She's burning up."

"Probably infection." Another voice. "Get her on the table."

The hands took me up again and the room spun around me.

Cold night air pinched at my skin as they worked at my armor vest and I kicked, reaching for my knife, but the sheath was empty.

"Stop." Iri's face came back into view.

I grabbed onto him, my fingers digging into the leather of his armor. "Get it out," I whimpered as hot tears gathered at the corners of my eyes.

"We will." He disappeared from view again.

Another shadow stepped in front of me and hands gently pressed around the arrowhead. "We should wait for Runa."

"She's with the wounded from Aurvanger. Just get it out of her." My brother's deep voice was too loud in my head. His hand grasped my arm and I wrenched it back, cursing. I needed him to take out the arrow, but the thought of him trying to comfort me made me sick.

The figure in front of me shifted and the firelight caught his face. Fiske.

I jerked back. "Get away from me!"

His hand came down over my mouth and I took his throat in between my fingers, compressing his windpipe. He knocked my hand away.

"Don't *touch* me," I hissed, writhing on the table.

"He's going to take it out, Eelyn. Quiet." Iri was behind me, tearing fabric into strips.

"He put it there!" I pinned my eyes on Fiske, the fury coursing through my body and my heart pounding like it was going to burst through my ribs.

Fiske looked down at me with no expression on his face.

"If he hadn't shot you in the shoulder, another arrow would have caught you in the heart and you would be lying dead in the forest right now. You should be thanking him."

I looked back at Iri, glaring. "*Thanking* him? I wouldn't be here at all if it weren't for him." I could hardly put the words together through the clench of my teeth.

"I told you to stop following us." Fiske wiped his brow with the back of his arm. His hands were wet with my blood.

"I can take the arrow out now or you can wait for Runa. It might be a while."

"Take it out." Iri's voice was tired, his eyes pulled with worry. It was a look I remembered well—one that had been painted on his face many times.

Again!

I could hear his voice echoing in my mind. The sun was setting over the fjord and it was almost too dark to see. Our father watched from the window of our home, silhouetted in firelight.

Again, Eelyn!

Iri was only a year and a half older than me, but I was always much smaller. I couldn't hold the shield well enough to fight with it. So he had taught me to fight without one, wielding my axe in my left hand and my sword in my right. He was bruised and bleeding, training me before our first fighting season.

Again!

That same look hung in his eyes now. He was wondering if I was strong enough.

Fiske stepped toward me and I watched him warily. I knew I didn't have a choice. I'd been sick and wounded before, but never in my life had I felt pain like this.

Fiske looked me in the eye as he came to stand over me. "It's going to hurt."

Iri handed me a piece of leather and I took it. "Just do it." I bit down hard on the strap, pulling in a deep breath and pinning my eyes to the rafters above.

Iri came around the front of me, hooking his arm beneath my neck to brace the back of my head and I held onto him with shaking fists. The arrow cracked behind me, releasing an explosion of white light behind my eyes and filling the whole room. I groaned into Iri's chest, twisting my hands into his tunic as Fiske dug at the front of the arrow until he'd caught it with his fingernails.

When he had it, he waited, letting me catch my breath. "Ready?" He looked down at me.

I pushed the air out in three hissing spurts, steeling myself before I gave a quick nod.

He yanked his arm back, pulling it free.

I bucked beneath Iri's weight and felt my body go limp as the arrow hit the floor. Fiske's hands quickly replaced the hole with a wadded cloth and clamped down on my shoulder so hard that I couldn't breathe. I blinked slowly, trying to see it, but my eyes weren't working.

"What in the name of Thora . . ." The high-pitched whisper of a girl trailed off and a pair of boots beneath a long wool skirt stopped at the door. "Iri?"

He stood, going to the door and leaving only Fiske's hand to keep me from rolling off the table. My head fell to the side and Fiske came back into view, his dark hair falling around his face as he worked at cleaning my shoulder. I couldn't feel the pain anymore. I couldn't feel anything.

"Who are you?" The words cracked in my chest.

He stilled, the hard angles of his face severe in the dim light.

The heat of a tear slowly trailed down the side of my face. "Who are you to my brother?"

His mouth pressed together before he answered, his hands stilling on the wound. "He's *my* brother. And if you get him killed, I will cut your throat like I should have done in Aurvanger."

SEVEN

I was alone when I opened my eyes. The thin blue light of morning seeped between the wooden boards above me in the barn. I sat up on the table and the throbbing began, making me tremble. I reached my hand beneath my tunic and gently touched the hot, inflamed hole in my shoulder. Below it, new stitches were sewn into the gash in my arm. I rolled my wrists on each other, feeling the raw, pink skin pull sharply where the rope had been.

My bare feet found the cold ground and I slid off the table to stand. My boots were sitting neatly on top of my armor next to the empty fire pit. The little idol of Iri I had tucked into my vest stood on the table next to me. I picked it up, running my thumb over the small face, and blinked, seeing him in the fog again. Feeling that lightning strike in my soul. That Iri was alive. And not just alive. He'd betrayed us. All of us.

The boy I'd shared my childhood with. The boy I'd fought side by side with. He was worse than any enemy. And the blood we shared was now poison in my veins.

Through the planks on the walls, I could see the silent Riki village stretch out down the slope, covered in a shallow snowfall. The deep green of pine trees reached up behind the houses like a thick wall.

I fought with my boots, grinding my teeth against the pain coming from the entire left side of my body. My ribs were stabbing again from the fall off the horse. Maybe rebroken. I made my way to the door and lifted the latch gently with my finger but when I pushed, the door wouldn't open; it was barred from the outside. I huddled down into the corner, wrapping my arms around myself and tucking my injured arm into my side tightly. I waited.

The village slowly came to life with the sounds of livestock calling for their breakfast and iron pots swinging on wooden rails over morning fires. The smell of toasted grains filled the air and my stomach ached. I closed my eyes and tried to push down the nausea boiling in my belly.

Iri's voice found me in the dark room after hours of sitting in the damp cold. The door opened, swinging out and pulling the daylight in. A gray-haired man wearing a clean black tunic stepped inside. He was too old to have been fighting in Aurvanger. His eyes surveyed me, crouched in the corner like a frightened animal.

"Is she even of use?" His lips moved behind his thick beard. "Runa says she had an arrow in her yesterday."

Iri stepped in behind him, ducking beneath the low door-frame and setting a bundle of firewood onto the floor. He was clean, his hair rebraided and his clothes fresh. "She looks strong. She's an Aska warrior."

He said something else I couldn't hear over the thoughts racing through my mind, like wind inside my head. Iri with the Riki. Iri acting like my captor.

The old man's eyes ran over me, thinking. "Runa also told me *how* she got that arrow in her."

The irritation in Iri's eyes wasn't hidden when they finally landed on me. "Fiske took her down."

"She'd probably just spend the whole winter trying to escape." The man shook his head. "No one will want her. I think it's best to get some coin for her when the traders from Ljós come in a few days."

I stood, keeping my back to the wall. The pain in my arm spread into my chest as I looked from Iri to the old man.

He went back out into the snow and my lip curled up as I set my furious gaze on Iri. "Trade me? To *who*?" I whispered.

He pulled the latch, clicking it into place, and set the fire-steel onto the table. "One of the other Riki villages."

"You can't do that."

"I'd planned to keep you here through winter, until I could get you off the mountain." He rubbed his face with his hands. "But you've made a mess of this, Eelyn."

"*I* made a mess of it? You're the one who brought me here!"

48

"Quiet." He looked out the crack in the door.

The blood in my body seethed, pushing through my veins and waking me up. "You're the one who abandoned your people and your god to serve our enemy, Iri."

His eyes snapped back to me and he made the distance between us fast, taking me by the tunic and pulling me toward him. "The Aska abandoned *me*. Left *me* for dead. The Riki saved my life."

I pushed him away with my uninjured arm and snatched the idol up from the table. I threw it at him. "I have mourned you every day for five years." The wave of it hit me, threatening to knock me down. "And you've been here the whole time! You haven't even asked about Aghi!"

Iri froze, the tension in his face falling and revealing something fragile, ready to break.

"My father." I took another step toward him, my voice shaking.

He looked to the ground. "*Our* father." His jaw clenched and the room fell silent. "I was afraid of what you might tell me."

"He's alive, Iri. He was fighting in Aurvanger. And he'd be ashamed to call you his son if he knew the truth."

He shook his head, refusing to fight me. "Do you think he'll come for you?"

"If I'm not back after the thaw, he'll come looking."

His eyes moved to the idol on the ground. "Did you tell him I'm alive?"

My father running across the field toward me, his eyes

glittering with fear, flashed in my mind. "I tried to. He didn't believe it. He thought Sigr had sent your soul to me."

Iri seemed suddenly far away, his eyes looking off into the dark corner of the room. "Maybe he did."

"Sigr didn't do this, Iri. Thora did." My voice flattened, my eyes narrowing. "You've *killed* your own people. What will you do when you die? You'll be separated from us forever!" The words buckled under the weight of their meaning. Even as I'd grieved for Iri, I always believed I'd see him again. That we'd all be together one day. But Sigr would never allow him to enter *Sólbjǫrg*. Not after what he'd done.

"You don't understand." His voice lost the last of its anger. He dragged his fingers through the scruff on his jaw before he picked up the idol from the ground, turning it over in his hand. "I saw you and . . ."

I leaned into the wall, trying to hold myself up as I watched the thoughts move over his face.

"I saw you and I thought I was about to watch you die. I thought my heart was going to stop beating inside of my chest." He swallowed hard, the place between his eyebrows wrinkling.

It wasn't what I was expecting him to say. The heat in my face pushed up, leaking out of my eyes. The tears stung in the cold. "We thought you were dead, Iri. We tried to get down into the trench for your body. We tried to . . ." I swallowed down the words. There was no undoing it. "We have to leave. We have to get back to the fjord."

His eyes shifted around the room. "I can't."

"*Why?*" I studied him, my voice rising again.

"I have to find a way to convince them to take you as a *dýr.*"

"No!" My voice filled the room, ringing in my ears.

"Quiet! If anyone knows I'm talking to you like this . . ." He sighed. "If they trade you, you're on your own. You won't make it back to the Aska. We have a couple of days before the traders from Ljós come. I'll figure something out."

I thought of my father, his blue eyes looking into me, heavy and wide with shame. I could feel the weight of a *dýr* collar around my neck.

"You know I can't become a *dýr,* Iri. I'll never be accepted into *Sólbjǫrg.*" I couldn't believe he would even suggest it. "I'll take my own life before I let that happen."

It was what we'd been taught our entire lives—*vegr yfir fjor*—honor above life.

He leveled his eyes at me, his voice dropping low. "If you take your own life, you'll leave our father alone in this world. But if you forfeit your pride and wait out the winter, you'll be back with him after the thaw. You'll go back to the Aska and earn back your honor."

I gritted my teeth, clenching my fists at my sides. Because he was right. "I hate you." The words released the full force of whatever I'd held back from him. The rage. The disgust.

But he took it. He let it roll off of me onto him, and he didn't fight it. He looked at me for a long moment, his eyes moving over my face like he was seeing me for the first time.

"I know."

EIGHT

I SAT BEFORE THE FIRE PIT, INCHING CLOSER TO WARM the numbness in my fingers and toes. I could wait for dark and break through the wall, but I had no idea where I was. And there was no way I would survive on the mountain with a sickness stewing in the muscle and sinew of my shoulder, writhing like a snake under the skin.

The latch on the door lifted again when the dark finally fell and I stood, backing against the wall. A small face crowned with dark winding braids appeared.

"I'm here to check your wounds and help you clean up." One hand clutched at the woven shawl draped over her shoulders and the other held a basket to her hip. "If you try to hurt me, I'd be happy to let you die of that infection." She nodded toward the spot of fresh blood seeping through my filthy tunic.

The girl was about my size, but she was too clean and soft

to be a warrior. It wouldn't take more than two breaths to have my hands around her neck.

She moved toward me warily, her large, dark eyes inspecting my face where I could feel the bulge on my cheek and the crack in my lip. She swung the basket onto the table and set a pot on the ground in front of the fire pit, watching me from the corner of her eye. When she handed me a small loaf of bread, I tore it into pieces with my grimy fingers and ate as fast as I could. The pain in my jaw was nothing compared to the hollow feeling in my stomach.

She set a jar and a stack of neatly folded cloths onto the table and then filled a carved wooden bowl with the steaming water, sending the smell of lavender and comfrey into the air.

I pulled my tunic over my head, trying to be careful with my shoulder, and lifted myself up with my only strong arm to sit on the table. The girl peeled the soiled bandage from the arrow wound and leaned in, examining it. Her fingers spread the skin slowly and I hissed.

"He's a good shot," she murmured. "Right in the center of the joint."

My jaw clenched against the throbbing. She may have looked clean and soft, but she wasn't weak-minded. And she knew I was dangerous but she wasn't afraid of me. She wanted me to know it.

She dipped a cloth into the fragrant bowl of water and pressed it firmly to the broken skin on my arm. I looked at the ceiling, biting down on my lip, and my hair fell down my bare back as she cleaned the wound. "This one looks okay. It's deep but it'll heal." She looked up at me. "Sword?"

I nodded, realizing that she must have been the one that came in last night. She'd stitched it cleaner than Kalda ever had. "Are you a healer?"

Her eyes shot up, as if she was surprised I'd spoken. "I'm learning."

She wrung the bloody cloth into the water as the door opened behind us, making me jolt. I turned to see Fiske standing at the opening. I sat up straight, keeping my back to him and pulling the length of my hair down over my shoulder to cover myself.

He stared at the hole in my shoulder. The hole he put there. In fact, they were all his marks. "Iri told you to wait for me, Runa." He shifted his eyes back to the girl.

"You took too long. I have others to tend to tonight."

He leaned into the wall, facing the side of the room as she went back to work.

"Let's get you cleaned up." She handed me another cloth and lifted the pot of hot water to the table.

I worked at washing the front of my body and she scrubbed down my back and neck. Once my skin was free of most of the dirt and blood, she braided my hair, still dusty and tangled, pulling the strands back away from my face. When she was finished, she picked up a clean tunic from the basket and helped me dress.

She unrolled a long cloth bandage and set my arm against me at an angle across my chest. "Hold here."

I obeyed, watching her wrap it around my body to hold the arm in place.

She stood back, looking at me. "I didn't come in here to help you wash the blood of my clansmen from your pretty blond hair because I'm kind. I did it because Iri asked me to. He's earned his place here and you're not going to threaten it."

I raised an eyebrow at her. "And what exactly did he have to do to earn his place?"

She picked up the basket, setting it back onto her hip. She didn't look back as she opened the door and Fiske followed her out. The latch slammed behind them and I looked down at my useless arm. If we'd gotten here a few days earlier, I may have been able to make it off the mountain before the first heavy snow. But I knew better. I could smell the cool burn of winter creeping into the village, closer every hour.

I would be a fool to try now. But if I could last the winter without getting a knfe in my heart, maybe I had a chance.

NINE

THE DOOR FLEW OPEN, SLAMMING ON ITS HINGES. I SAT up on the table, searching the dark. Hands grabbed me before I could make out the forms in the shadows. I fought, trying to shift myself free, but a thick arm wrapped around my body, throwing my ribs into agony and sending the world turning sideways.

The hands pulled me by my tunic out the door, into the snow and I trudged down the path barefoot, kicking it up as I stumbled. I tried to get my bearings, but there was nothing but white below me and the dark mist surrounding the village.

"Where are you taking me?"

The man glanced over his shoulder before he reached back and slapped me. My head flew to the side, my mouth filling with blood. "Speak again and I'll put another arrow through you, Aska." I bit back the acid on my tongue.

We walked through the dark to the end of the village, where the sound of a hammer on an anvil pinged, echoing up the silent mountainside. The orange glow of a forge lit beneath a thatched canopy ahead.

The man shoved me forward and another one caught me, pulling me into the tent. He wrenched my head up by my hair and a Riki with a leather apron looked me over, holding iron tongs in his hand. He turned, fishing something from the forge, and my eyes went wide as he lifted an iron *dýr* collar up before him. I pushed back, trying to back out of the tent but the two men had hold of me. The blacksmith hammered the glowing hot collar on the anvil, bending and stretching it to size as I fought, shoving into the bodies behind me.

"If you're still, I'll be sure not to burn you," he instructed, his eyes on my neck.

I looked around the tent, searching for something to fight with. There were tools everywhere, but nothing within reach. The hand in my hair pushed me forward, forcing my face to the frozen anvil, and the other man leaned all his weight into my body to keep me still.

I screamed, thrashing, but they were too strong. The luminous metal ring moved closer as I kicked, but my bare feet only slid on the icy ground. Another Riki took hold of my shoulders and I was pinned, completely powerless. I grunted and spit as the blacksmith slowly spread the still-hot collar with the tongs and carefully positioned it around my neck. I kicked again, this time finding a leg, and I slipped. My skin sizzled as the metal touched me and I sucked in a choked breath, freezing.

"Hmph." The blacksmith hovered over me, his brow scrunching. "I told you to be still."

My face slid on the anvil, slick with snot and silent tears, as they held me in place, letting the collar cool. It was too late. The weight of the warm metal sat heavy around my neck.

Down the path, a torch lit in the dark and they pulled me back out into the snow. When we stopped, one of the men hooked the collar in his fingers and slid a length of rope through the circular opening, securing the other end to the trunk of a tree.

He left me shaking there as he went to the group of men standing near the torch stuck in the ground. They were talking and laughing, wrapped up in bearskins against the morning cold.

I reached up and touched the burn that was now scalded above my shoulder, trying to make out my surroundings. It looked maybe an hour before dawn, but the stars were still strung out across the sky, colors dancing behind the trees to the north.

The first sound of a cart made me stand up straight, pulling against the rope to see down the path, where a caravan came around the trail between two large, jagged boulders. The last cart pulled a line of cattle behind it. I knew what was happening as soon as I saw the Riki greet each other. These were the traders from Ljós. The stone in my chest grew heavier. They were going to trade me.

The village was still dark and quiet, the sunlight only just beginning to creep up the sky. Iri couldn't know. Or maybe he'd changed his mind and decided to let them get rid of me.

My eyes went back to the caravan, trying to gauge my chances. I looked down to my feet, buried in the snow. The deep ache of cold was already pulsing up my legs. I couldn't take them without weapons and I couldn't outrun them barefoot. I sorted through every scenario in my mind, searching for an alternative. But there was nothing. No chance.

Two more *dýrs* were brought out and tied to the trees behind me, probably Riki criminals. The woman stared off into the forest, her face blank, and the man shifted on his feet as goats bleated beside me, reaching their noses over the railing of their pen toward my trembling hands.

Another group came down the trail to join the men already gathered. They spread out as the light lifted, starting at the far end and making their way down the line of trees to see the goods that had been laid out for trade.

Including me.

I kept my eyes on the ground, the voice in my head saying everything I didn't want to believe. I was going to be dragged into the forest and dumped in some Riki mountain village as a *dýr*. I would never see the fjord again. I would never see my father. Mýra. Not in this life or the next. My heart broke inside of me. The hope of getting home seemed so foolish now, eaten up by my anguish.

All because of Iri.

Boots stopped in the snow in front of me, and a deep laugh rang out. "She's a little thing, isn't she?"

The burn in my face scorched like a summer sun. The leather of his armor vest stretched as he rocked back and forth on his heels, clicking his tongue before his shadow moved on the snow.

Two more Riki stopped in front of me and I pinned my eyes to my feet, refusing to look up.

"How much for her?" one of them called back to the torches.

"Four *penningr*," a man shouted back.

I could feel myself sinking deeper into the snow. It was the same price I'd paid for the goat we sacrificed the night I saw Iri. I tried to blink back the flare in my eyes. It was a cruel joke. Like Sigr was looking down on me and laughing. He had to be.

The two Riki moved on, taking more interest in the livestock than in me, and a man bigger than the others stopped before me.

"What's wrong with her?" He flung a hand toward my shoulder.

The old man who'd come to look at me in the barn came to stand next to him. "Injured from battle."

"She's Aska?"

"That's right. Not much good for work right now, but she'll heal before the thaw."

My hands balled into tight fists. I wanted to reach up and

strangle him with the rope. I wanted to watch the light leave his wrinkle-framed eyes.

The big man stepped closer as the old man walked away. "Turn around."

I took a step back. "What?"

His hand shot out, snatching me by my bruised jaw, and he yanked me forward until the collar choked me, putting his face close to mine. I knew what he was going to do before he did it. His fingers caught me behind the knee and he ran his hand up the inside of my leg. I pressed myself against the rough bark of the tree but he moved with me, letting his body push against mine.

"Get off me," I growled through my teeth.

A smile pulled at his lips behind his bushy beard. He flung me around, turning me to face the tree, and pushed me into it, his eyes falling down the back of my body like a hot iron. "You're coming with me." The words rode on a laugh.

He let go of me and the shaking stopped, my body filled with the hot fever of hatred that flowed through my veins when I swung my axe and sword beside Mýra in battle. An injured arm wouldn't keep me from driving a blade into this man's gut.

He walked back to the torches and I wondered if I'd ever seen him. If I'd ever killed anyone he loved. The breath filled my chest, my eyes narrowing. It wouldn't take long to find an opportunity to kill him. When I did, the others would kill me.

But that would be alright. Sigr might see honor in that.

The collar pulled around my neck and I flinched, turning

to see Fiske standing on the other side of the tree. His armor vest was loosely thrown over him, the laces of his boots undone. The length of the rope was wrapped around his fist and he pulled me forward.

"What are you doing?" I jerked against the rope.

He didn't look at me, turning back toward the village and pulling me with him. "I just paid for you."

A voice shouted behind us.

"Don't turn around." Fiske kept walking.

Arguing echoed between the trees, but it died down as we walked and slowly turned into laughing. I glanced back and Fiske yanked the rope.

"I said don't turn around."

The first sliver of sun peeked over the pines as I hobbled behind him, the pain in my frozen feet now shooting up my legs in spasms. We rounded the bend in the path where the snow was melting into the mud and the Riki working outside their homes turned their heads, watching me. Fiske didn't look at them, his eyes forward as he led me down the middle of the village back toward the small empty barn they were holding me in. He was cleaned of the grime from battle, half of his hair pulled up into a knot and the rest falling down on top of the orange fox fur on his shoulders.

He stopped and I bit down hard to keep my teeth from chattering together as he opened the door and pulled out his knife. He cut the rope from my collar and stood to the side. "Go ahead."

I stepped past him into the barn, and stood, shivering

with my arms wrapped around myself. The cut on his ear from where I threw my blade at him was still red, scabbed over beneath his hair.

His eyes dropped down to my feet and he cursed under his breath. He took the pile of wood from the table and started the fire before he pulled a stool from the wall and set it beside the pit. I sat down, pulling as close to the heat as I could and setting my feet up on the warmed stone circling the flames. They were pale and numb, aching, but probably not frostbitten.

Fiske dropped a bearskin beside me as I massaged my legs with my hands to summon the warmth back into them. I sat, staring into the fire and feeling its heat against the tears running down my face.

"How did you know I was out there?" I steadied my voice.

He looked like he didn't want to answer. "I heard you screaming. In the blacksmith's tent."

I closed my eyes and swallowed, thinking about the way I'd cried and begged the night they pulled the arrow from my shoulder. I had never begged for anything in my life. The humiliation of it seared hotter than the infection in my shoulder or the burn on my neck. His pity cut into me, bleeding me of my pride.

"I've agreed to keep you until the thaw." His voice filled the empty space when he finally spoke.

"*Keep* me?" My words were ice.

"If you run, I'm not coming after you. You'll die out there within a day. Maybe two."

"Where are we?"

"Fela."

I'd heard of it. It was only one of several Riki villages on the mountain. "I'll take you to my home tomorrow."

I sniffed. "Is that where Iri lives?"

He hesitated. "Yes, and our family doesn't know anything about you. If you want to stay alive, it needs to stay that way."

"Why didn't Iri buy me?"

He leaned into the wall. "The Riki can't know who you are. Stay away from Iri."

I studied him, trying to read the look on his face. Fierce, but pleading. He loved Iri—I could hear it folded beneath each word. "Why did you agree to take me?"

He ran a hand through his hair. "Iri is my brother."

"Iri is a prisoner you kept as a pet," I muttered. I could feel the change in him, the edge of him sharpening. "I won't run. But if you think I'm going to act like a *dýr*—"

He didn't wait for me to finish. He pushed the door open and left, leaving me sitting before the fire. I stared at the closed door as he locked it and watched his outline flit through the light coming through the slats.

When he was gone, I reached into my pocket and pulled my idol of Iri free. The wood was smooth and shining where I'd held it in prayer under every moon that rose in the sky. I carried it against my heart as I fought. I slept with it beside me. We became warriors together. And long before that, we were friends.

It was Iri who'd wrapped his arms around me in the dark

when I dreamed of the white-eyed Herja who'd slit our mother's throat. It was Iri who'd held me together when I was cracked down to the bone with the pain of losing her. I ran into my first battle with my brother at my side. I washed the blood of his first kill from his hands and pretended not to see the gleam of tears in his eyes. He'd been stronger than me in every way, but we had taken care of each other. And honoring him had been where I'd found my own strength after he was gone.

I dropped the idol into the flames, tears catching in my chest.

I let him go. I erased him. Every memory. Every small hope.

Because the Iri I loved was gone. The boy who had once known every shadowed corner of my life was dead the moment he spilled the blood of our people. That boy was gone just as our mother was, but his soul was lost.

I watched the charred black catch the edge of the wood, eating its way across until the idol was just a part of the fire. Turning to smoke and gathering up above me. It stretched and curled around itself, reaching out into the air.

Until it was nothing.

TEN

I DIDN'T SLEEP FOR FEAR THAT THE DOOR MIGHT OPEN again.

The burn under the collar came alive around my neck, stinging deep down into the skin. I pulled on my boots, sitting in the empty barn alone, my eyes on the closed door. I'd spent the hours with a broken piece of firewood clutched in my fist, finding the veins beneath my skin that would bleed the life out of me the quickest. If I killed myself, Sigr might accept me. I'd never have to be a *dýr*. But Iri's words haunted me. I imagined my father as an old Aska, alone in our home on the fjord. He'd already lost my mother and Iri. I was all he had. The thought of abandoning him was too much to bear.

I could make it through winter. I could make it back to Hylli, to my father and Mýra. I could earn back my honor.

Footsteps crunching in the snow brought me to my feet

and I stood to face Fiske as he opened the door. When the light spilled in, the snow was falling softly, some of it caught in his hair.

The door closed behind him and he looked at me for a long moment, his eyes searching for something in mine. "Iri says I don't need to worry about you being a danger to our family."

Iri was a liar. I wouldn't hesitate to kill every one of them if I thought it would get me home, but it probably wouldn't.

"I saved your life. I'm hoping that's good enough reason to believe him."

I pressed my tongue to the top of my mouth. "By my count, you've tried to take my life more times than you've tried to save it."

I pushed past him, opening the door and ducking out into the open air. I fell to my knees, scooping up a handful of snow and holding it against my neck where the skin was blistered. A long, hissing breath pushed out of me as I tried to breathe through the sting.

He started down the path ahead of me and my feet followed him in the direction we'd walked the day before. I studied the incline. The village crawled up above us, houses set beside and behind each other in uneven rows. At the top of the hill, their ritual house sat, much like the one in our village. The smoke from the fire was floating up from its roof, fading into the fog that hugged the treetops.

Again, the Riki stopped to stare as we walked in the falling snow, stilling their hands on their work to watch me follow Fiske like a dog through their village. I didn't meet their eyes as we passed them. I was disgraced. Weak. And every one of them knew it.

The house stood on a hillside near the tree line. It was bigger than some of the others, with long thin logs stacked together to form the walls and a thatched roof. Fiske didn't wait for me to enter. He opened the door and disappeared through it, leaving me outside.

There was nothing keeping me from walking straight into the snow-piled trees. And there was nothing keeping a Riki from burying their knife into me. I'd probably killed several people from this village. And more likely than not, I'd have to kill more before I left this place.

I stepped through the door slowly, my hand instinctively reaching for the knife that hadn't been there in days. Iri sat, bent over a wooden table with a hammer and a stack of animal furs. He glanced at me from the corner of his eye before returning to his work, but I could see the tension in him, winding his muscles tight beneath his tunic. I wanted to pick up one of the burning logs in the fire and throw it at him.

"Ah." An older woman stood at the table in the middle of the main room with her hands pressed into a ball of dough on a kneading board. She wiped the flour on the sooty apron that wrapped over her red wool skirt, looking at me. Her dark hair was grayed near her hairline, braided into one long strand that wrapped up over her head, but her eyes were a sparkling blue like Fiske's. "You're the Aska, then?" Her gaze dropped down, inspecting the arm still wrapped to my chest. Her lips pressed together. "What happened there?"

My eyes moved to Fiske, who leaned against the wall, eating.

"I shot her." He didn't look up from his bowl.

The woman's eyes widened. "And then you bought her?"

He tipped his chin in an answer, still not bothering to look over at us.

A creak sounded above me and two big eyes peered over the edge of a loft, watching me beneath a muss of dark hair.

"I'm Inge." The woman tilted her head to the side, thinking. "I should take a look at your arm. Are you hungry?"

I shook my head in answer, looking away from her.

She pulled the wooden spoon from the pot and tapped it on the rim, smirking. "Halvard, come down here."

Footsteps tapped above us and a small boy leapt down from a wooden ladder that reached up to a sleeping loft. His eyes didn't leave the collar on my neck as he moved across the room.

Inge patted his back, handing him the spoon. "Come stir while I take a look at the Aska's arm."

I took a step back toward the door.

Fiske finished, setting his bowl down, and Iri stood to follow him. They went outside, leaving the door open. Through the doorway, I watched Fiske reach down into a pail and set a big silver fish onto a wooden table. He kept his attention on me as he pulled his knife out and cut down its belly. On the other side of the table, Iri did the same.

Inge set a bowl down on the table and prepared a bundle of herbs, soaking them the way Runa had. When she came toward me, I pressed my back into the wall.

She stopped, dropping her hands. "I only want to clean it for you."

Of course she did. I wasn't of use with my arm like this.

I moved toward the table, eyeing the room. The house looked lived in, probably at least a couple of generations old. Some of the wall slats were newer wood, recently replaced, but almost all were grayed with many winters and rains. A long counter ran along the right wall with food stored in barrels beneath it and vegetables strung up on hooks. Beyond the fire, three large trunks sat closed, probably where the weapons were kept.

Inge unwrapped my arm as I sat down slowly, holding it firmly in place until it was free. I dug my fingers into the edge of the bench as she gradually lowered it and set my hand in my lap. The skin covering my shoulder was a dark purple, still swollen but not as red as it had been two days ago. I tried to slow my breaths and blinked back the prick behind my eyes. I could tell by the way she handled me that she was a healer. Maybe the one Runa was apprenticing with. She was focused, gently cleaning the skin before filling the wound with something that looked like beeswax. I lowered my face to smell it.

"It's what's in the pot." She nodded to the fire.

The boy was standing over the flames, stirring slowly and watching.

"This is Halvard." She leaned in closer to my arm and I shifted back. Her nearness made me uncomfortable.

When my arm was out of the tunic, her fingers followed the skin up my neck to where I could feel the burn radiating. She walked to the door and stepped one foot outside so she could crouch down and gather a handful of snow into a cloth. I watched her fold it in on itself.

"Here." She pressed it to the burn and lifted my hand to hold it while she moved down to the gash. "Runa didn't tell me she tended to you." She looked at the stitches. "It looks good. We'll cut those out next week. By then, your face will look better." She took my hand into hers, turning it over and eyeing my skin where it was blistered from being tied to the cart. "And these. But the shoulder will take longer."

When I said nothing, she leaned down to meet my eyes. I wanted to reach up and take a handful of her hair into my fist. I wanted to slam her face into the table.

She slid my arm back into my tunic and repositioned it against me before she wrapped it again. "You'll stay here with us; I'll make you a cot up in the loft. I'd stay clear of anyone outside the house if I were you." She stood, making her way to a large iron pot on the other end of the table, and spooned something into a wooden bowl. She looked up at me, biting the inside of her lip before she glanced over her shoulder to Fiske, who was still watching us from outside as he cleaned fish. When she spoke again, her voice lowered. "I don't know why Fiske took you on, but from the looks of it, you'll be traded soon enough. Until then, you'll help me around here.

You don't have to talk. But if I'm feeding you, you do have to work."

She put the bowl down in front of me, setting her hands on the curved hips below her small waist. She waited for me to look at her. "And if you bring trouble into this house, Aska, you won't make it off this mountain."

ELEVEN

THEY'D BEEN LIVING WITH AN ASKA FOR TOO LONG.

I stared at the cot that Inge made up along the opposite wall from the others in the loft. I'd expected to sleep with the animals. Maybe they wanted me to know they weren't afraid of me. Or maybe they wanted to keep me close enough to watch. Either way, they were foolish. I wasn't Iri.

I went up as soon as they sat to eat supper. I couldn't sit across the table from my brother and pretend not to know him. I couldn't pretend that I wasn't thinking every moment of how to kill every last one of them. I rolled onto my side and stared at the wall, where the cold was coming in through a crack. I lifted my hand and fit my fingers into it.

"Did you see Kerling today?" Iri spoke, breaking the silence.

"I did." Inge's delicate voice was the only feminine thing

in the house. "Vidr did the right thing by cutting off the leg. He'll manage and it'll heal. His pride, on the other hand . . ."

"He's lost his leg." Fiske's voice rose in rebuke.

"But not his honor." Inge's words turned sharp. "Gyda needs him. The baby will be here soon."

"What will he do without his leg? He can't fight anymore. He can't farm," Halvard said softly.

"He'll raise goats," Fiske answered. "They'll be fine."

Another long silence stretched out before Inge spoke again. "Sit down and let me look at you, *sváss*."

"I took care of it already." Fiske sighed.

"Sit," she urged again, and I heard the scrape of a stool on the stone floor followed by the sound of her unbuckling his armor vest.

From what I could tell, Inge's husband was dead and I could probably guess how. Most clansmen died in the fighting season, but others died in raids or of illness. Fiske was obviously the man of the house, but Inge wasn't helpless if she ran her home and worked as a healer while he was gone during the fighting season. The span of years between Fiske and Halvard could mean there had been more children. Or maybe Halvard wasn't hers the way Iri wasn't hers.

"Are those teeth marks?"

I burrowed deeper into my blanket, remembering the way it felt to sink my teeth into Fiske's flesh. I could still taste his blood in my mouth.

"You didn't come home in such good shape last time." Her tone lifted on a smile. "You sure you did much fighting?"

Halvard and Iri laughed and I swallowed down the nausea climbing up my throat.

"I did plenty of fighting," Fiske shot back.

"Is that where the Aska came from?" Halvard spoke and the others fell silent, the house filling with the sound of the wood crackling in the fire as the sap popped in its grooves.

I lifted my head, quietly pulling myself to the edge of the cot to look through the planks of wood to where they sat below. Halvard was filling clay jars with the salve they'd been making over the fire. He looked to Inge for an answer.

She sat at the table beside Fiske. His tunic was pulled off and she was cleaning his arm where I'd bitten him. The rest of his skin was covered in scrapes and cuts and bruises.

"Yes," Fiske answered.

Halvard looked up at him, securing the lid to a jar. "Why didn't you kill her?"

Inge leaned over him, wiping at a cut on his neck. She looked small next to his large, solid frame. Fiske glanced at Iri and Inge watched their wordless exchange from the top of her gaze. "Sometimes we bring them back. You know that."

"Well, I'm glad you didn't kill her. She's pretty."

Iri sat across the room, a smile breaking onto his face and I cringed, my forehead wrinkling. I didn't want to think about seeing myself in his face. I didn't want to think about our mother. About what she would think of Iri now.

"Her hair looks like yours, Iri."

My heart skipped ahead of my breath and the line of Iri's

shoulders hardened. Fiske stood up, taking his tunic into his hand.

Inge was watching him. "Stay away from her, Halvard."

"Why?" He set down the jar, his eyebrows coming together. "She's just a *dýr*."

"She's not just a *dýr*. She's Aska," Fiske corrected.

"Iri's Aska," Halvard muttered, his shoulders slumping.

"She's dangerous, Halvard. Stay away from her." Fiske waited for the boy to look at him.

He nodded, reluctantly.

Inge was still watching Fiske as she packed the supplies back into the basket on the table. "Which is why it's interesting that you brought her here."

He didn't respond. Instead, he slipped the tunic back over his head and picked up his axe before he opened the door and went out into the night. Inge's eyes traveled over to Iri, but he didn't look up either. A few minutes later, the hollow pound of an axe and the splintering of wood was echoing against the house.

I pushed back from the edge of my cot and lay back down when the fire pit was nothing but smoldering ashes. Halvard climbed the ladder and I huddled down into my blanket, hidden in the darkness. He flopped down across the loft, fidgeting for a few minutes before his breaths stretched out longer and deeper. He fell asleep with his hand hanging out of his blankets, his fingertips touching the floor.

The door below opened and closed a few minutes later, and Iri lifted himself up over the edge of the loft, stepping over Halvard. He crouched low, looking at him, before he brushed a hand over his hair and stood back up, coming toward me.

"She's gone," he whispered, sitting down beside my cot.

He looked down at the collar around my neck, his eyes shifting to avoid mine. "I thought we had more time. I'm sorry."

I didn't answer. The last thing I wanted from him was his sympathy.

"It's only until the thaw, Eelyn. Then we can find a way to get you home. Back to Aghi."

I rolled onto my back to face him. The glow from the fire pit was too low to see his eyes. "Hylli is home to *both* of us, Iri."

He looked away. "Fela is my home now."

The tightness in my chest strangled me, and I was glad he couldn't see my face. The only thing that could be worse than losing Iri was knowing that he'd *chosen* to leave. He was dead all over again. I was alone again, but differently.

"What happened to you?" I whispered. "What happened that day in Aurvanger?"

He looked at me for a long moment, until the door opened again and he stood, making his way to his cot. I pulled up the blankets, staring at the outline of his face as he lay down on his back. The arch of his brow and the angle of his nose were the same as they were when we were children.

Fiske climbed the ladder and settled onto the cot beside mine, prying his boots off and sitting up in the dark. He pulled in a long breath, rubbing his face with both of his hands before he worked his tunic back off and raked his hair up, tying it in a knot.

He lay down, staring at the ceiling a long time, his hands folded on his chest. I watched the thoughts cross his face one at a time until his eyes closed.

My fingertips found the collar and I tried to imagine what my father's face would look like if he could see me. I blinked and the dread spilled over, drowning the quiet. Because the only thing worse than knowing I was a *dýr* was the thought of my father knowing it too.

TWELVE

I STARED UP INTO THE DARK LONG BEFORE THE OTHERS awoke, hearing Iri's voice in my mind. A man's voice. I closed my eyes, trying to see the boy I'd run on the beach with as a child. I tried to remember what his voice had sounded like then, but I couldn't summon it to me. Memories suddenly felt more like dreams, moments stuck between waking and sleeping.

When I heard Inge moving below, I climbed down the ladder, hooking my good arm into each rung, and stood beside the fire pit. My eyes drifted to the stale bread sitting on the table.

"Good morning." She handed me the fire-steel and I looked down to where it sat in my open palm. My other arm was still tied to my body.

"Oh." She turned back when she realized. "Sorry, I suppose you can't do that."

She reached out to take it back and I closed my fist, turning away from her and walking to the wall beside the door to gather up the wood. She raised an eyebrow at me before going back to the grains on the table. I set up the kindling with one hand at the edge of the fire pit instead of the center. I struck the one piece of the fire-steel against the stone until it sparked, but the kindling didn't catch. I moved the kindling closer and tried again. This time it lit and I picked up the burning bundle and set it in place before it could snuff out.

"Can you show me how to do that?" Halvard watched me from the edge of the loft with sleepy eyes and hair standing up around his head. He slid down the ladder in only his pants and the memory of a young Iri pushed its way back into my mind, barefoot and dirty-faced.

I rubbed the heel of my palm against my chest, as if it might erase it.

I looked away, turning toward Inge. She was sifting the grain into a bowl, her eyes narrowing on me. "Can you please heat the water?"

I found the kettle and when I turned around, Halvard was standing next to me, holding out his hand. Inge watched us as I gave him the kettle and he hopped down from the edge of the fire pit. He fit his fingers into the grooves of one of the flat stones that made up the floor and lifted it up carefully. There, beneath the stone, water was running in a dug-out channel under the house.

I'd never seen anything like it. He looked up at me proudly, using a cup to fill the kettle, and handed it back to me, smiling. Inge poured the grain out onto a large hot cooking stone, toasting it with a wooden paddle. The house filled with the warm nutty smell and my stomach pinched with hunger.

Iri and Fiske stirred above us and Inge smiled, shaking her head. "Like bears in the winter," she muttered.

Halvard set out wooden bowls and Inge filled them with the grain before pouring the hot water over them. Iri and Fiske climbed down the ladder, their hair unbound and faces drawn with sleep. Iri scratched at his jaw as he sat down, his eyes squinted against the light.

Halvard scooted over on the bench to make another seat but Inge took the fifth bowl and handed it to me. "Over there." She nodded toward the corner by the door.

I looked into the bowl, the heat lighting in my cheeks. Iri gave her a look, but she ignored him. Why should she let a *dýr* sit at the table? She didn't trust me. She *shouldn't* trust me. And why did I care? I didn't want to sit with them.

I picked up a stool, setting it down hard on the stone and sat with my bowl in my lap, taking a bite of the grains. My lip still stung fiercely, but I was hungry enough not to care.

"I'll take Runa and the Aska to gather the yarrow for *Adalgildi*. You're both needed to bring in the ale from the mountainside cellar," she said, glancing up to Iri and Fiske.

Fiske stared at her, his spoon hovering over his bowl.

She looked at me before meeting his eyes. "You think I can't take care of myself?"

"What about me?" Halvard spoke through a mouth full of food.

Inge smiled. "You can come with us, *sváss*."

I listened as they made plans for the day, dividing up responsibilities. When Inge stood, she leaned down to kiss Iri on the cheek, running a hand through his hair. It set my teeth on edge. A spark, threatening to eat up the dry, angry parts of me. As she passed Fiske, she did the same and they both relaxed under her touch, leaning into her. Fiske and Iri were grown men, hardened by battle, but they were soft with her.

I faced the wall as I finished eating, unable to stomach it. I didn't remember as much of my mother as Iri had. We lived most of our lives with only our father, but I didn't like Inge touching him. I didn't like the tenderness between them. Inge acting like Iri's mother was an insult, but Iri acting like Inge's son was blasphemy.

My fist tightened around my spoon as I took my last bite and I stood, washing my bowl and returning it to the crate Halvard pulled them from. Iri met my eyes as he ducked out the door behind Fiske—a warning to behave.

I leaned into the wall and waited as Inge lifted two large leather-handled baskets up onto the table and took two pairs of iron shears from the wall. If she wanted me to eat in the corner like a goat, I wasn't going to go out of my way to help her.

Behind me, the door swung opened and Runa came in, brushing snowflakes from her dark hair and her skirt. She was bundled up in a wool wrap, her cheeks flushed pink.

When she smiled, her full lips stretched over straight white teeth. "Good morning."

"Runa!" Halvard ran to her, wrapping his arms around her waist.

Her gaze lifted to me, moving over my face to my shoulder. As soon as they landed on the *dýr* collar, her eyes flitted away. "You look better." She held out a green wool cloak in her arms. "I brought this for you."

I stared at it.

"For the cold." She pushed it toward me.

Halvard took it from her and shoved it into my arms. "Aren't you going to put it on?"

Inge came around the table with the hood of her own cloak pulled up over her head. She handed one basket to me and slid the other onto her hip.

They walked side by side with Halvard running ahead and me following behind. We followed the path through the houses and I watched out of the corner of my eye, taking note again of how the village was laid out. Between Inge's house and the ritual house, a row of houses lined the path, except for the blacksmith's tent and what looked like the village cellar. The wooden door was set into a rocky cliff face.

At the last house on the path, a man stood with his son and daughter before an elk strung up from a tree. Its black, empty eyes seemed to follow me as I walked, its tongue hanging from its mouth. The man lifted his knife, showing the boy where to cut. Behind them, a woman gathered eggs into her apron. She watched me, clutching the hem of her skirt tighter in her hands.

As we made our way out of the village, the trail grew

thicker, overrun by the forest. We stepped carefully into footsteps that were already punched into the snow and climbed farther up. The village looked small from above, the dark wooden structures nestled together with smoke lifting up from the rooftops.

The path cut down sharply and we followed it, walking until the snow began to thin. As the sun rose above us, the warmth came back into my body, maybe for the first time since I'd arrived in Fela. But winter was only just beginning and days like this were numbered. Maybe it was the last one.

Inge and Runa talked quietly, taking turns carrying the basket, and I listened, lugging mine with one hand on my sore hip. They talked about an old woman with a cough, a child with a lame leg, and a few men brought back from Aurvanger who probably wouldn't heal from their battle wounds. Again, they mentioned a man named Kerling.

I watched carefully, memorizing the path. We weren't far from the village, but we were moving up again, not down. As the trail narrowed between two steep rock faces, I maneuvered the basket in front of me to wedge myself through. When it opened back up, we were standing in a large clearing covered in white and yellow stalks of yarrow. They reached up from the ground as high as my waist, pushing and pulling against each other in the breeze.

Inge and Runa set down their basket and settled onto the ground, reaching for the stalks nearest to them. They cut with their shears at an angle, pulling them up out of the thick brush.

"Here." Inge reached for the basket I was holding and I set it down beside her. "Remove the leaves. We'll keep them," she said, gently placing the cut stalks into the basket.

"They're for *Adalgildi*." Halvard found a place on the ground next to me. "Do the Aska have *Adalgildi*?"

I ignored him, stripping the leaves from the yarrow and piling them between us. He did the same with the stalks from Runa's basket, where the stack of flowers crisscrossed each other like fallen trees. He snapped one of the stalks in his hand and pried the bloom off, careful not to smash the tiny petals. He held it up between us. When I didn't move, he pushed it at me. "It's for you."

He grabbed my wrist and turned my hand over so he could set the flower down into my palm like an egg in a nest. He smiled at it.

Inge stood, moving farther into the clearing, and Halvard followed after her. I looked down at the bloom in my hand until I felt Runa's eyes on me. She was staring, her gaze trailing over me slowly.

"What?" I couldn't smooth the bite out of the word, pulling the flower into my cloak.

"Nothing." She blinked. "You just—with that green cloak and your hair—you look just like Iri." Something sad fell like a veil over her voice, the lift in her mouth turning down at the corners.

So, she knew who I was. At the very least, she suspected.

I dropped my eyes and went back to work. I didn't care if she thought I looked like Iri. I didn't care about their offerings

85

or their customs. The Aska were home with their families, mourning their dead, and I was in Fela, cutting flowers for the god of the Riki.

I eyed the shears in Runa's hand. If I wanted to, I could kill the three of them right now.

I could set this field of yarrow on fire and let myself burn with it.

THIRTEEN

THE HOUSE WAS FILLED WITH TOWERING HEAPS OF YAR-
row and long woven garlands of cedar by morning. The door
stood open, letting the colors of early sunlight stream inside,
and the smell of herbs grew thick in the air.

I untied my arm, stretching it carefully so I could try to
use it. It was painful, but it would only grow stiff if I kept it
bandaged. I set the tops of the yarrow in large, flat baskets as
Inge instructed me to and watched from the table as she
pulled clothes from the trunk against the wall. I eyed the two
trunks next to it, trying to guess which one held the weapons. There was no way they wouldn't keep them in the house
and I'd already checked the loft. Fiske and Iri wore theirs during the day and slept with them beside their beds at night,
but Inge must have weapons too. And Halvard.

She laid clean tunics hemmed in golden thread out on the
table. They were dress clothes similar to the ones the Aska

wore for ceremonies. "You'll need to clean and oil them. Then shine the buckles." She dropped their armor vests, scabbards, and sheaths down in front of me.

I finished with the yarrow and picked them up off the floor, sitting beside the fire. I scrubbed the dirt and blood from the leather with a brush until it was clean and then I oiled them, rubbing the shine into the creases with my fingers the way I did with my father's armor and mine. My arm ached and burned with the movement, but it felt good to use the muscles.

Iri pulled his tunic off, reaching for the dress clothes, and my hands froze on the scabbard in my lap. The scar reaching across the side of his body was a thick, gnarled thing, pink and shiny against his skin. It was the wound that I'd seen bleeding out as he lay at the bottom of the trench. I rarely saw scars like that. They were the echoes of wounds that people didn't actually survive.

"Will Kerling come?" Iri looked out the door to the small house that sat across the path. Beside it, posts were driven into the ground for what looked like a barn, but it was unfinished. A small garden patch was nestled inside the gate, full of rhubarb and leeks.

Inge shook her head. "No." She pulled the bench out from under the table and she worked at Fiske's hair, braiding it back against the scalp before pulling the length of it into a neat knot and securing it with a leather tie. "Aska, can you do Iri's?" She nodded toward him and my fingers curled around the leather strap.

He sat down and I stood, coming behind him to take his hair into my hands. He didn't look up at me, but he didn't flinch under my touch, instantly making me feel like I was going to cry.

"Do you know how?" Halvard asked, looking up at me from where he sat on the ground.

Inge laughed. "She has hair, doesn't she?"

"I used to do my brother's," I answered. The breath caught in my chest.

Inge and Halvard both looked at me. Iri stilled, sitting up straighter.

"What happened to him?" Halvard's voice turned wary.

"Halvard," Inge scolded him, her brow furrowing.

I pulled the hair into three measured sections. "He's dead," I said flatly.

Halvard went quiet.

I braided the thick, waving strands back away from his face, taking the pleats all the way to the end of his hair and then tying them. I used to braid Iri's hair all the time just like this and then he would do mine. Remembering it was like swallowing a stone.

Iri sitting before our fire, laughing.

Iri lying in the snow, bleeding.

I blinked. Fiske sat in front of him, leaning forward on his elbows and looking at me, like he could see the memories cast behind my eyes.

I looked away, brushing off Iri's shoulders, and brought the braids to lie down his back. He stood, taking the Riki armor vest from the table and fitting it over the fine tunic. He didn't look at me as I reached up to buckle the sides, his eyes strained behind the strength painted on his face.

I tightened the straps around his thick torso, remembering. I did the same thing before battle five years ago, in the darkness of our father's tent. Hours later, Iri was gone.

Once he was dressed, he picked up a round, flat black stone from the table and rubbed his thumb over its surface where worn letters were carved. He looked at it for a moment before tucking it into his vest.

"You did a good job on these." Inge worked at Fiske's armor. "They're cleaner than they've been in years."

Hearing her say it made me wish I hadn't done it.

When they were dressed, Inge looked them over carefully, turning them each around and inspecting them.

Halvard still watched from the floor, his face sleepy. "When do I get to go fight?"

"Never." Iri half-smiled.

In five years, he'd be old enough. But the young ones only finished off the fallen on the battlefield. It would be ten years before he was allowed on the front line.

Inge held out a folded length of cloth to me, tied with a strand of twine. "Here."

I didn't take it.

Her face twisted, confused. "It's a dress."

"For what?" I looked down at it.

"For *Adalgildi*." Halvard stood, unfolding the length of it to show me. It was a plain black wool dress with long sleeves and a long, full skirt. Little white bone buttons ran up the front torso in a simple, neat line.

I swallowed, shaking my head. "No."

"Well, you can't wear *that*." Inge's eyes dropped down to my tunic, armor vest, and pants. The same clothes I went to battle in.

"I'm not going."

The edge came into her voice. "I didn't ask."

I looked at Iri but he was looking at Fiske.

My stomach dropped, my mouth going dry. I couldn't go to a Riki ceremony. Especially one honoring their warriors. Sigr wouldn't like it.

"She'll offend her god." Iri spoke my thoughts aloud.

"All the *dýrs* go. You'll have to serve. And you can't go into the ritual house like that."

I stepped back. "No."

"Aska." Fiske's booming reproach cut into the room, his eyes fixed on me, and I flinched.

The others, too, were staring. Halvard's mouth hung open. The blood drained from my face.

Fiske had his hands resting on his belt, his chest pulling beneath his fitted tunic. "You're going to the ceremony. You'll serve. You'll wear the dress."

I gritted my teeth, hearing the seething of my soul inside my head. Because I didn't care if a collar hung around my neck. I wasn't their *dýr*.

"And if I don't?" I stared back at him, my nostrils flaring.

The cold, hard set of his eyes bore down on me with his

91

ADRIENNE YOUNG

answer: I'd be punished. By him. And if I wasn't punished for deliberately disobeying, Inge would know something wasn't right. All of the Riki would.

Behind him, Iri was looking at me, his eyes tight. Begging me to obey.

I twisted the dress in my sweaty hands and swallowed hard before I turned for the loft.

Inge watched me climb. "I told you," she whispered. "She's got fire in her blood, Fiske."

I pulled my clothes off, throwing them onto my cot, and stepped into the dress. I hadn't worn one since before the fighting season, when our clan sent off the warriors to battle. I clasped the buttons and tied the waist, cinching the fabric around my body. The neck was wide and open, letting the collar sit completely visible.

I looked down at it with a sneer. At least it was warm.

When I climbed back down the ladder with the length of the skirt gathered in my arms, Iri and Fiske were gone and Runa was rolling the cedar garlands into circles and piling them on top of each other. She smiled at me softly.

"Runa, do something with her hair," Inge said, pushing past me to the loft.

Runa dropped the garlands and came to the table, waiting for me. I glared at her before I sat. When she touched me, the tension shot through my whole body. I closed my eyes, feeling her hands in my hair, pulling at it with hooked fingers to unravel the old, tangled braids. She brushed it out, taking the ends in her hands and pulling the comb through as I stared into the fire.

When she stopped moving, I looked back at her. She was staring at the strip of hair along the right side of my head that was shorn over my ear. "Is that how Aska women wear their hair?" she asked.

I reached up to rub my hand over it out of habit.

She mussed the strands until it was thick and wild on top and then she braided behind my left ear, taking it around the back of my head and then over my right shoulder. She was slow and precise, taking care to braid it correctly with thin, intricate strands. When she was finished, she tied the end and stood back to look at me.

She picked up the jar of *kol* from the table and opened it. "The Aska wear this, don't they?"

I looked from the jar up to her, trying to figure out what she was doing. Why she was being kind. But her face didn't betray her thoughts. She dipped her fingers into the jar and then ran them around my eyes, darkening the skin and then dragging her thumbs down the center of my cheeks in a line. Something about it made the twisting in my muscles let go a little. It felt familiar. I closed my eyes, remembering Mýra in the dark of our tent, painting the *kol* onto my face. And then I opened them, the vision stinging too badly to hold in my mind.

Runa went back to her work on the garlands and I came to stand beside her, taking one into my hands and winding it up the way she had. Halvard shoved the door open, running in and then stopping short, his mouth falling open.

Inge came down the ladder, dressed in a dark purple dress.

"Look at her, Mama." Halvard was still staring at me.

Behind him, Fiske and Iri came through the door and they, too, stopped to look at me, stiffening. I kept my eyes down, working at the garlands and trying to cool the red blooming over my face. Letting them dress me up for their feast was humiliating. And seeing them look at me like they liked it made me want to cut my own hands off.

Inge handed Fiske and Halvard baskets, pushing them out the door. Then she pointed to the others on the table. "Bring them up."

Iri picked up a basket and handed it to me. "You look pretty." The smile on his face made him look like a little boy.

I looked him up and down before my eyes met his, the anger inside of me coming back to life. "You look like a Riki."

FOURTEEN

I STOOD AT THE ENTRANCE OF THE RITUAL HOUSE IN THE falling snow, holding the basket piled high with yarrow. The huge archway was a detailed carving of the mountain, the trees etched into it in slanted patterns and the face of Thora, mouth full of fire. Her wide, piercing eyes stared down at me, her teeth bared. In each outstretched hand, she held the head of a bear.

The walls were constructed of huge tree trunks, much bigger than the trees that surrounded the village. Through the doorway, a blazing fire burned in the center of the chamber and elk antlers holding candlesticks hung down from the ceiling. The heat poured out the door, warming the back of me as clusters of snowflakes clung to my dress. Out in the distance, a storm moved toward Fela, carrying a heavier snowfall within its dark clouds. One that would seal me into the village for the winter.

Another *dýr* held a basket of yarrow on the other side of the archway. Her eyes stayed on the ground, her body perfectly still. She wore a gray wool dress similar to mine, her hair braided back tightly. The collar around her neck was smoothed from years of wear and her blank, empty face said the same thing.

The Riki made their way up the incline in the snow, and my gaze flitted to the forest. A horde of my enemies was moving toward me, weapons strapped to their bodies and I stood there holding a basket of flowers. What was to stop one of them from throwing me on the fire?

My shoulder ached under the weight of the basket, the weak muscles straining under the skin, and I shifted, trying to adjust it to the other side.

They arrived by families, men and women walking with their children or the elderly. The first group stopped before entering, each taking a yarrow bloom into their hands and cupping it gently before them. I tried not to look up into the angry eyes cast down on me, the hatred burning through their stares. But it was quickly followed by something that looked like satisfaction—justice—as their attention fell to the collar around my neck.

They hated me like I hated them. But they'd won. And they knew it.

"Gudrick," a soft voice called from behind us and the man before me looked up, a smile breaking onto his toughened face.

I turned to see an older woman in an amber dress standing behind me, holding a braided reed cage. A white snow owl with large yellow eyes peered out at me from inside. The long strands of wood-beaded necklaces hung around her neck meant that she was the Tala, the clan's interpreter of Thora's will.

The children ran to her, sticking their fingers into the cage, and she ushered them into the warm ritual house. They went inside, one family at a time, and walked down an open aisle to the fire, where they stood together for a silent moment before dropping the yarrow into the flames. The smell of the offerings burning filled the air with a floral, charred scent. It pushed out the doors and wound around me.

Dýrs moved about, refilling my basket when the yarrow was gone and helping to carry things inside for the arriving Riki until the path was clear. The village below looked empty, except for the house across the path from Fiske's, where fire smoke still rose from the roof and light glowed in the window.

Inge appeared and took the basket from my arms, nodding toward the doors. I hesitated, looking up at it again. Going into their ritual house felt like a grave betrayal.

"Aska," Inge prodded me and I followed the other *dýrs* beneath the archway where it was loud and the air was so warm it made my cold skin tingle. The doors closed, creaking on big iron hinges, and the Riki quieted. The men and women found their seats on long benches circling the fire in rows that reached to the back of the chamber and the children flooded to the front, finding space on the ground. I found a place along the back wall with the other *dýrs,* my hand pressing into my throbbing arm. More hard eyes landed on me.

Everyone quieted as the woman in the amber dress stood, raking her fingers through her waist-length golden hair, wild with thick streaks of silver. "Vidr, come."

A large man with a coarse black beard stood and the room followed. He smiled, taking his place beside the Tala with his hand on the hilt of his sword. When the faces of the Riki looked up at him, it was clear he was the village leader.

"Welcome," the man bellowed. "Welcome home." He motioned for them to sit and they obeyed, sinking onto the benches almost in unison.

The Tala handed him the cage and he nodded to her, setting it on the altar before the fire. He lifted the lid, reaching inside with his hand to pull the owl free. As it flapped its wings, the woman set a large wooden bowl and a bronze dagger before her.

She lifted the blade, looking into the face of the owl. "We give thanks to you, Thora, for bringing our warriors home." Her voice rang out over the Riki, finding me in the back.

Vidr held the bird as the Tala placed the tip of the dagger to the owl's breast and carefully pushed it in between the bones. A screech broke the silence as the bird went still and Vidr held its body over the bowl as the blood ran out.

The Riki pounded on their benches, their knuckles knocking against the wood. The sound beat like wings in my chest. When the blood was finished draining, he laid the still bird down on the table and took his seat.

"Welcome to *Adalgildi*." The Tala's voice reverberated in the ritual house. But instead of turning her attention to the men and women on the benches, she sank down onto the stone altar and leaned forward, looking into the faces of the children. They straightened, sitting on their heels and whispering to each other.

"We've gathered together this evening to honor our Riki warriors." She looked out over them, her eyes gleaming with pride. "We burn the yarrow in remembrance of those who did not return home. We give thanks to Thora for their lives and their courage." The sound of fists knocking against wooden benches echoed out again, making the room feel smaller. "To understand the honor deserved, we must remember the story of Thora. We must remember *why* we fight.

"Thora was born of the mountain, in the great eruption that created our home," she began, her hands extending out around her small frame. "She came forth from the flame and ash. From the melted rock, she created her people and placed them on the mountain to dwell. She named them Riki for their strength and power. But peace was short-lived." Her voice lowered. "Sigr, the god of the fjord, saw what Thora had done and his heart was filled with envy. He sent his people up into the mountain to tear down what Thora had built. A bloody rivalry was born and Thora swore eternal revenge on Sigr. She sent the Riki down to the inlets of the great sea to destroy the Aska. Every five years, since that day, we have met them on the battlefield to bring glory to Thora." She clasped her hands in front of her.

It was a different history than the one the Aska told, but the end was the same. Our hatred of the Riki was written onto our bones. Breathed into us by Sigr. What had started as a quarrel between the gods turned into the hunger for revenge—a blood feud. Every five years, we lost those we loved. And we spent the next five years counting the days to the moment we could make the Riki pay for our pain. It was a long-burning fire inside of me.

"Our warriors have brought honor to Thora this fighting season. They have cut down the enemies of our god. The same as you will do one day. All of you." She stood back up, the hem of her skirt floating over the stone. "And Thora is pleased."

Shouting erupted in the chamber, and I pressed myself into the wall, watching from the top of my eyelashes.

"Yes, Thora is pleased and we must now honor the warriors who have brought this great favor to our people. Come."

The children got to their feet, funneling down the aisles and finding their families.

As the floor cleared, the Riki warriors across the ritual house came forward, their families looking up at them, and my eyes found Iri, who stood beside Fiske on the far side of the room. They filled the aisle as the Riki watched them, many with tears in their eyes. *Dýrs* carried the baskets of cedar garlands from the back of the room and set them down at the feet of the Tala. She crouched down, picking one up and holding it out before her in her open hands.

"We honor you, Riki, as you have honored Thora. *Lag mund*." Fate's hand.

The man before her bent low so she could lift the garland over his head and set it onto his shoulders. As he stood, she dipped her finger into the bowl of owl's blood and lifted it to touch the place between his collarbones. He bowed before her, peeled off the line, and returned to his seat, hands touching him as he went. Below his throat, the deep red stroke of blood glistened on his skin.

She repeated the words, looking at the woman next in line and setting the garland onto her shoulders. After the Tala had blessed her with the blood of the sacrifice, Fiske came to the front. She touched his face, speaking to him softly. "We honor you, Riki, as you have honored Thora. *Lag mund*." He looked down at her, coming low so she could set the garland on him, and she painted him where the collar of his tunic opened. Instead of going back to his seat, he stepped aside, letting Iri come forward.

The Tala's smile pulled wider, looking up into Iri's fair face. "We honor you, Riki, as you have honored Thora. *Lag mund*." The sound of it shot around inside of me like a flying blade, cutting deep.

Because Iri wasn't Riki. He was Aska.

He wasn't hers. He was mine.

I held my breath, wringing my hands together in front of me until the skin burned.

I remembered the way my father looked at Iri and me when we held the funeral rites for our mother's soul. I remembered the way his eyes said that we were everything. We were everything until Iri was gone. And then the sun of my father's world grew dimmer again, still rising and setting on me. I'd become both his son and his daughter, carrying his name and honor. It was a heavy mantle, but I was the only one to bear it. And I knew that though he'd never say it, some part of him held me responsible for Iri's death. Because I was.

I was his fighting mate and that made him my responsibility. It was my job to keep him alive. I should have given my life before his could be taken. The guilt haunted the shadows of my every dream. He was there, in every nightmare. I'd gone into the fighting season, ready to avenge my brother. But Sigr was waiting for me in Aurvanger, ready to pour out his wrath upon me. And now I was being punished for my weakness.

I had failed. I knew that the moment Iri went over the edge.

The Tala brushed a strand of hair from his face before he turned back down the aisle. I watched him, the pride spread over his face like sunlight. I brushed a tear from my cheek, and a feeling like a finger dragging over my skin made me blink. I looked up to where the Tala stood, and for a moment, I thought her eyes were on me.

FIFTEEN

THE CEREMONY BROKE AND THE RIKI POURED INTO THE hall at the back of the ritual house like fish spilling from a net. Inge came to get me, positioning me beside a barrel of ale, and leaving me to serve. I kept my eyes down, trying to stay invisible as they lined up in front of me. Whatever pride I'd had within me felt unreachable. I took their cups, filling them and handing them back in a repetitive motion and ignoring the curses on their lips.

Voices filled the room as the Riki sat at long tables before spreads of roasted venison and stew, eating together. Iri sat with Inge, Fiske, and Halvard along the far wall. Runa sat at the other end of the same table with a man and woman who looked to be her parents and three younger children.

"Hello." The Tala stood before me with her cup in her hand, her gaze set heavily upon me. "You're the Aska they brought back from Aurvanger, aren't you?" Her head tilted to the side curiously.

The others stood nearby, listening, and I watched them draw closer, their hands going to their weapons. I stiffened.

"You're very beautiful, even with all of that." She waved a hand at the healing bruises on my face, a smile curling on her lips. "What's your name?"

I shifted from one foot to the other as I took the cup from her hand, not answering. Her eyes studied me as I filled it. When I handed the cup back to her, she stood, unmoving, still watching me.

"Tala." A large round woman came to her side, whispering in her ear, and the Tala nodded, her concentration on me broken and pulled in another direction. She glanced at me one last time before she stepped away. The Riki standing nearby were still staring.

"Aska." Halvard broke through the bodies before me and handed me a cup, smiling wide. "Did you see Fiske and Iri?"

My attention was still on the Riki watching me.

"When I'm old enough to fight, I'll be honored too." He folded his arms up on top of the counter.

I had said those very words to my father. When Iri and I were children, we sat at the entrance to our village and watched the Aska go off to fight. We couldn't wait to join them. We were eleven and twelve when we finally got our wish. In only five years, Halvard would get his.

He took the cup from me and ran off, sloshing the ale as he went. When he reached his table, he climbed up onto the bench beside Fiske and whispered in his ear. Fiske's eyes shifted to meet mine across the room as Halvard handed him the ale. He took a long drink, looking at me over the rim of the cup.

Another *dýr* took my place when Inge asked me to clear the tables and I took an empty basket, filling it with dirty bowls and spoons. I moved carefully through the room, making sure I didn't touch or look at anyone. When I came to clear Iri's table, Fiske was sitting alone with his empty cup, leaning against the wall.

I gathered up the mess, dumping the meat bones into one side of the basket and stacking dishes into the other. Iri stood down the wall beside Runa and I stopped as soon as I saw him, freezing with a bowl clutched in my hands. He stood so close to her that her skirt brushed against him. My widened eyes traveled down and I swallowed down the burn of bile. His hand was dropped by his side, his fingers winding into hers.

I looked down to the table, the sight stinging inside my head like the hot *dýr* collar against my skin. When I looked up again, Runa was laughing and I dropped the bowl into the basket, letting it clatter against the others.

I shoved off the table, stalking across the hall and weaving in and out of the Riki. I burst through the doors and dropped the basket into the snow. The dishes tumbled out onto the ground and I pinched my eyes closed, trying to stay balanced as the world spun around me. The cold air burned in my dry throat, my muscles twitching.

I'd wondered what could break the bond between an Aska and his clansmen and cause him to turn against his people. What could make him leave his own family behind. I'd always thought of Iri as strong. Wise. But my brother was a fool. He'd given us up for a Riki girl. And if Iri could do a thing like that, then what was I doing here? I'd followed him into the forest. I'd gone after him. Risked everything. For this.

He hadn't just become one of them. Iri was *in love* with one of them.

"What are you doing out here?"

A Riki man stood at the entrance of the ritual house, his hand gripped around the handle of his axe. Snowflakes fell, catching in his red beard, and I looked down at the basket toppled over at my feet.

"What are you doing out here, Aska?" he snarled.

I crouched down to pick up the dishes and bones, setting them back into the basket carefully. His boots crunched in the snow, coming toward me. I stood, holding the basket between us. When he took another step, I had to step backward.

He looked down to the buttons on my dress. "Didn't know there was a lady under that armor vest."

I tried to step around him but he moved, blocking me. My eyes landed on the knife at his hip.

"If I'd known, maybe I would have bought you myself." He smiled as his fingers tightened around the axe handle. "Maybe Fiske would take a good price for you."

He dropped his face next to mine and when I felt his hot breath on my skin, I reached, snatching the knife from its sheath and finding his neck with its cold edge. I pressed the tip of the blade beneath his jaw and looked him in the eye, the twitching in my body slowing. It brought me back to the fight that filled me. I listened to the sound of his breath bursting in and out in surprise and pushed the blade a little farther.

The amusement in his eyes was gone, his hands going up and his body stiffening against the knife. Calm flooded into every dark place within me. I wanted to press until the soft skin gave way to the blade. Until I felt the warmth of his blood on my numb skin. I wanted to feel anything but the betrayal of my brother. This is where I belonged. Spilling Riki blood. And Iri was Riki now.

"Aska." My eyes snapped up to see Fiske standing in the archway of the ritual house. His eyes moved from the man to me and back again. He stalked toward us.

The Riki's eyes were boring into me, his breaths still heavy. He clenched his teeth, his face turning red as Fiske reached us. His hand clamped down hard onto my arm, and he wrenched the knife from my grip. He dropped it to the ground before he yanked me toward the trees.

SIXTEEN

I STUMBLED, TRYING TO KEEP UP WITH HIM, BUT HE didn't slow. Fiske's grip on my arm sent a shooting pain into my shoulder, making me dizzy. When we were far enough into the forest that I could no longer see the ritual house, he stopped, releasing me.

"Do you *want* to die? Stay away from the other Riki."

I held my arm to my side, glaring at him. "If you wanted me to stay away from them, why did you make me come here?"

He looked back the way we came, his voice dropping lower. "What was the Tala saying to you?"

I clenched my teeth. "She was admiring what you did to my face. I should have taken off my dress and let her see the rest of your work."

He flinched at the words, moving a step back. "If you

don't start acting like a *dýr*, you're going to keep drawing attention to yourself. To both of us."

"What do you mean *act* like a *dýr*?" I picked up the collar around my neck and let it drop back down against my skin. "I *am* a *dýr*. I won't pretend to like it. If you want to punish me so I don't embarrass you, you can drag me back to the ritual house by my hair and beat me to death. I'm sure your clansmen would enjoy it. It would be a better end for me than knowing I'd spent the entire winter shining a Riki's armor of my clansmen's blood because my brother is a fool," I whispered hoarsely, my chest rising and falling beneath the fit of the dress.

He glared at me, his pulse moving at his neck where the stroke of ritual blood was dried on his skin. The blue of his eyes glinted in the faint light. "You want to go?" He launched me toward the trees. "Go!"

I turned in a circle, nothing but snow-covered trees as far as I could see.

The building fury in the center of my chest exploded and I shoved into his chest with my fists. He didn't budge. I hit him again, harder, and he snatched my wrists up with both hands, holding me before him as I tried to wrench free.

"I shouldn't have listened to Iri," he muttered. "His concern for you is going to get him killed."

"So be it. He's betrayed me and dishonored the Aska. He deserves to die." I spat.

His face changed, a flash of darkness igniting in his eyes.

His fingers tightened around my wrist as he pushed me back, pinning me to a tree. His axe slid from its sheath smoothly before the cold blade pressed to my throat.

"Threaten my family again and I will kill you," he breathed. "I'll kill you and then I'll wait for the thaw. I'll go down to the fjord and kill your father while he sleeps."

My eyes widened, my mouth dropping open. I looked into his face, trying to measure the hatred there. But it was something else. Something more ferocious than hate.

It was love. For Iri.

"Iri would never forgive you," I grunted.

"I care more about keeping him alive than I do his forgiveness. I will leave you dead in this forest and tell Iri you ran." He drifted closer.

"Then do it." I leaned into the blade, meeting his eyes as a sob broke from the words. And for a moment, I thought he would. I almost wished for an end to the cracking, crumbling ache in my chest.

I lifted my chin defiantly, as more tears fell down my cheeks. I wouldn't beg for my life. But in the next breath, his eyes lost their blaze, traveling over my face. I held his stare, not moving as he leaned in closer to me. His breath brushed across my skin, making me shudder. I didn't blink.

"I don't have to." The blade lifted from my throat suddenly, and he stepped back. "You'll find your own end before the snow melts because your pride and your anger are more important to you than your own survival."

I drew back, the words stinging. Because they were true.

More true than I wanted to admit. "I'll be gone before the thaw."

"Good." He looked at me a long moment, his brows pulling together before he turned, leaving me. The axe was still clutched in his fist as I watched him trudge up the hill in the deep snow to where the smoke of the ritual house was rising above the treetops.

I caught my breath, trying to slow the tears before I followed, stepping into Fiske's footprints until I was standing before the ritual house doors. Thora looked down on me, her eyes hungry.

I went inside with the basket of broken dishes on my hip and made my way to the stone trough where the other *dýrs* were working. The bowls tumbled into the water and the slave standing beside me looked up. She moved away, watching around us warily.

Across the room, Fiske sat beside Iri at the table with Runa. The Tala was standing over her, her fingers combing through Runa's hair. By the fire, the red-bearded man stood beneath the hanging antlers and watched me. His fingers were pressed to the trickle of blood trailing down his neck from his beard.

I turned away from them, plunging my hands down into the hot water and scrubbing. Fiske was right. I wouldn't last in this village the whole winter. I couldn't wait for the thaw. I had to find a way home.

SEVENTEEN

Inge left before dawn to gather garlic and sage in the forest, leaving me to make breakfast for the others on my own. Halvard insisted on helping, waking almost as soon as I did and making it impossible to search the house for weapons.

"Will you show me now?" He stood close to me, holding out the fire-steel.

I looked past him, to where a bowl of blackberries sat on top of a cabinet.

He followed my gaze, laughing when he realized what I wanted. He retrieved the bowl and set it down before me. "Please?"

I picked up one of the berries and popped it in my mouth. "Like this." I gathered the kindling into a pile at the side of the pit.

He watched carefully, perched on the stone beside me. "I've never met an Aska before."

I picked up the fire-steel and lifted it up to strike.

"Iri says you live on the fjord."

The fire-steel slipped, and I scraped my knuckles on the stone.

He fetched it from the floor and handed it back to me. "I've never seen the sea."

I struck it again, this time catching a spark. Halvard cupped his hands around the kindling to protect it from the cold air. Once it was burning, he picked it up and moved it to the stack of wood and I went to the pot. I ate the berries as he tried on his own.

"My father said the Aska hang seashells over their doors." He struck the fire-steel against the stone.

I stopped stirring, looking up to him.

"Why do they do that?" The third time, the kindling caught and he looked up at me, pleased with himself. He climbed up onto the table and sat cross-legged, watching me stir.

I stared into the pot. "They catch the wind, making music."

His eyes twinkled as he tried to imagine it.

The sound of blades clanging together rang outside where Iri and Fiske were running through fighting maneuvers as the sun came up. Their grunting and labored breath found us through the open window.

If I were home, Mýra and I would be doing the same, keeping up our strength and skill until the next fighting season or whatever threat may come against Hylli. We spent our mornings on the fishing boats and our afternoons on the hillside running drills. By the time the snow began to melt and I got out of Fela, I would probably be too weak to even swing my sword. I'd always been a skilled fighter even if I was smaller than many Aska warriors. When I got back to the fjord, I would have to start over.

When Iri came back inside, he was alone. He came to the fire and helped cook, turning the grains over on the stone. He watched Halvard and me talking, smiling at the corner of his mouth.

"Do all the Aska look like you and Iri?" Halvard looked between us.

I turned my back to Iri. "Some. We all look different, like the Riki do."

"Then how do you tell your people from our people when you're fighting?"

"Sometimes, you can't." I shot Iri a look, hoping he understood my meaning.

And he did. He looked back at me, his face hardening. "The Aska armor is a red leather with bronze metal. The Riki use brown leather and iron," he answered.

Halvard slid down from the table and took the spoon from me to push the fish around in the pot that hung over the fire. "I promise not to kill you if I ever see you in battle." He stopped stirring and looked up at me.

I stared at him, unable to help the smile pushing onto my lips. I tried to picture him on the battlefield and then wondered how long Halvard would live. In five years, he'd be old enough for the fighting season. But there was something soft about him. Something that wouldn't hold up well in a fight. I wondered what I would do if I saw him there, on the other side.

The smile melted off my face and I swallowed.

I set the bowls on the table, taking my own and retreating to the stool in the corner. Iri picked up the fourth bowl, pouring it back into the pot. "Fiske isn't here."

"Where did he go?" Halvard looked disappointed.

Iri bent over his bowl to scoop a large bite into his mouth. "Checking the nets."

My fingers tightened around my spoon, my heart skipping a beat. If Fiske was checking nets, there had to be a river nearby. And rivers ran down the mountain. Into the valley and on to the sea. If I could find the river, I could find home.

Inge came through the door and dropped a large crate on the floor before she went back outside. "Iri, I need you to help Kerling inside."

He stood, going through the door and walking down the path to where a man with a long blond beard stood beside a pregnant woman. I realized she must have been the woman they spoke of, Gyda. His arm was draped over her shoulder and she leaned into him, keeping him balanced. Iri met them on the path, taking the man's other arm, and they hobbled up to the door slowly.

"It's good you're out!" Inge smiled, standing to the side so that Iri and Kerling could get inside.

Kerling kept his eyes to the floor, his face twisted up in pain and sweat beading at his hairline. One pant leg was tied up to the knee, where the lower half of his leg was missing. I'd seen it before. Probably an axe or a fall that crushed the bones. It could have even been an infection.

The woman came through the door and stood behind Kerling. When her hands fell on his shoulders, he shrugged her off, scooting to the edge of the bench and lifting his amputated leg up to rest on the seat. Inge sat beside him, slowly untying the pant leg, and she pushed it back to reveal red, swollen skin, puckered together in zigzagging rows of stitching.

"Compress, Iri." She leaned in closer to inspect the wound as Iri got to work, pulling the kettle from the fire and opening a large wooden box of herbs on the shelf.

"How are you feeling?" She looked up into Kerling's face.

He met her eyes, gripping the sides of his leg with his fists. "Like half a man."

Inge looked up to Gyda, whose face was cast to the floor. "I don't know how you survived that wound. Thora has favored you."

Kerling stared into the fire. "Or cursed me."

Iri pulled the cloth from the bowl of steaming water, looking at Kerling. Beside him, Gyda looked at me. Her furious eyes were filled with tears, her teeth set on edge. I took the unfolded cloths from the other end of the table and sat beside the fire, folding them one at a time and setting them into my lap with Gyda's stare still burning into me.

Iri dressed Kerling's leg in a fresh bandage and helped him outside. When they were through the door, Inge put her hands on Gyda's belly, pressing gently. "It will be soon."

Gyda didn't answer, but her face fell, the corners of her mouth turning down.

"I'll be with you. There's nothing to be afraid of." Inge smiled.

But that wasn't true and if I knew it, then Gyda knew it too. A woman was as likely to die in childbirth as she was to die in battle. And Gyda looked as if she'd seen a fight before.

"He doesn't want the baby anymore," she whispered.

Inge sighed. "Why do you think that?"

Gyda's hands went to the curve beneath her belly. "He doesn't want anything anymore."

Inge looked outside, to where Kerling and Iri were making their way back to the house across the path. Before she could speak, Gyda turned and left, following after them.

Inge stood at the door, watching her. The strain in her eyes reached down to the straight line of her mouth. Her fingers were coiled around each other. I'd seen it happen before in Hylli, the wounded losing their will to live. She probably had too.

Inge cleared her throat. "Have you crushed garlic before?" She rolled up the sleeves of her dress and closed the door.

"A little," I answered. "For cooking." I watched her pull

an entire crate full of the little white bulbs from the shelf on the wall.

She set a large stone pestle and mortar on the table in front of me. "We'll peel and crush them. Then we'll bottle it all." When she placed an iron knife on the table, my hand twitched at my side. "I'll peel it, you crush it." She smirked. She knew better than to give me a knife. "How many years are you, Eelyn?"

I tried to read her, but her eyes were on her work. It was the first time she'd said my name. I didn't like it. "Seventeen."

"Do you have family in Hylli? That's where you're from, right? Hylli?"

I nodded, studying her. How did she know where I was from? I know Iri didn't tell her. "Only my father."

She was quiet for a few minutes and when the sharp, acrid smell of the garlic began to fill the house, she stood and went to the door, propping it back open to let the air in.

"Did you know that Iri is Aska?" she asked, sitting back down.

I picked up a handful of the garlic cloves and set it into the pestle, trying to hear what she wasn't saying. What was carefully buried beneath the words.

"He and Fiske nearly killed each other five years ago."

My eyes snapped up from the table.

"It was the last fighting season. They were fighting and fell over the edge of a deep trench."

I swallowed, blinking.

"Fiske broke a leg and an arm and Iri's side was cut open from the blade of Fiske's sword. My husband searched for Fiske for two days before he finally found him. He thought he was dead." She sucked in a breath. "But he wanted to burn his body. So, he scaled down the wall of the trench and, when he reached him, he saw that Fiske was alive." Her eyes lifted to mine. "So was the boy he'd been fighting. Just barely. And Fiske wouldn't leave Iri behind. He begged his father to save his life." She wiped a tear from the corner of her eye. "Iri was so badly wounded that no one thought he would live."

I tried to clear my eyes of the burn that was gathering there. "How did you save him?"

She set the knife down onto the table and looked at me. "They brought him in, and the cut was so deep that his organs were coming through the opening of the wound. I was sure he would die. But then he didn't. Somehow, the skin and the muscle were cut but his organs and arteries remained intact. I stitched him up and it took a long time, but he healed. And as he healed, Fiske healed."

"So, why isn't he a *dýr*?" I asked. The sharp words crossed the table between us.

She paused again. "He was going to be. But he was so injured that we had to keep him here, in our home, and care for him day and night. And I'm not sure how it happened, but he became a part of our family. Fiske's love for Iri became ours." Her eyes shined again.

"So Iri is Riki now?"

She nodded. "He is. Iri left his past behind. It took time, but the Riki accepted him. The gods are funny that way."

I narrowed my eyes at her. "What do you mean?"

"I mean, sometimes they make families in peculiar ways." She stood, pulling more garlic from the crate. "*Fjotra*," she said, under her breath.

"*Fjotra* is the blood bond. They aren't brothers," I corrected her.

"That's *munstrǫnd fjotra*. *Sál fjotra* is a bond between souls."

I stared at her.

"This kind of bond is formed when a soul is broken. It's formed through pain, loss, and heartbreak. They're bound by something deeper than we can see. And that made Iri family."

I stopped trying to hold back the tears that were waiting to fall. Because I knew exactly what she was talking about. It was what I had with Mýra. A tether born of tears.

Iri and Inge didn't share blood, but Iri looked at Inge as if she were his mother. She felt like he was her son. And I didn't need to ask her how she'd been able to love him. Iri was pure of heart in a way that I had never been. And he was brave. Not afraid to love or give of himself. People had always been drawn to him and I had been proud to be his sister. For the same reasons that Inge loved him.

A shadow came through the door and I looked up to see Runa coming in with a cloak pulled up over her head. She looked at me a little warily as she set a small bundle of wood onto the table. I recognized it immediately—sacred wood. My hands stilled on the mortar before I dropped my eyes back down to the garlic, remembering the way she touched Iri at *Adalgildi*. The way she looked up into his face, her cheeks pink and her eyes warm.

She took a basket of sage from the table and washed the branches in a bowl of water. When she was through, she dried them with a cloth carefully and tied bunches of them together, hanging them on the wall beside the fire.

"What's all of this for?" I asked.

"Healing," Runa answered. "The garlic is for illness, wounds—that sort of thing. The sage is used for skin, teeth, stomach . . ."

"And those?" I nodded to the bundle of raspberry vines. All the berries were gone.

"They're for Gyda. We'll use it when the baby comes." She tightened the twine on another bundle of sage and hung it. "Do you have a healer in Hylli?"

I nodded, not meeting her eyes.

"I've been apprenticing with Inge for almost four years."

"She's ready to be on her own." Inge smiled proudly.

Runa blushed. When she turned toward the fire, I reached up slowly to take a piece of the sacred wood from the table.

"We need more jars." Inge sighed.

I dropped my hand back into my lap.

"I'll be right back."

I went back to grinding the garlic, still keeping my arm pulled into my side so I didn't have to use the joint.

"So, you and Iri are . . ." I wasn't sure what word to use.

"Yes." But the sweetness was missing from her voice. She was ready to defend herself.

"And that's why he . . ."

"Maybe it was part of it. I don't know."

I leaned onto the table, looking at her. "Then why aren't you married?"

"We will be. My father wanted to wait until he was back from Aurvanger." Her voice changed, the words finding a softer tone. "He was going to tell you."

I went back to work. I didn't want to know what Iri planned to do. He'd left. He'd taken a new family, and he didn't owe me anything anymore.

EIGHTEEN

A PIECE OF SACRED WOOD AND A SMALL, DULL CARVING tool sat together beside my bed the next morning. Inge must have seen me try to take it and put them there. It wasn't the first time I realized that she saw more than she seemed to.

I sat beside the garden with my legs crossed, watching thin curling strips of wood peel up off the crude block as I dragged the carving tool over it. The shavings fell down onto the ground in front of me, scattered on top of the snow. Fiske stood with Halvard on the side of the house, watching him practice his axe throw. He'd kept to himself since *Adalgildi*, tending to his duties in a manner that I was beginning to recognize as his. He hung in the shadows, like he wasn't really there, save for the presence that followed him. It was thick and heavy, silent but alive. And it seemed to be everywhere. All the time.

Fiske stood back, watching Halvard closely as he stepped

forward, letting the axe in his hand sink down behind his head and then snapping his arm forward and letting it fly.

It hit the trunk of a pine tree with a loud pop. The sound was so familiar that it tugged at the tangled knot of memories inside of me. I bit down on my lip, watching him as he repeated the throw over and over, Fiske quietly instructing him until he moved to the other hand. I could tell by the way he gripped it that it wasn't as strong.

Halvard sighed, hanging his head back as the axe's handle hit the tree with a ping, falling to the ground.

"Again," Fiske ordered, walking out to the tree and retrieving it.

Again.

Iri's voice echoed in my mind.

Again, Eelyn.

Halvard shook out his arms before he lifted it again, but he didn't argue. His elbow sunk forward, sending the axe out. It missed, this time the blade hitting at an angle and sliding to the left.

Fiske walked back to him with the axe in his hand, his eyes looking over my head to something behind me. I turned to see Gyda standing across the path. Her long black hair was braided over each shoulder, the ends trailing down to where her hands wrapped around her swollen belly. She stared at me, her eyes narrowing with the same hatred they'd held the day before.

I brushed the wood shavings from my lap, taking the

hooked metal over the top of the wood to round it out. The idol my father had of my mother was so worn that the wood had turned a dark, slick gray. He held it in his calloused hands every night, whispering prayers for my mother's soul, and I'd do the same for Iri. Then we'd switch, kneeling in the fire-lit dark of our home on the fjord. I lifted the wood to my nose and breathed in the crisp, raw scent of it. I'd always believed my mother's soul made it to *Sólbjǫrg*. That she and Iri were together there.

Fiske made Halvard throw the axe until he hit his mark three times in a row and when he finally dismissed him, Halvard ran to me, sliding on the snow and landing on the ground beside me. His knees touched mine as he leaned forward, inspecting the idol.

"Is it your brother? The one who died?" His thick eyelashes flickered as he looked up at me. His eyes were as blue as Fiske's, but different. Dark. Like a storm.

"My mother." I handed it to him and watched him turn it over in his hands gently.

He smiled.

"What?"

He shrugged, handing it back to me. "I like it."

"Don't you have one for your father?"

He shook his head, pulling his mouth to the side of his face.

"Why not?"

"It's not our way," Fiske interrupted, coming to stand over us.

My eyes dropped back down to the half-finished idol. I had the head and shoulders done but the rest was still just a block of wood. Halvard reached into his vest and pulled something into his hand. When he opened it, a round, flat stone sat in the center of his palm. It was etched with words I couldn't read, the same as the one I'd seen Iri tuck into his vest before *Adalgildi*.

"What does it say?"

"*Ala sál*. Soul bearer," he said, proudly. "It's my *taufr*."

I picked it up and turned it over in my hand. "What is it?"

"It protects me."

"How?"

"You give it to someone you want to protect. It tells the gods that you bear another's soul. My mother made it for me."

Fiske's shadow slipped over me as he headed toward the house. He took the net from where it hung on an iron hook. He was going to the river.

"I—" It slipped out just as he stepped onto the path and I clamped my mouth closed, clenching my fist around the idol in my hand.

But he was already looking at me, turned with the net swinging beside his leg. "What is it?" The words were missing the anger they usually held.

I bit my lip again. "I can help you with the fish."

He looked surprised and for a moment, I thought maybe he could see through me. That maybe he knew what I was up to. His weight shifted back and he looked at the ground before his gaze rose to the trees. His hands twisted in the net. "Alright."

Halvard groaned, falling back from where he sat and landing backward in the snow with his arms out wide around him.

"Come with us." I stood up off the ground and tucked the idol into my vest.

"I have to stay for Gyda. In case she has the baby." His eyes moved to her house, but she was gone.

I gave his leg a soft kick with my boot and when he looked at me, I grinned. I pulled the hood up on my cloak and followed after Fiske, trying to catch up to him.

He didn't slow for me. I shortened my strides as I reached him, staying on his heels as the path pulled up out of the village and the trees multiplied. The pines were so tall that I couldn't see the tops. They moved in the wind, the branches of each tree bleeding into one another as the trunks creaked. I kept my eyes up instead of down, tracing the shape of the trees and marking a path in my mind that I would recognize even in deep snow.

The path snaked through the forest until I could hear the river. We came up over the ridge to see it carved into the ground like a vein under the skin. It rushed past, the spray of it rising up into the air around us, and I let my hood fall back, studying it. It wound down the slope, crossing in front of us and disappearing. The water had to make it to the sea eventually. If I followed it, it would take me down the mountain and into the valley.

"It's not the way down," Fiske said beside me and my eyes snapped up. "Try if you want to, but you won't make it."

I looked back to the water. He had to be lying. The river had to lead down the mountain.

He walked down the bank until he reached two large flat stones in the water and he made his way across. I picked up my cloak and stepped carefully as the water roared past. When I made it to the second stone, he reached for me and I took his hand as I jumped, landing in the deeper snow on the other side.

We walked farther down to where a large wooden post was buried in the ground with a length of rope tied around it and disappearing into the frozen surface of the water. He pulled his axe free and broke up the ice, then crouched down and untied it, his fingers prying the wet rope from the knot.

We used nets in the fjord all the time, but never like this. It was standing up on its side, tied across the width of the river like a hide stretched in the sun. "It's a net?"

"Yes." He grunted, freeing the rope and winding it tightly around his hand as he lifted it slowly against the weight of the current. His face tensed, the muscles in his neck pulling and his shoulders tightening as he hoisted it up, but it was caught. The bottom of the rope was snagged on the branches of a fallen tree.

"It's stuck."

He looked down, still holding the net against the rush of the water. "Can you reach it?"

I unclasped my cloak, tossing it onto the snow, and came

around his legs to squat down between him and the trunk of the tree disappearing under the surface.

I took a deep breath and plunged my arm in, following the rope down so far that the water came up to my shoulder. I found the end and yanked at it, gritting my teeth.

The rope went slack and Fiske shifted his weight until the net full of silver fish rose up out of the water. I took the other end of the net and we pulled it onto the bank, setting the fish into the snow.

They laid on their sides, wide eyes looking up at me and mouths gulping air as Fiske got down onto his knees to replace the net with the one we'd brought with us.

"It means fish."

He looked up at me, his brow furrowing as he stood.

"Your name. It means fish, doesn't it?"

A sharp snap sounded behind us and I turned, my heart coming up into my throat as I stepped back, toward the water. In the trees ahead, an enormous brown bear stood on his hind legs, looking at us. My hand found Fiske's arm and clamped down hard onto it, my fingernails digging into his tunic. He looked over his shoulder and dropped the ends of the net, sending the fish sliding over the snow.

The hollow pump of the bear's breaths echoed, sending white puffs fogging the air around his snout. He came down onto his front feet and took a step toward us, his nose in the air. Fiske's whole body went rigid, his eyes lighting up with something I knew well. It was the same thing pulsing through every inch of my body—death coming close. Whispering in my ear. I'd known that feeling since I was a child, watching the Herja slither out of the forest toward Hylli.

Fiske's hand wrapped around my arm and pulled at me slowly as the bear moved closer. "Don't run." He said it so softly I barely heard him over the sound of my heartbeat in my ears.

There was nowhere to run anyway. The ice-crusted river ran behind us and the bear stood before us, coming closer. Fiske moved me behind him and my heels sank into the water as he shifted in front of me. I leaned to the side to look around him and held my breath. The bear was so close to us that Fiske could reach out and touch him. The sunlight turned his brown fur golden at the tips and it fanned out around his heart-shaped face, his shining nose wet at the end of his snout. He leaned in, sniffing Fiske's chest, and I tightened my grip on his armor vest, my fingertips numb against the woven leather. I peered over his shoulder and my heart stopped altogether.

Because the bear's eyes were set on me. Wide and deep and open. Looking right at me.

He stepped closer, nosing around Fiske. I gulped down a breath as the bear stilled, his huge paws sunken into the snow and Fiske's back pressed into me. I set my mouth against the back of his shoulder and stared back at the creature. It was as if he was going to speak. As if he had something to tell me. His black eyes glistened, boring into mine, and the chill of it ran down my spine, tingling in my fingertips.

Without warning, he dipped his head down, took a fish

into his mouth and turned. He didn't look back as he walked, the colors of his thick hide shifting in the light.

Fiske relaxed against me but I still held onto him, feeling like I might fall over. Like the tremors in my legs would send me through the ice. We waited for the bear to get out of sight before we moved. Before we breathed. When Fiske finally let go of my arm, he turned, looking down at me. He stilled, his lips parting as he took a step back, a question in his eyes.

The fish flicked their tails on the ground between us and when I looked back down the bank, the forest was empty. Nothing but tracks were left, winding a trail through the trees.

NINETEEN

In my mind, I traced the path through the forest to the river.

I sat in the corner and ate, looking at the wall.

I kept to myself.

I went about the chores without instruction from Inge.

I obeyed. Like a *dýr*.

Iri stayed close to me, rarely leaving the house, and I continued to ignore him. When he and Inge spoke about the betrothal, I went to feed the goats. When he offered to help me carry in the firewood, I pushed past him, carrying it on my own.

I dropped to my knees in the garden on the side of the house, working the soil with a small spade and tearing out the dead roots of autumn still trapped beneath the earth. The cold, rocky ground broke beneath my blows and I raked out the garden's remnants, one plant at a time. Soon, it would be time to sow again. My father would be doing the same, turning manure into our garden and getting it ready for turnips and carrots. I sat up onto my heels, rubbing the place between my eyes with my thumb and looking up to the smear of white clouds stretching across the blue. It seemed impossible that it was the same sky that hung over the fjord. Home felt an entire world away. But it was only snow and ice between me and Hylli.

Across the path, Gyda was hanging clothes over the fence that bordered their garden. On the other side of the house Kerling sat on a tree stump, one hand on his knee, above the missing leg. His pale face turned up toward the sky and the light caught the blond in his beard, making the hairs shine like threads of gold. He'd been sitting there all morning, staring out at the trees. It wasn't until that moment, seeing him with his eyes closed and the sun on his face, that I remembered him from the journey back up the mountain from Aurvanger. He was one of the men lying in the back of the cart.

Iri's shadow fell over the broken ground as he came to stand over me.

"Is he your friend?" I asked, still looking at Kerling.

Iri followed my gaze across the path. "He is." When I didn't look up, he lowered down onto his haunches and waited, folding his hands together. "Eelyn."

I brought the spade down with both hands and its edge cracked against a buried rock.

"Look at me."

When the rock was pried free, I tossed it to the side, almost hitting him.

"I know you're angry."

But I wasn't angry. I was aflame with fury. I was filled with something so dark it was poisoning me from the inside out. I lifted the spade again, pointing it at him. "How could you do it? How could you be here all this time living a new life with a new *family*?"

He looked down at the ground between us. "I can't explain—"

"I know about Fiske," I snapped. "I know he was there that day. That he went over the edge with you."

He looked around us warily. If there was anyone nearby, they would have heard me. But I didn't care.

"Tell me what happened." The tears came back up and it made me even angrier. Because as much as I wanted to, I couldn't pretend that I wasn't hurt. I couldn't hide that I was cut deep with what he'd done.

He sank onto his knees beside me, taking the spade, and started digging. "That day, I got separated from you in the fight. Fiske came out of the trees behind me and opened up my side with the first swing of his sword. You were fighting in the distance. I could barely see you in the fog."

I stared at the ground, remembering the shine of his blood and the smooth pearly skin where the scar stretched around one entire side of his body.

"I dropped my axe and stumbled forward, trying to hold the wound together. Before I knew it, I was going over the edge. I reached out and caught Fiske's armor vest and pulled him over with me. I remember hearing you scream. But I couldn't move. I couldn't make a sound." He pried another rock from the earth. "When I woke, Fiske was trying to climb the wall with one arm and one leg. He used his knife, fitting it into the cracks of the rock to lift himself, and every time, he fell. He thought I was dead. So did I. I could *feel* my soul dying. I remember it. I remember every thought that came into my head and every feeling. When night came and I finally closed my eyes, I thought it was the end." He stopped, staring into the dirt. "But it wasn't. I woke again and it was morning. I thought I was dreaming. Or maybe that I'd made it to *Sólbjǫrg*. But Fiske was kneeling beside me, packing snow against my wound." He sniffed, wiping his eyes with the back of his arm. "He looked down at me. His face was pale, his eyes red and swollen. He said, 'We're not going to die, Aska.'"

I stared at him.

"For two days, he kept me alive. His father found us, and when he called down from the ridge, he swore to me that he wouldn't leave me behind. And he didn't. When they pulled us out of that trench, we were brothers. Sigr abandoned me that day, Eelyn. Thora saved my life. I was reborn. I came here to Fela and I didn't know it for a long time, but I was becoming one of them. Inge became my mother. I fell in love with Runa. Thora honored me. She gave me favor."

And though I couldn't imagine it, maybe I did know what he was saying because I could see it. He'd found a place here and he fit.

"You still have Aska blood in your veins. You still belong to *my* family."

"I will always be your brother. I was born Aska. But I'm something else now."

"You're either Riki or Aska, Iri. You can't be both. You told Runa who I am."

He didn't meet my eyes. "Yes."

"How long until she tells someone and they come to kill us both?"

"She would never do that."

"Well, I'm not going to stay long enough to find out. I'm going home. With or without you. I'm not going to wait for the thaw."

He raked a hand through his hair. "Then you'll die."

"*Vegr yfir fjor,* Iri. Honor above life." My voice turned weak. "Didn't you think about me?"

"I've thought of you every day." He watched as I wiped the tears from my face. "Fiske's father gave me a choice to be traded back to the Aska, Eelyn."

"*What?*" I could feel the words prying my mind open.

"I couldn't go. I couldn't leave this place." He reached to take my hand. "The path of my soul has taken a turn, just as yours has."

"This is *not* the same." I glowered at him. "I want to go home."

"I know. But you will never be the same. You will never be the same person you were." He paused. "You are seeing the truth. I see you thinking it, every day."

"What truth?"

"That they're like us."

I put my face into my hands, trying to escape what he was saying. Because it made me feel like the world was turned sideways. Like everything I'd ever been taught didn't fit into the shape of this world.

"What are you thinking now?"

The weight of it fell from my head, down into the rest of my body. The words were small but they were true. "I'm thinking that I wish you'd died that day."

TWENTY

FISKE DIDN'T RETURN UNTIL DARK. HE CAME THROUGH the door with Iri, carrying a basket full of cleaned fish and keeping his eyes off of me. He hadn't looked in my direction since we went to the river and for some reason, he hadn't told the others what happened.

Iri, too, had turned cold. I could see the anger wound tight around him. But I meant what I'd said. More than I wished I did.

Inge took the basket from Fiske and nodded toward me. "I need you to take the stitches out of Eelyn's arm." She filled another basket with the jars of garlic we'd made. "We have to get these to the cellar and then we're going to Runa's."

Fiske's tight gaze was fixed on Inge.

"You've done it a hundred times. We start on the barn at dawn." She brushed past him and Iri and Halvard followed her outside.

I stood against the wall, looking at Fiske as the door swung shut. He pulled his scabbard up over his head and laid it down beside the fire. I didn't like being alone with him. I wished Halvard had stayed.

"Kerling's barn?" I asked.

He nodded. "He set the posts for the frame before we left for the fighting season. They'll need it finished so they can buy goats before the baby comes." He sounded tired, the words riding on a deep breath. "If you sit, I'll take them out."

He walked to a wooden box on the shelf and lifted the lid, fishing out a small metal tool, and I sat down close enough to the fire to keep warm. Every day was colder than the last and my clothes weren't made like the Rikis'.

He sat down in front of me, straddling the bench and scooting closer. I pulled my arm from the sleeve and into my tunic, but when I tried to lift it up out of the neck, I couldn't. The muscles around the bone were still too weak and it was too painful to lift that high. He caught my fingers and I flinched, leaning away from him. He let me pull against his hand until the arm was free and I let go, the sting of him still hot against my skin.

I turned to the side so he could reach the stitches. I wanted to remind him it was his sword that had cut into me in the first place, but I stared into the fire instead. I didn't want to look at him. I didn't want to feel him touch me. He picked up the tool and pressed his fingers against my skin before he slid it under the first stitch and carefully pulled against it until it broke.

"It was you. That day," I said. "It was you in the trench with Iri. Inge told me."

He broke the next stitch and I winced. "Yes."

"Where is your father now?"

His hand dropped down to his leg and he looked at me. "He's in *Friðr*."

I knew the word and what it meant. Peace. It was where the Riki went when they died.

"He died last year of fever." And though his voice didn't change, something in the set of his mouth did. Something behind the eyes.

"Why did you do it?" I asked. "Why did you save Iri's life?"

He sat up straighter, letting the silence between us stretch out and pull like the thoughts in my mind, trying to find a place to land. "Because we were dying. Because it was the end. And at the end, life becomes precious."

He looked at me for a long moment, his eyes running over my face, and I could feel it—his gaze dragging over my skin. Like he could see Iri there. Or something else. The red stung beneath my cheeks.

He pulled the last stitch free. "Iri . . ." But then he stopped.

I pulled my braid down around the front of my shoulder. "What?"

"Iri never planned to stay here," he finished. "Not in the beginning."

"I know." I twisted the ends of my hair around my fingers. "But he did."

He helped me work my arm back into my tunic. I shivered, suddenly cold.

"I don't belong to you," I told him.

"No, you don't." He looked at the floor. "But you aren't going to make it through the winter without me."

"I told you. I'm not staying." I met his eyes again and this time, I didn't look away. I waited to see something I hated. Some trace of the man I'd tried to kill in Aurvanger. But I couldn't see past the soul who had saved Iri's life. The soul who had packed snow against his wound and wouldn't leave him behind.

"We should uncover that." He looked at the bandage over the burn on my neck.

I reached up, touching it.

He pulled it back slowly and the cold air on the skin tingled.

"Does it hurt?" He leaned closer.

My stomach dropped, pulling my heart down with it, and the pulse in my veins beat unevenly. He was too close to me.

I stood, the bench scraping on the stone beneath us. He looked up at me, and I tried to find something to say. But there was too much. It was all buried too deep. I couldn't reach it.

"Everything hurts," I whispered.

I climbed the ladder and went to my cot, tears filling my eyes until I could barely see. I wanted to go home. I wanted to hear my father's voice and see the fjord. I wanted to erase the scars lifting on my skin below the collar and go back to that moment I saw Fiske on the battlefield. I wanted to tell myself to run.

I sat down on the cot, curling up on my side and tried to stay quiet as I wept. But the thing writhing inside me was too angry to be calmed. It was too hurt to be hushed. It was a living, breathing thing and it was trying to swallow me whole. And maybe it would. I cried until I couldn't cry anymore and only the sound of the fire remained.

Below, Fiske's shadow reached up the wall from where he sat by the fire in the empty house. Listening to me cry myself to sleep.

TWENTY-ONE

Dawn fell on the village as Fiske was returning from the river. Halvard pulled a chest of tools from the wall and opened it, laying them out next to each other on a stretch of hide. Once Fiske had checked them, Halvard rolled them up over his shoulder, walking lopsided against its weight. He swung the door open and I could see the Riki were already gathering across the path, greeting each other in the morning cold.

Inge handed me the basket full of fish, still chilled from the river's water. "They're cleaned. When the sun is overhead, you can cook them and bring them over."

I bristled, my eyes drifting back to Kerling's house where the number of clansmen was multiplying.

Inge, Fiske, and Iri followed Halvard out the door. The Riki were already getting to work, their furs pulled tight around them. Children ran down the path, chasing the chickens, and

I leaned into the wall, watching them through the window. The men hauled giant logs in from the forest and the women settled onto the ground planing them. They bent low over the fallen trees, scraping at the raw wood in long, even strokes.

I cleaned out the iron pot on the fire and shoveled the ashes from the pit, listening to them. When the deep-throated laughs of a few men echoed out into the village, my hands stilled on the hard edge of the table and my heart twisted. It was all too familiar. Too much like home.

I went around the back of the house where I couldn't be seen and washed the clothes Inge had piled in a basket. My hands turned pink in the cold water, my knuckles stiff as I raked them over the washboard. I'd be doing the same thing if I was home. Fishing with my father or doing chores with Mýra. I wondered what she was doing now. I wondered if she was training with a new fighting mate.

Winter was my favorite time of year on the fjord, when everything was dusted in a sparkling crust of ice. Each blade of grass glistened in the sunlight. It was what I'd always imagined Sólbjǫrg to be like. I'd pictured my mother there, sitting on a hillside with her skirt spread out around her, almost every night.

I hung the clothes on the railing of the fence, smoothing out the fabric as it flapped in the wind. When I came around the house again, the Riki already had planks going up along one of the walls of the barn. The structure extended off of the house, just big enough for ten or fifteen goats. If they were diligent, Kerling and Gyda could get by trading on what they grew in their garden patch and what the goats produced. It was clear Kerling wasn't a blacksmith or a healer. He had been raised a warrior. Gyda too. Maybe she would join the next fighting season in his place. Maybe I'd see her there.

I took the basket of fish from the table and started on the fire. They were perfectly cleaned, their skins smooth where the scales were removed. I stuffed the cavities with herbs and salt and set them onto the hot coals to let them cook.

The rich, savory smell filled the house and I could feel the twinge in my chest again. This, too, was like home. I looked out the window, to where they were lifting more boards, stacking them on top of the lower ones to lift the walls. In Hylli, we'd often work on the boats of the Aska who were too old. We'd care for their animals and my father had me check their fish traps on the dock when I checked ours. The Riki, too, took care of their own.

I pulled the fish from the fire when the skin was crisp and lifting up from the flesh and piled them into a large wooden bowl. I steeled myself before I opened the door and walked out into the midday sun with the bowl on my hip. My eyes fixed on Inge, where she stood with another woman, winding rope. The path widened as I passed the gate and a figure in the corner of my eye made me draw back. I stumbled, almost dropping the fish, and a hand shot out to catch me by the arm, steadying me.

Kerling.

He stood beside Inge's gate, leaning into the post. When

I had my balance, I stood, staring up at him. But his attention was pulled toward the barn that was lifting up plank by plank from the ground. He was watching the Riki work, hidden in the shade cast by the tree.

The pain and humiliation of his injury was plainly painted on his face. He was dependent upon his clansmen in a way that no one wanted to be. If it were my father, he'd feel the same.

"Thank you," I whispered, trying not to show the pity I had for him.

His eyes drifted toward me, as if he was suddenly aware of my presence, and I turned, crossing the path until I passed the gate before his house. The banging and sawing stopped as the Riki noticed me and each head turned as I made my way toward Inge. Someone stepped into the path before me and I stopped, staring into the face of a woman with hair as red as Mýra's.

The bowl slid from my hip and I looked up to see Fiske taking it into his hands. He nodded, dismissing me, and I bit down onto my lip, meeting the eyes of the Riki who were still staring at me. I turned on my heel as pain curled in my chest and I swallowed it down, making my way back toward the gate. The sounds of work picked up slowly, followed by the soft tune of a song rising on a woman's voice. The others joined in, singing as they swung their hammers and scraped the wood. Ancient words on an ancient melody.

My lip quivered, fresh tears springing to my eyes as I reached Inge's gate. And there, still tucked into the shadow, Kerling still stood.

TWENTY-TWO

I STARED INTO THE SIDE OF THE MOUNTAIN AS IRI SPOKE.

Inside the house, Inge was rolling up blankets for him and Fiske. The morning was stark and the fire was still warming the house, but Iri was up before the others and waiting for me when I came down.

He leaned in close to me, buckling the axe sheaths to his back. "We'll be back tomorrow."

They were going hunting with some of the men from the village. He was leaving me. Again. And I wouldn't be here when he returned. I'd wait for a chance to get to the river and I'd take it. I wouldn't look back.

"Stay here in the house." He set his hand on my shoulder but I shoved him off.

I wasn't going to ask him to stay. I'd learned to take care of myself a long time ago.

I helped Inge pack their saddlebags as Halvard stood at the door, pouting.

"Why can't I go?" He leaned out to catch snowflakes in his hand.

"Next year." Fiske gave him a reproachful look and Halvard slumped against the wall. "Someone needs to check the nets while we're gone."

Halvard nodded reluctantly, happy to have a duty, but he still crossed his arms over his chest.

Iri had the horses ready when we came outside with the bags. He and Fiske kissed Inge and she ran her hands over their faces. "Be careful, *svóss.*"

Iri met my eyes one last time before he lifted himself up onto his horse, but I kept them cold. Hard. I wasn't going to give him an unspoken good-bye any more than he would beg for one. He turned his horse and started down the path toward the others. They disappeared around the bend and I rubbed my palm against my chest.

It would be the last time I'd ever see him. In this life or the next.

I picked up the milk pail and went to the goat pen, pushing my shoulders back, ashamed of the pain still twisting behind my ribs. I didn't need him.

Iri was a traitor.

But we were bound together in a way that even I didn't understand. And the worst part had been realizing that there was maybe nothing he could do to change that. I wanted to forget him, but maybe I never would. I wanted to let him go, but I might never be able to.

I sat, ignoring the ache in my throat, and a goat pushed his head through the pen, nudging me until I ran my palm over his forehead. It had only been two weeks since I was brought to Fela. There were still at least six more to go before the snow stopped falling and started melting. I could make it home in time to help my father plant. He'd never have to know about Iri. And if Sigr had mercy on me, maybe I'd forget him too.

"What did you do?" Gyda stood behind me with a stack of wood gathered in her arms. "What did you do to get them to keep you alive?"

I turned back to the goats and filled the pail. I didn't want to make up an excuse. I didn't want to lie. I felt sorry for her and Kerling, and I hated myself for it.

"Thora will bring her vengeance on you," she uttered. "For all of us."

She walked away with her skirt clenched in her fists and I looked into the dirt, feeling the weight of the collar and thinking that maybe she already had. Maybe it was Thora who'd brought me to Fela, like Iri said. Maybe it was Thora who'd fit the iron around my neck.

I looked to the tree line. If I made it to the river and had Riki chasing me in a forest I didn't know, I wouldn't have time to get down the mountain before they caught me. I'd have to wait until I wouldn't be noticed. Then I'd leave this place behind.

When Halvard was asleep, I sat beside the smoldering fire with the sacred wood, pulling the carving tool toward me slowly to shape the feet.

"Who are you making it for?" Inge asked quietly from across the fire.

I blew the dust from my hands. "My mother."

The thing I remembered most about my mother was her hair. I remember it catching the sun and thinking that it looked like it was moving even when it wasn't.

"When did she die?" Inge leaned forward, propping her chin up onto her hands as she watched the tool cut into the wood.

For a moment, I thought I should lie. I didn't know what Iri had told her about our mother. But it wasn't right to lie about her. I wanted Inge to know about the woman she'd replaced.

"I was six. My mother wasn't a warrior." I answered the question I knew she was asking in her mind. "She was killed during a Herja raid."

Her eyes widened and she stiffened. "The Herja?"

"Yes."

"I've heard the stories. I thought . . . people think they're a myth."

I dragged the tip of the metal across the bottom of the block slowly. "They aren't stories."

The night the Herja came was the first night I saw my father break. Iri and I ran, because that's what he told us to do. He shoved us to the door and pushed us out into the dark.

We ran up the hill and into the forest. We didn't stop running until morning broke and when we returned, hobbling back on bleeding, bare feet, we found him holding her on the beach. His hands tangled in her hair. I would never forget that sound—the primal roar that tore from his throat and echoed through our village.

"I'm sorry," Inge said, watching my face.

"I don't remember her well." I shrugged. But I could still hear the sounds of screaming in the dark. The smell when we burned the bodies. I could still feel the chill on my skin from when I first saw the Herja.

"You do." She sat up. "Even if you can't see her when you close your eyes, our bodies and our minds remember things that we can't. They hold onto things. And you'll see her again. When you reach *Sólbjǫrg*."

I stopped carving, surprised.

She smiled. "That's where your people go after death, isn't it?"

I looked into her eyes, wondering what she was thinking. What she wanted from me. "I'm not sure I'll make it to *Sólbjǫrg*." Saying it out loud made the fear inside me wake up again and I wished I'd held my tongue.

Her head tilted, resting on her shoulder. "Why is that?"

"Because I'm a *dýr*." I dropped my gaze back down to the idol. I didn't want to see whether she felt sorry for me or not. "I've lost my honor."

She was quiet a long time, watching me carve. I listened to the pop and hiss of the fire and tried to forget she was there.

I imagined my mother's face. Her dark, deep-set eyes. Her straight, square teeth.

"We find things, just as we lose things, Eelyn." Inge stood. "If you've lost your honor, you'll find it again."

I kept my back to her as she went to the ladder and climbed up into the loft. I couldn't try and explain it to her. I couldn't tell her that I'd abandoned my clansmen on the battlefield to chase after the brother who didn't even want me. Or that it was me who left Iri in that trench.

I held the idol up in front of me. The crude shape was simple. My father was the one who could carve. But it was still her. It was still something.

I looked back up to the dark loft where Inge and Halvard slept. If my father were here, he would tell me to take the carving tool, climb the ladder, and kill them both. I lifted the small iron hook, turning it around in the firelight before I set it down, and touched the face of the idol with my fingers.

"Sigr, keep the soul of my mother safe in *Sólbjǫrg*. Protect my father. Do not take your favor from me." The words bent and turned around each other. I sniffed them back. "Don't forget me."

TWENTY-THREE

INGE FILLED HER BASKET AND PUT ON HER CLOAK AS Halvard settled down to sleep. "I want you to go to the mountainside cellar. We need to store the sage and I need you to get some vinegar from the barrel." She took my cloak from the hook on the wall and handed me an empty jar.

"You're not going with me?" My brow lifted.

"I have patients to tend to. The cellar is below the ritual house. You'll see the door in the rock face." Inge took up a small torch from beside the door and lit it in the fire before opening the door. But she paused, looking back at me. Her lips pressed together as thoughts flitted behind her eyes. "Good-bye, Eelyn." She turned before she'd even said my name, stepping out into the darkening village.

I stood, staring at the door, my mind jumping from one thought to the next. She was letting me go. She was giving me my chance. My heart raced past my mind and I ran for my boots. I fit them on clumsily before pulling my cloak around me.

The door creaked open and I looked down the empty path, turning the jar over in my hand as my pulse picked up. I could take some food from the cellar and slip into the forest. There was still some sunlight left and if I hurried, I could make it to the river. No one would notice I was gone until morning.

I loaded up my arms with the bundles of sage and watched. The village was quiet, but the Riki were still awake, behind closed doors. I lit the other torch and stepped out the door, walking quickly. Inge stood in the candlelit doorway of Gyda's house.

I headed toward the ritual house, staying to the side of the path, and avoided the gaze of anyone who passed. The blacksmith stood in his tent, pounding against his anvil and sending orange sparks out around him in the growing dark. I cringed at the sound of the embers sizzling in the snow, remembering the burn of the collar on my neck. He glanced up as I passed before he turned back to his hammer.

The cellar was carved into the side of the mountain, with a large wood plank door set into it. I gripped the sage with one arm and pulled at the cold iron handle, opening the door against the snow. I pushed my weight into it until I could fit through the opening. It was dark and damp, the sound of melted snow echoing in the space as it dripped from the rock ceiling. The walls were stacked with barrels and crates—food, ale, medicines. The village's winter stores were stocked high, with grain packed into woven bags and set up on top of wooden stands to keep them off the ground.

On the back wall, salted meat hung on metal hooks. I stuck the torch in the mount that hung on the wall and opened my bag, filling it with a small sack of grain and shoving clean bandages into it. I reached up for the meat, and almost slipped, catching myself on a basket of ginger root and sending the pieces rolling across the floor. I cursed under my breath, lifting onto my toes until I had ahold of a long strip of venison and pulled it free.

The sound of the door made me stop, my hands freezing on my bag. A red-bearded man stood in the opening, leaning against the rock wall with an axe in his hand. The man from *Adalgildi*.

"What are you doing in here, Aska?" I could hardly see his lips moving beneath his thick beard.

I stood, slipping the meat into my bag, and took the jar from the pouch inside. The barrel of vinegar was sitting open behind me with a wooden ladle hung on the wall beside it. I turned my back to him, taking the lid from the jar and filling it to the top.

"I said what are you doing in here? Stealing?"

I dropped the jar back into my bag and walked across the cellar floor, taking the torch from the wall and waiting for him to move.

"Did Fiske cut your tongue out?" He hooked one of his fingers into the collar and jerked me forward.

"Don't touch me." I pulled away from him.

He smiled, one eyebrow lifting. "I need something from you before you go." He reached out and put his hand on my waist. His rough, stained fingers set against the line of my hip, and his eyes met mine.

I knew these eyes. I'd seen them in battle and other places too.

His voice was calm when he spoke. "You're a *dýr*, Aska. You'll do what I say or you'll be punished."

"I belong to Fiske. If you want something, you'll have to ask him for it." The words were rotten in my mouth.

I waited for his anger. For him to push harder. But the man looked down at me with something that looked like relief on his face. And as quickly as I realized it was coming, his hand was flying through the air. It cracked against the side of my face and I fell into the wall, dropping the torch. The bag on my shoulder fell open and I caught it, gripping the jar in my hand and swinging my arm wide. My shoulder popped as it caught him in the face. The glass shattered, the vinegar exploding from the jar, and he howled, clawing at his eyes with his hands. I jumped over him, running for the door, and he caught my foot. I hit the ground hard, trying to crawl away as his other hand clasped around my ankle.

He cursed, pulling me back. I kicked until my heel found his chin and he pulled again, harder, until I was underneath him. He took my face in his hand, squeezing. His eyes were red, glassed over with the burn of the vinegar. "You'll pay for that, Aska."

Fingers hooked beneath my collar and he dragged me

down the path. I clawed at his arms, choking as my feet slid around me. He towed me past the ritual house and into the forest. Deeper. Farther. When he finally stopped, I tried to stand, but he pushed me back down, grabbing the collar again and threading a thick rope through it.

"Stand up," he spat, yanking me forward.

I searched around us again, but it was too dark. I couldn't tell how far from the village we were. Even if anyone saw us, they wouldn't help me. If I screamed, no one would come.

I stood shakily, my hair wet and cold, suddenly wanting Iri so badly that my insides ached. I could see him, riding away on the horse. Trying to meet my eyes. Trying to reach me.

He pulled me to the trunk of a wide tree and wrapped the rope around it, pulling it tight. I was pinned in place, my face against the rough bark.

"What are you doing?" I tried to pull away.

He took my hands above my head and tied them tightly, followed by the tops of my legs so that I couldn't move. Around us, the snow began to fall. He pulled the knife from his belt and I squirmed, fighting harder against the ropes.

"Don't!" I screamed.

He stood back, watching me fight, a smile lifting the lines in his face. When he stepped toward me, I grunted, feeling the skin still healing around my wrists break open against the rope. He pressed the tip of the blade to my back, holding it there and watching me. I tried not to breathe, my heart stopping in my chest.

"We're not in Aurvanger, Aska. You're not a warrior here."

He caught my tunic with the knife and pulled it up, cutting into the fabric.

He tore the cloth from top to bottom, taking the knife to the arms next. When the blade ran through, he pulled at the pieces and dropped them on the ground in front of me, leaving me naked from the waist up.

I pulled at the rope, my teeth clenching, but I could barely move, scraping against the trunk of the tree.

"You're going to freeze to death. Slowly." I couldn't see his face in the moonlight as he stepped back and looked at me. He stood there, silent, his breath slowing. "You're going to close your eyes and never wake up. If you do, it will only be to wish you were dead." He dropped the end of the rope onto the ground and walked back down the path, into the dark.

I pulled at the ropes harder, trying to wiggle my legs free, but it only bit against me. It wouldn't budge. I grunted and spit, fighting against the knots until something moved in the trees and I froze, trying to make it out. I waited for my eyes to adjust, my breath puffing out around me in white bursts. A woman. She twisted her fingers into her necklace, looking at me.

The Tala.

She stood, motionless, in the dark.

I waited for her to say something. To do something. But she only looked me in the eye, so still that she could have been carved out of ice. I gave up struggling, leaning into the tree, and looked back at her. A drip of blood trailed down my cheek. And then she blinked. The look on her face didn't change as she turned and started down the path. Leaving me tied to the tree in the falling snow.

TWENTY-FOUR

I WAS IN THE FJORD.

I could see the ice-blue water. The clouds moving in its reflection. My feet pressing into the smooth black pebbles. My arms wrapping around myself against the wind. The vision came over me like a cold wave. The cliff face jutting up from the water like a wall. Green moss climbing down it in long, bright strands. I could see it.

I let my weight fall against the tree, trying to hold the sight of Hylli in my mind. The edge of the forest beside the village. A shadow moving in the trees. I squinted, trying to focus my blurred vision.

The figure stalked in the distance, watching. Thick furs and the shine of silver. The white, empty eyes of a Herja. I blinked.

"Eelyn."

He was there, in the trees. He was watching me. The

Herja had come for my mother and now they'd come for me.

"Eelyn?" Something stung across my cheek. "Eelyn!"

The sunlight was suddenly gone. Black moved on black and hands pulled at me. My skin was numbed against the snow on the ground. I closed my eyes again, trying to leave it. Trying to get back to the fjord.

Fiske's face was looking down into mine, his hands on me. But I couldn't feel them.

"Herja," I croaked, looking back to the trees. But there was no one.

Above his head, the moon blinked through the branches overhead. "What?"

"I want to go home, Fiske." My words ran into each other and I could hear the weakness in them. The brittle sadness breaking on each one.

And then I was falling. The world bumped and swayed around me as he lifted me up off the ground. I could hear his breath. I could feel his skin. His arms wrapped around my limp body, holding me together.

I opened my eyes again and the trees floated past above. The sound of crunching snow filled my pounding head. I curled into Fiske and pinched my eyes closed until I could see the fjord again. Fog touching the cliffs. The smell of sea-water. But the Herja was gone.

A door opened and suddenly we were inside. The familiar firelight of the house swallowed me, but I couldn't feel its warmth.

"What happened?" Halvard ran to us.

"Get the water on." Fiske was setting me down and surveying me in the dim light.

I was wrapped in his cloak. "Where's Iri?" I whispered.

"Looking for you." He pulled a blanket from the trunk and moved me closer to the fire. "Find him." Fiske pushed Halvard toward the door and shoved him out. When he came back, he crouched down in front of me. "Who did this?"

I pulled the blanket tighter around me, searching his face. He looked different. There was something shining in his eyes that wasn't there before. Or maybe it was. I had never seen them so closely.

"Who?" he asked again.

But all I could think was that he was still too close to me. That I wanted him to move away. "It was the man from *Adalgildi,*" I whispered.

"What did he do?"

I closed my eyes. I tried to disappear.

"Did he . . . ?" The question broke off and his eyes dropped from mine.

I shook my head in answer, coiling my arms around my bare body.

Fiske stood, his boots pounding against the stone as he walked to the wall. He lifted an axe from the hook and opened the door. "Don't tell them where I'm going." And then he was gone.

★   ★   ★

I OPENED MY EYES WHEN THE DOOR OPENED AND THE weight of more blankets pressed down on top of me. Iri was asleep next to the fire, his head propped up on his saddle-bags.

Fiske came through the door quietly, and I opened my eyes enough to watch him hang the axe back on the wall. He pulled his armor vest and tunic off and went to the basin of water to wash his face, raking his fingers through his hair. The cuts and bruises from the fighting season were healing, leaving smooth skin over the form of him, broad on top and narrow in the middle, like Iri. He set his hands on the table and leaned into it, looking into the basin as a single drop of water trailed to the end of his nose and fell into the water.

I stared at the blood-spotted tunic crumpled on the floor.

"Fiske?" Inge came down the ladder with her hair long and unbraided over her shoulders. "Where have you been?" she whispered.

When he didn't answer, she took his arm and pulled him to face her.

"Thorpe." He didn't look at her.

Her voice dropped lower. "What did you do?"

He tied his hair back, coming to the fire and sitting to take off his boots. "Reminded him not to touch what doesn't belong to him."

Inge watched him for a moment before she gave a small nod, but worry hung heavy on her face. "I'll speak to the Tala tomorrow."

"*I'll* speak to the Tala." The room fell silent.

"Fiske . . ."

He stilled, looking up at her.

But she didn't speak. She only looked at him, her eyes falling from his head down to his feet and meeting his eyes again. Like she was trying to uncover something.

He stood, walking past her to the ladder. She watched him until he was out of sight and then turned back toward the fire. She didn't move for a long time and when she finally closed her eyes, her mouth was moving, a silent prayer on her lips.

I sunk lower into the blankets. Because Inge didn't know that I was the past Iri had left behind. I was what she should be praying against.

And it was only a matter of time before she did.

I LAY IN THE LOFT AS THE OTHERS WENT ABOUT THEIR day.

No one talked to me.

No one asked me to do anything.

I pulled my legs up and hugged them into my chest, still trying to feel the warmth down in the center of my frozen bones. Where I felt empty.

When the sun grew brighter, I pulled the blankets up over my head and listened to my heartbeat. Iri climbed up the ladder and stood over me, his worry filling the room. I pretended to be asleep and when he climbed back down, I let myself breathe again. I stared into the dark of the blankets, trying to remember what that feeling was—the feeling chewing at the edges of me while I stood in the dark of the forest tied naked to the tree.

I had never been so vulnerable. So full of fear.

And I had never hated myself until that moment.

I remembered the light reflecting off the snow. The sound of my quick breath in the silence. Thinking that if I died, I wouldn't reach *Sólbjǫrg*. Then, the all-consuming shame of being *afraid* to die for the very first time in my life.

I could see the reds and oranges and yellows of the battlefield. The heat and the sting of pain. The burn of a war cry in my throat. I could see myself, alive. Strong.

I blinked.

And there was only the white and cold and quiet of that forest. There was only loneliness. There was only the very barest part of me, waiting for the end to come. It crept toward me in the dark. It came for me. And when it overtook me, my last thought was *I don't want to die.*

I had never known real fear until the moment I saw Iri in Aurvanger. I had never considered there was more to life than the most basic explanation—that the gods were willing over us. That they were giving and taking their favor.

But I was without my clan.

I was alone in that forest.

Sigr had turned his eyes from me. I could feel it. And I could only think of Iri, just a boy, dying slowly in the cold. Of my mother, the life drained from her flesh. All her fight gone.

And the Herja, floating in the dark like a harbinger, watching me.

There was a knock at the door below and my eyes refocused.

"Inge." A warm voice floated up to me and I crawled to the edge of my cot to peer through the cracks of the loft.

The Tala came through the door and everyone stood. Inge took the Tala's hands into her own and squeezed them. But that worry was still there, hanging over her. It made her look heavy on her feet.

"I have good news." The Tala stepped over the threshold and into the house. "Runa's father has accepted Iri's request to marry her." She gripped Iri's arm and smiled.

Relief pushed its way over his face and he looked up to meet Inge's eyes.

"You're worthy of it, Iri." Inge smiled.

The Tala nodded. "The two of you will make a very good match."

The sweetness in Iri's eyes reached inside me and touched the raw pain of losing him again. The urge to cry swelled behind my tongue.

"Thank you." He nodded.

"You'll need to get everything in order, of course. We'll make the preparations as soon as you like."

The Tala smiled again and I studied her. She seemed genuinely happy and the others looked at her with a fondness. A trust. But all I could think of when I looked at the Tala was the way she'd watched me in the forest. The way she walked away from me, leaving me to die.

She sat at the table, folding her hands in her lap, and her

manner changed a little, the room going silent with it. "We do need to talk about what happened last night." Her eyes went to Fiske, who stood on the other side of the fire. "Do you have anything you'd like to say?"

Fiske didn't seem nervous like Inge was. He stood straight, looking the Tala in the eye. "I went to speak with Thorpe last night after I returned from the hunt and learned that he'd tried to kill my *dýr*."

"You *spoke* with him?"

Fiske's face bore no expression. Beside him, Iri looked into the fire, his hand twitching at his belt.

She tilted her head to one side. "Thorpe abused your property and he had no right to take what belongs to you. He brought the consequences upon himself."

That was the Aska way too. When you broke the law, you paid for it. There were no judges or rule keepers. Only the Talas attempt to keep the peace in a village. When someone wronged you, you dealt with it yourself. If you didn't, you were a target for others looking to take advantage.

Fiske nodded. "Thank you."

"Thank you," Inge echoed quietly.

"However, I would like to advise you, Fiske. You've chosen to take on your first *dýr*. And you didn't take just any *dýr*. You took an Aska. May I ask why?"

Fiske jerked his chin, stretching his shoulder. "My mother needed help with the house."

"What is it?" Inge looked concerned.

The Tala watched Fiske for a long moment. "I had a

dream about her. I'm unsure of what it means, but I feel that Thora has her eye on this Aska."

Iri's jaw clenched.

"You seem very upset by Thorpe's treatment of her."

"I need her to work. If Thorpe had killed her, he would have had to pay me for her, just like he would for killing a sheep or a horse."

The pit in my stomach grew, widening until it was something I could fall into. Something that could make me disappear.

The Tala looked up to Inge. "I would suggest trading her to another village after the thaw. Somewhere they won't know what she is. She draws too much attention as an Aska to be useful. And I will also remind you that you're expected to choose a wife, as Iri has. I hoped it would be this winter, but it looks as if that's not going to happen."

Fiske hesitated before shaking his head. "No."

"Alright. Next winter. Agreed?"

"Yes," Fiske and Inge answered together.

"I'm very glad to hear that." She stood, smoothing out her skirt. "Inge, I'd be happy to help find you another *dýr*. I know you need the help."

"Thank you." Inge hugged her, her chin resting on the Tala's shoulder.

They walked to the door arm in arm and I sank back into the cot, burying myself again.

I closed my eyes and welcomed the dark.

TWENTY-FIVE

I SAT BESIDE INGE IN THE MEADOW, DIGGING UP BULBS OF fennel in silence. The sun was high and heatless, reflecting off the frozen ground. I pushed the spade into it, prying the earth up and raking through it with my hands.

The skin around my wrist was raw again, the bruise on my face sore when I moved my mouth.

Inge picked up a bulb and dusted it off with her fingers. "I'm sorry about what happened."

I sat back on my knees, taking it from her and setting it into the basket beside me. It wasn't her fault, but I wanted to be angry at her anyway. I'd had my chance to get to the river and now it was gone.

She watched me, setting her hands into her lap. "I think we should talk." She picked at the dirt beneath her fingernails. "About Iri." She looked up to meet my eyes. "I know who you are, Eelyn."

I recoiled, my mind pulling thoughts so quickly I could hardly follow them. I searched the meadow around us instinctively, looking for a threat. But we were alone.

She didn't move, watching me. "I haven't told anyone."

The beat of my heart knocked in my chest. I tried to read her. Tried to decide what she was planning to do about it. How much she knew. "How?"

"When Fiske brought you home, I knew there was more to it than what he told me. When you mentioned your family and your age I had my suspicions. I thought you might be the sister he told us about. But I wasn't sure." She pulled in a long breath and let it out.

I stood, walking out a ways until I had a good view of the meadow. If she'd planned to trap me, this would be a good place. I had nowhere to hide. "He told you about me?"

"He did, but he didn't have to. You look just like him."

"Did he tell you I was his fighting mate?" My eyes were still on the tree line.

A sad smile lifted on her lips. "No, he didn't."

I faced her. She sat with her skirt spread around her in the grass. I swallowed hard. "I lost him in the fight. I turned around and he was just . . . gone. I was looking for him." I sucked in a breath. "And I saw him just as he went over the edge. I couldn't reach him." I sank back down beside her. "What are you going to do?"

"I thought that if I let you escape, the danger would be gone. But I was wrong. It took years for this village to trust Iri. If the Riki knew that he and Fiske are lying about who you are or that they are trying to help you, they would kill them. I won't tell the Tala or anyone else. After the thaw, you'll run away. You'll go back to the Aska and we won't come after you." She went back to digging and the pain surfaced on her face. The fear.

"He's not leaving. He won't come back with me," I said.

"I know."

"I—" I bit back the strangled sound in my voice.

"What?" She sat up.

"Thank you—for what you did for Iri."

When I looked at her again, her eyes were filled with tears. "You're welcome."

"Mama!"

Halvard ran toward us from across the meadow and Inge stood quickly, taking her skirt into her hands. "Halvard?"

"It's Gyda!" He jumped up and down, waving her to him.

She smiled widely. "It's time." She held a hand out to me.

I looked at it, the soft, slender line of her fingers, splayed out and waiting. She looked down at me, the smile still broad on her face.

I lifted my hand and almost pulled it back before I let her take it. She pulled me up beside her, brushing the grass off my pants like a mother would do to a child.

"Let's go." She lifted the basket onto her arm and started toward the trees.

The length of her dress parted the tall dry grass as she walked, her arm swinging at her side as she ran after Halvard. Her long dark hair fell down her back in one intricate braid.

It didn't matter how much I didn't want to see it or how hard I tried to remember what I'd always been taught. Inge was a mother. And whatever the difference in blood, she loved Iri as if there were none.

I WATCHED OUT THE FRONT DOOR, ACROSS THE PATH TO Gyda's house, where Inge and Runa were inside. The labor had already been going for hours, but it was Gyda's first baby. They could be there all night.

Halvard finished eating and climbed the ladder, leaving Fiske, Iri, and me by the fire. I pulled a pair of Halvard's pants into my lap and started mending them where he'd torn a hole in the knee.

"I'll stay until the thaw," I said, pulling the needle through the wool.

Iri sat up, leaning forward. Beside him, Fiske glanced at me, his gaze lingering for only a moment.

"I'll stay until the thaw and then I'll go home."

Iri nodded, smiling. "Alright."

If Inge wasn't going to tell anyone, there was no sense in me taking the risk now. I would stay out of sight and out of trouble. I'd go home and face my shame and try to find a way to earn back what I'd lost in the eyes of Sigr.

Runa came through the door, her face flushed from the cold, and fetched a wooden box from the shelf. I filled a bowl with the stew we'd eaten for supper and handed it to her.

She hesitated, looking at it and then behind me to where Iri sat. She took the bowl, smiling. "Thank you."

I sat back down, starting on the pants again, embarrassed. I hadn't thought about it. I'd just done it.

"Did the baby come?" Iri caught her hand as she passed and pulled her to him.

She smiled, touching her nose to his. "Not yet." Her fingers slipped through his grasp and she went back out the door.

Halvard's snoring rumbled in the loft and Fiske and Iri sat in front of the fire, mending opposite ends of a net. I listened to them, talking about the next hunt. The next fighting season. The next visit from the Riki traders. Making plans.

Their lives would go on when I left. I would fade like a bruise or a memory.

Fiske rubbed the salve into the broken skin on his knuckles that appeared after he went to see Thorpe. I ran my fingers over the wound on my arm and the same sting that had crawled over me when he touched me ignited again, making me feel too warm by the fire.

A screech echoed through the air outside and we all straightened, Iri and Fiske falling quiet. I stood, looking out the door, into the dark village, but I couldn't see anything. It was quiet again.

"Maybe it was Gyda." I leaned into the doorpost.

Iri relaxed back into his seat, throwing another log onto the fire. "Eelyn's good with nets."

I looked back at them. "What?"

"We need a new net made. Can you make it?"

I looked back out the door, remembering. Sitting on the dock with salty rope in my hands. Tying knots and repairing broken strands while Iri cleaned fish beside me. I nodded.

Another scream rang out and Iri shot to his feet and froze. Listening.

Then another. And another.

I knew that sound. We all did. Screaming in the middle of a clear night. Wood breaking. Metal clanging.

They were the sounds of a raid.

TWENTY-SIX

As soon as I thought it, the warning bell sounded in the ritual house and Iri and Fiske moved like one person, going for their weapons on the wall.

I pulled the door, leaving it cracked open just enough to peer out. The only thing I could see was the warm glow of the fire in Gyda's house across the path. When I turned back around, Fiske was holding my weapons in his hands. They hovered in the air between us. My sword and my axe. My knife.

I stared down at them, my mouth falling open.

"Fiske?" Halvard's sleepy, wavering voice came down from the loft.

He pushed the weapons into my hands and I clutched them to my chest as that still quiet poured into me. That sure, steady thing I knew. The fight inside of me. The whistle sounded again and the bellowing grew, getting closer. Fiske looked at the door and then back to Halvard.

"Go." I dropped the scabbard over my head, tightening the straps. "I'll stay with him."

He looked at me and then back up to Halvard. "Get across the path to Gyda's when it's clear." He waited for me to nod.

Iri went to the door, sliding his knife into his belt and taking an axe into each hand. I swallowed hard, turning back to the fire, and they slipped out into the dark, where more wailing echoed in the village.

I fit the axe onto my back and it centered me. Brought me back into myself. The familiar weight of my sword at my hip was an anchor.

Above me, Halvard peered over the edge of the loft. "What's happening?" Tears glistened in his eyes.

There was no point in coddling him. He knew what a raid was. "Where are your weapons?"

He disappeared over the ledge and a few minutes later, he came down the ladder with his scabbard fit to him. He went to the trunk against the wall and pulled out a belt with a knife in it.

He handed it to me. "It was my father's."

I pulled it around his waist, tying the leather into a knot because it was too big to fit him. But it would do. He could reach it and that was all that mattered.

I knelt down in front of him, looking up into his eyes. "Have you ever killed a man?"

He shook his head skittishly.

"Do you know how? Where to strike?"

"I—I think so."

"Show me."

His small, shaking hand lifted, pressing to my neck. I nodded. Then he dropped it down to my stomach, my side, my lower back.

"That's right." I tried to smile. "Are you better with a sword or a knife?" I knew he wasn't very good with the axe. I'd seen it.

"Sword." He lifted his chin and tried to pull the nerves back inside.

"Alright. Take a deep breath and listen to what I'm about to tell you."

He obeyed, inhaling slowly and standing up straight in front of me.

"In a moment, someone will come through that door. They will try to kill us or take us, but I'm going to kill them before that happens."

He nodded.

"If they kill me, or they take me, it will be your job to kill them. Understand?"

"Yes."

I uttered the words that had once been said to me, the night my mother died. "You run into the forest. You don't stop until morning. No matter what."

The sound of screaming echoed in my head, taking me back to that night in Hylli. Running barefoot in the trees. Iri before me. My father's deep, grinding voice behind me.

Run!

Halvard's eyes danced over my face. "Alright."

"You don't try to help me. You don't come back for Inge or Fiske or Iri. You *run*. You leave them behind."

The night Iri pulled me into the forest was the same night I'd become a warrior. If he survived, this would be that night for Halvard too.

The tears smarted in his eyes again.

"Don't cry," I ordered, standing. "If you die tonight, you'll see your father in *Friðr*. Right?"

He smiled, sniffing. "Right."

The door creaked and Halvard's face fell, his eyes going wide. I turned to stand in front of him, sliding my sword from its sheath slowly.

A figure stood in the open doorway.

And I knew right away. My sword almost fell from my grasp, my heart stopping. A wildfire of fear ran over me and I tried to pull air into my lungs. I blinked.

Slick, shining furs. The glint of silver. White, dead eyes.

Herja.

My eyes ran over him. His long stringy hair fell down around his face and he stared down at me with no expression. I eyed the sword in his hand and stepped back slowly.

"It's just a *dýr*," he called back over his shoulder, his eyes on the collar around my neck.

Another man came into view behind him, glancing inside, and then disappeared.

"Stay back, Halvard," I said calmly, my heart finding its rhythm again.

He obeyed, moving toward the wall on the other side of the fire, his small sword in his hand.

The Herja took a step toward us and the blood ran faster under my skin. Reaching every muscle. I watched his movements carefully, sinking into my feet and finding my balance. He looked around the house, his eyes taking stock. What he wanted to take. And who he wanted to kill.

I watched, waiting for it.

One breath.

He pulled his knife free.

Two breaths.

He took another step.

Three breaths.

He leapt toward me and I reached for the pot on the fire, taking it by the handle and flinging it toward him. It hit him in the chest, knocking him over, and he howled, the hot stew burning his dirt-smeared skin. He slid on the wet stone, looking up at me with shock lighting on his face.

Then he was moving again. I tightened my grip on my sword and pulled my axe free as he stood, using the momentum to swing it around and catch his armor vest. But he was still standing with his sword rising up over my head. I swung again, this time for his legs, and he barreled into me. I hit the floor, losing the sword, and the axe slid, hitting the wall next to Halvard. I scrambled after it as more screams rang out in the dark.

Maybe Runa. Maybe Inge.

"Eelyn!" Halvard yelped behind me and I rolled as the sword came down on the stone next to me, sending sparks flying out around us. I grabbed the axe, sitting up, and snapped it down over my head. The hot pain in my shoulder erupted again as the axe flew, cutting through the air and sinking into the man's thigh. His sword dropped to the ground, clanging.

I sprang to my feet, getting to it before he did, and reared it back before piercing it down into his side with a shriek. He coiled in on himself, crying out, and the other Herja appeared in the doorway again, looking from me to the man writhing on the ground.

He ran toward us, his sword ready at his side, and I lifted the axe from the man's leg and threw it. It spun in the air until it plunked into his ribs. It was a bad throw, but it hit him. He fell to one knee, trying to stand, and I ran to him, taking up the sword on the ground and running it through his middle.

He grabbed onto me, blood pouring from his mouth, his gnarled fingers pulling at my tunic as he fell forward onto me. Halvard ran to the door, slamming it closed, and came to help roll the man to the side. I stood, my chest heaving and his blood dripping from my hands.

I took up my axe and sword.

"You alright?" Halvard looked at me with wide eyes.

I nodded, going back to the door. The village was alight with fire, roaring up where it consumed the houses below. Across the path, Gyda's door was still closed. The forest was dark as pitch, but I could see the tree line. I tried to think. I could run into the trees and get to the river. It was dark, but it was worth a try. No one would come after me. No one would even notice.

Terror paled Halvard's face as he looked out over the fires burning in the homes down the path. He'd probably make it to Gyda's. He was small and hard to see in the dark. Maybe they wouldn't even see him. But the thought made my tongue stick to the roof of my mouth, a chill running up my spine. I growled, my hand tightening around my sword. Even if Halvard made it, Kerling couldn't defend the others.

I couldn't leave now.

"Come on." I wrapped one arm around him and held him against me as I flung the door open and we ran out into the dark, swords drawn.

The firelight from the house spilled out onto the snow before us and a shadow came from the trees. I broke off from Halvard, shoving him toward the light coming from Gyda's. I let my arm swing back and snapped it forward, bringing my sword in front of me. I drove it into the Herja, shoving her to the ground as I passed, one eye still on Halvard.

"Eelyn!" he screamed as footsteps sounded behind me.

I turned back to swing the axe around me and another woman fell into it, stumbling to the ground as the moonlight reflected off the silver armor. I pulled it free and brought it down again, into her back just as Halvard appeared, almost running into me.

He ran ahead and when another man came on our heels, I stopped short, bending low to let him fall over me. He rolled across the snow, his sword flying, and another man hit me from behind. I drove my sword behind me, catching him in the gut, but the other man was back on his feet. I didn't have enough time.

He ran at me and I closed my eyes, curling in on myself.

But it never came. The blow. I heard him hit the ground in front of me and opened my eyes to see him facedown on the ground, a knife stuck in the back of his neck. Behind him, Halvard stood, his hand still lifted from the throw.

"Run!" I yelled, getting back to my feet.

Halvard turned as a figure knocked into him. A Herja wrapped his arms around his body, hoisting him up and running as Halvard flailed in his arms.

"Halvard!" I shouted, my feet digging into the deep snow as I ran.

But the Herja was ahead of me, moving faster. When he reached the trees, I pumped my arms harder. I was losing him in the chaos as more Herja poured into the forest, re-treating.

I turned back to the village, my eyes darting from one side to the other as bodies flew past me. "Iri!" I screamed. He couldn't possibly hear me. He couldn't possibly be close enough. "Fiske!" I screamed again, until my lungs felt like they were bleeding.

Behind me, Halvard's screams echoed in the dark.

Something sounded deep inside my chest. Something grinding, breaking against me, like the crack of an avalanche. Something so desperate and angry that it could tear me open.

Hands grabbed me and I turned, swinging my axe, and Fiske ducked.

I gulped in a breath, dropping the axe to the ground and grabbing hold of his armor vest. "Halvard—they have him!"

He looked down into my face, trying to understand. Trying to put it together. "No."

I didn't have enough breath left to explain. I pointed into the trees.

He picked up my axe and shoved it back into my hands. Without hesitation he took off, and I ran after him. We weaved in and out of the trees, the snow thinning beneath our feet as we went downhill. Behind us, no Riki were coming and I knew what that meant—that whatever was going on in the village was bad enough to let the Herja leave alive.

We came up on the last of them on light feet, staying low to the ground. Fiske threw his knife, dropping the first man as it stuck in his throat, and I took the second, sliding on the frozen ground as his blade flew over me. I reared back and stabbed him between his shoulder blades. He arched, throwing his head back, and landed on his side. When I turned around, Fiske already had another one on the ground.

We closed in on the swarm of them moving down the wooded slope a few minutes later and stayed in the thick of the trees, melting into the dark. They walked in a long line, their armor vests shining in the moonlight.

We stopped, crouching close together behind a fallen, rotting tree, and peered up over it. The Herja were pulling the captured Riki by ropes tied around their necks, like leashes. I cursed under my breath, trying to make out Halvard's body, but there were so many Herja I couldn't see him. A horse brayed and my eyes shot to the animal at the back of the line. Three figures were being pulled behind it, one of them limp and dragging. I lifted up onto my knees, my eyes going wide.

Fiske breathed heavily beside me. "Can you see him?"

I dug my fingers into the bark of the tree. "I think the small one behind the horse is him. I'm not sure."

"I can't see him." He swallowed the words. "Maybe they . . ."

"If they wanted to kill him, they would have done it in Fela. The Herja take people when they raid. You know that."

But he also knew why. If the stories were true. The Herja sacrificed the ones they captured. We'd found the blood-drained bodies in the forest after they came to Hylli.

He looked at me, the same thought like a storm on his face. A long breath pushed between his lips and he set his forehead against the tree, closing his eyes.

"We can get to him, but we can't get the others," I whispered. "There are too many of them."

He looked at the snow, thinking. "We'll take Halvard. We'll come back for the others."

I nodded. "And then we'll kill every last one of them."

TWENTY-SEVEN

WE STAYED LOW, CUTTING EAST AND HEADING DOWN the slope parallel to the Herja as they moved deeper into the forest. The cold found its way through my armor as we crept closer and I kept my eyes on Halvard, being pulled by the black horse at the rear. When the line had spread enough that they were falling behind, I stopped, pointing in the right direction.

The moonlight came through the trees and lit Halvard's face in a quick flash. His nose looked broken, a stream of blood pouring down onto his tunic. I winced against the sting behind my eyes. Probably his first broken bone. Maybe his first glimpse of violence and the life the rest of us lived.

As soon as Fiske caught sight of his brother, he tensed, almost launching himself forward. I grabbed hold of his arm, lowering him back down to the ground. But he was all angles and sharp edges, his eyes strained. The construction of his face shifted and pulled, sending my heart into my stomach. He was afraid. And it looked so foreign on him.

I let my fingers wrap around his arm, squeezing, and he came back into himself, pulling his eyes from Halvard's shadowed form and setting them on me. He sunk back down, slowing his breaths, and I held his gaze until I knew he wouldn't fly down the slope swinging his sword.

We were far enough ahead to see Halvard as he struggled to keep up with the horse, stumbling along the trail with his fingers hooked into the rope around his neck to keep the slid-ing knot from tightening. If he fell, it would choke him.

A woman was tied beside him and they walked alongside the bloodied body being dragged over the trail. Whoever it was, they were dead.

We didn't move. We didn't make a sound.

I searched for a stone on the ground and when I'd found one about the size of my palm, I stood.

Fiske's hand caught my wrist, stopping me. "I should go."

"I've got him, Fiske," I whispered. I was smaller and faster, less easily seen. As soon as he came out of the brush, they'd spot him.

He looked at me for another moment before he let me go, and I lifted one foot. I moved slowly, avoiding the patches of light on the forest floor. Fiske followed behind me with one hand pressed to my back.

The clouds moved overhead and darkened the forest again as the horse neared us. Fiske pulled the knife from his belt, sinking down, and I raised the rock in my hand. As soon as the next group of Herja passed, I swung my arm back and flicked my wrist, sending the rock skidding over the brush between the trees, like it was skipping on water. It crossed in front of the horse and the animal reared up, its nostrils flaring.

Halvard steadied himself against a tree and the horse stamped the ground nervously as the other Herja continued down the path. I slipped my knife from its sheath.

The two Herja walking behind caught up, one of them taking the reins and clicking his tongue to calm the animal. "Cut that one free." He nodded toward the dead Riki on the ground.

I took one step as the second man obeyed, crouching down to saw at the rope with the blade of his axe. The riggings rattled and I cut left, going wide around the horse to across the path still shrouded in darkness. Ahead, the Herja still moved down the slope.

I came up on the first man's side fast. By the time he heard me, it was too late. I leapt up, hooking my arm around his neck and pulling the knife across his throat until blood spurted out in a pulsing stream. Fiske dropped the other man beside him and Halvard's eyes found us in the dark. He instantly began to cry.

Down the path, more Herja were coming.

"Shh." I reached him, cutting through the rope in one motion and shoving him toward Fiske. He picked Halvard up and the boy's arms and legs wrapped around him as he started back up the slope.

Then I saw her.

Standing on the trail, with a rope around her neck, the Tala was watching me. I stopped, looking around us. The forest was still quiet except for the footsteps of three Herja coming closer. And she stood there, like she knew what I was going to do. I wanted to leave her tied to that horse like she'd left me. Until she was the next body dragging over the forest floor. I wanted to punish her. But there was something knowing in her eyes. Calm. Like she'd been waiting for me.

Before I could think, I turned the knife over in my hand and threw it to her, handle first, and she caught it. Her gaze was still heavy on me as I pivoted on my heel and a few seconds later, I could hear her following behind, falling into step with me as I caught up to Fiske on the slope.

We got low again, watching the men catch sight of the horse. As their voices grew louder, I reached back toward the Tala and she placed the knife into my open hand. I sat up on my knees, taking a breath and squaring my shoulders before I lifted the knife up to my sight line. I aimed, taking my time, and then let my arm sink back, sending it forward with a snap.

It flew like wind, silent until it stuck into the back of the man on the right and he fell flat. The other man paused, looking up to us. And then he ran.

I slid down the decline, pulling the knife from the first man's back, and looked up, tracking the second one.

Then everything stopped.

Everything went still. The sound of breathing roared in

my ears. The trees swirled around me. I squinted, trying to focus. Trying to will what I was seeing into something else. But there was no mistaking the hilt of an Aska sword. The red-tinged leather of an Aska scabbard. And that could only mean one thing. That the Herja had been to the fjord.

I didn't think. I didn't breathe. I ran.

I pulled the last bit of the energy within me up and out of myself, throwing my body forward into the trees. Toward the fleeing shadow. He turned back as he ran, watching me gain on him, just long enough to lose his footing and slam into a tree. He rolled when I came down on him and I pinned him with my knees, clutching his hair in my hands to make him face me.

"Where did you get that sword?" My panicked voice was a hoarse whisper.

He looked up at me, clenching his teeth.

"Where did you get it?" I slammed his head back into the ground and he groaned.

Fiske and the Tala reached us, coming to stand over me. There was no one in sight, but if he shouted, the Herja might hear him.

I couldn't kill him. Not yet.

I reached across my body and let all my weight fall with the butt of the knife, knocking it into the side of the Herja's head. He went still beneath me, his head rolling to one side.

"It's . . . these are Aska leathers," I sputtered, my throat tight.

"I know." Fiske set Halvard down and the Tala slid one

arm around his shoulders, pulling him close. "We'll take him."

He grabbed one leg and I wiped my face before I grabbed the other. We dragged him through the forest, the Tala and Halvard walking ahead.

"They've been to the fjord." I grunted against the Herja's weight, my legs weak.

"Maybe."

Before I could answer, the sound of Fela reached us through the trees.

The first of the morning light rose up over the mountain, turning the village the deep purple of a day-old bruise. Smoke trailed up from some of the homes still burning and bodies were strung out along the main path. Every few steps, the snow was spattered red.

The Tala looked over her shoulder to Fiske, her lips parting.

We dragged the Herja until we neared the house and I swallowed hard. It was quiet and I didn't know what that meant. What it might do to me. The sky and the earth were both pulling at every piece of me, making me feel thin. Like I was going to rip in two.

I dropped the leg of the Herja and pushed through the door. Inge's scream broke the silence. She lunged forward, catching Halvard in her arms and sinking to the floor, her face so twisted and broken I almost couldn't recognize her.

My eyes darted around the room until they found him.

Iri.

Standing at the end of the table, his face red. His eyes wet. Hair sticking to the side of his face.

A sob broke loose from my chest and I ran to him. I fell into his chest and his arms wrapped tightly around me, lifting my feet from the ground. I tried to breathe, taking the air in slowly and willing my heart to calm.

He let me go, reaching for Fiske and kissing the side of his face. The air in his chest hissed out as he pulled him into his arms. "I thought . . . we thought . . ." He shook his head. "We couldn't find your bodies."

Behind him, Runa leaned against the wall, her knees pulled up into her chest. She stared into the fire blankly, a trail of tears striping her soot-covered face.

Inge still sat on the floor, her arms wrapped around Halvard and crying into his hair. She whispered into his ear, holding him close, and he nodded against her, sniffing back the tears. The dried blood crusted down beneath his nose and a ring of raw skin encircled his neck where the rope had been. When she pulled back from him, she looked at it, pressing on each side of his nose with her thumbs as he looked up at the ceiling. A dark bruise had already bloomed under both eyes.

"What is this?" Iri looked down to the Herja lying outside the door.

Inge gasped, pulling Halvard closer.

I ran a hand through my hair, my fingernails scratching against my shorn scalp. "They've been to the Aska."

His face went slack and his eyes widened, filling with

whatever had been there when I came through the door. Asking the question that I couldn't answer.

I leaned into the table, rubbing my face with my rough, blistered hands, and looked around the room, my muscles jumping around my bones. My blood still running fast. It was the way my body slowly calmed after battle. The way my mind raced in a million directions, trying to find something to latch onto. As my breaths grew longer, the pain began to surface in my shoulder again. I pulled my armor vest aside to look at it.

"Let me see." Inge finally let Halvard go and rose to her feet.

Runa still sat against the wall, silent.

"Her father." Inge met my eyes, speaking lowly.

My stomach roiled, my mind hovering over the only thought in my head. *My* father. The Aska.

Fiske set a hand on Inge's shoulder. "You should go up to the ritual house. The wounded will be there."

My eyes were still on the Herja's boots in the doorway.

Inge nodded, looking to Runa. "You're right."

Runa stood, still empty in the eyes. She went for the basket on the table and pulled it onto her arm, waiting for Inge with a blank stare falling on the door. But Inge didn't move until I looked at her. She waited for my eyes to lift and when they did, she took my face into her hands and pressed her warm cheek against mine, her breath running over the side of my face. She held me, folding her arms around me and pulling me tightly against her.

"Thank you," she whispered.

And the glacier inside of me cracked. It roared as it broke and fell into the icy waters around my heart. "You're welcome."

TWENTY-EIGHT

I HELD HALVARD'S HEAD IN MY LAP ON THE TABLE SO
that Fiske could set his nose. When the tears slid down the
sides of his face, I brushed them away with the back of my
hands.

Iri helped him stand, pulling the tunic over his head, and
I went back to the doorway, counting the bodies as the Riki
dragged them out onto the path and separated them. There
were more Riki than Herja. Of that, I was sure.

I stood over the Herja we dragged through the forest,
waiting. He was a big, hard-looking man, his clothes soiled
deep and shredded at the edges. They'd been traveling for
some time, living on the move. But the Aska leathers weren't
as worn. If they'd been to Hylli, it had been recent.

"My mother doesn't want him here. She's afraid." Fiske
tried to unbuckle his armor vest, wincing at it with his arm
half lifted over the fire.

"Here." I reached for him.

He turned, giving me his side, and I took his wrist and set his forearm up onto my shoulder to hold it up. I pulled at the clasps gently, prying the side of the armor vest open and ducking down to lift up his tunic at the side, over his ribs.

He pulled in tight breaths as it came into view—a wide spread of dark blood beneath the skin. I lifted my hand to feel the bones with my fingertips and his head tilted back, his eyes pinching closed. I'd spent a month nursing an injury just like this in Aurvanger. "They're broken."

He laughed, surprising me. "I know."

I straightened, looking up at him. I hadn't really seen him smile before. The side of his face pulled, revealing a dimple at the corner of his mouth, and I looked away, feeling my cheeks flush. I set his arm back down, unclasping the other side of the vest and helping him work it off with my eyes on the ground.

"The night I found you in the forest . . ." His voice dropped to a whisper.

I took his vest into my arms. "What?"

"You said 'Herja.'"

The sound of a grunt came through the door and my eyes snapped back up to the boots. Moving.

I dropped the vest on the table and stepped one foot in front of the other, pulling the knife from my belt. When the sunlight hit my face, I stepped into the snow and looked down at him. He rolled over, holding the side of his head that was bleeding.

"Iri!" I called into the house and the Herja's eyes popped open.

Iri came through the door, pulling the Herja by his armor vest and sliding him over the ground to sit up.

I waited for him to look back at me. His head hung, his eyes studying his surroundings. They landed on the *dýr* collar around my neck just as Fiske stepped out of the house, one hand tucked into his bruised side.

"Where did you get the Aska armor?" I crouched down in front of him, speaking quietly.

His eyes still travelled past me, looking around us. He was trying to gauge his chances.

I gripped the knife tighter in my hand. "Where did you get the armor?"

He pressed his lips together, leaning his head back. A small smile lifted at the corners of his mouth.

I dragged my arms up over me and slammed them down, sinking the blade of the knife into the thick of his thigh. He howled, writhing as I yanked it free, and he looked up with spit flying out of his mouth, gaping at me.

"Why do you have Aska armor?" I yelled, flinging the blade to the side to flick the blood onto the ground.

His breath punched in and out of his lungs as he bit down, glaring.

I stabbed him again, finding the flesh in the other leg and going deeper. He shrieked louder, and I twisted the blade. The knife pulled up again, tearing through the skin and muscle, and he lunged for me. Iri got hold of his vest, rolling him onto his back, and I kneeled over him. But the ferocity in his face was only growing.

I grabbed his hair, holding his head to the ground, and tossed my knife to Fiske's feet. Iri held him in place and he squirmed beneath me, kicking. I listened to the sound of my heart over the sound of boots crunching in the ground behind me. A growing crowd of Riki stood on the path watching, their faces drawn with horror. They'd heard the stories, but they hadn't seen a Herja until last night. To the Riki, they were only legend. To me, they were the demons who killed my mother. Destroyed my father.

Before he could roll again, I pressed my thumb into the inside corner of his eye and dug until I could feel the warm, wet muscle and tissue. He bucked and I leaned all of my weight down onto him as I pried my thumb up, popping his eyeball from its socket. When I had it clasped in my hand, I yanked it free.

His mouth opened wide, the cry trapped in his chest.

"Where did you get the armor?" I screamed, pressing my thumb to the other eye.

"We raided the Aska!" he wailed, choking.

"When?" I stood up off of him. "When were you there?"

He sat up, cupping his bleeding eye socket with his bound hands. "A few weeks ago."

The sway returned to my voice. "What happened?"

When he hesitated, I picked up my knife and slashed it across the meat of his arm. He fell to his side, trying to crawl away as voices rose behind me.

"We raided six of their villages, along the fjord."

The words cut deep into my gut. They stuck me to the ground and held my heartbeat in place.

"And the Riki? How many villages?" It was the Tala's voice.

She stood beside Vidr, their village leader, before a swelling crowd. The sky swayed above us. I shook my head, trying to quiet the sound roaring within it.

The Herja looked down to his blood-covered hands. "Four Riki villages. Fela is the fifth."

The Tala looked back to Vidr, the graveness of it not hidden on her face. If they'd been able to raid that many villages in only a few weeks, there were many of them. *Too* many. The panic flooding my mind drowned out the sound of his hoarse voice, rattling off the names of villages they'd been to and ones they hadn't yet attacked.

"Send riders. Warn the others." Vidr barked out orders and a set of footsteps broke into a run down the path. He stepped forward, his feet beside mine. "Where is your camp?" He looked down at the Herja.

I stood, trying to think as quickly as my thoughts could move. But they were stuck. Sewn to the image of my father. Covered in his own blood. Floating in the blue-gray water of the fjord. I turned to face the Riki gathered behind me, watching. My hands twitched at my sides and I realized I was still holding the Herja's eye. It was warm and slick in my palm. I dropped it into the snow and my knife fell from my other hand. Iri picked it up, going back to the Herja.

I took a step back, stumbling, before someone caught me by the elbow. I looked up to see Fiske standing beside me, his hand taking my upper arm and gently pulling me toward the house. The cold air burned against my hot skin. I blinked again, trying to focus, rubbing my eyes with my numb hands. Outside, the Riki were shouting. Angry, bloodthirsty, vengeful. And I knew that Iri was probably dragging the Herja to the ritual house. They would find out where the camp was and then they would string him up. They would make him suffer.

Fiske pulled my scabbard and sheath off and I stared into the fire. He watched me, making me feel like I was going to break into pieces. Like he was waiting to see it.

"I have to go to the Aska," I whispered. "Now. I can't wait for the thaw."

The shouting outside was getting farther away.

"I have to go," I said again.

"I know." He didn't look away. He didn't blink. "I'll go with you."

I stared at him.

"You can't get off the mountain before the thaw unless someone shows you the way. I'll go with you. I'll take you to Hylli."

He was right. But I wanted to say no. To ask why. I wanted to run as far from Fela as I could. As far from the deep whisper inside of me that spoke when Fiske looked at me the way he looked at me now. The way he did at the river. Like he knew something I didn't.

TWENTY-NINE

"FISKE." I COULD HEAR THE WARNING IN INGE'S VOICE.

They stood facing each other, both with their arms crossed. I traced the resemblance of their faces with my eyes. I'd never noticed how much he looked like her. Eyes rimmed with dark lashes. The square of their faces.

Iri leaned into the table, watching Runa, who lay asleep against the wall with her back to the fire.

"We'll take her to Hylli," Fiske repeated. "And then we'll come home."

"You're needed here." She looked between them.

"We'll come back to fight."

Inge looked into the fire for a long time, breathing evenly. She was still in the same bloodstained dress, the lack of sleep carved deep into her face, with her hair a mess around her.

Fiske didn't move, waiting.

She reached up and touched her lips with light fingers,

like she did when she was thinking. She didn't look in my direction, but her thoughts drifted toward me. She was asking questions. Wondering.

I moved past them, climbing the loft and leaving them below. Halvard was still asleep on his cot with a bearskin pulled up over him and I stopped, hands on the top rung of the ladder. Gyda was lying on her side with her body curved around a small wiggling lump and Kerling was folded behind her, peering over her shoulder. She held the tiny thing to her, pressing it against her bare skin and kissing its head.

Kerling's face had changed. The barrenness in his eyes was gone. He was missing the weight that usually showed there. Gyda looked up at me and I froze, lifting my foot to climb back down. But instead of the bitterness I'd seen in her eyes the days before, her face was smooth. Quiet. When she looked back down to the baby, trailing her fingertips over its soft dark hair, Kerling pressed his face into her back, closing his eyes.

I found my braid with my hand and wound it around my knuckles, watching them. As if it all hadn't happened. The raid. The battle in Aurvanger that took his leg. The blood feud that burned in their hearts for me and my people. There was no room for it in that moment. There was only a beginning. And its light hid everything else. It was so beautiful that it hurt, touching every wound uncovered inside of me.

I quietly climbed back down the ladder, leaving them in the dim light of the loft, and walked outside to wash the blood off my face and arms. I could hear Inge and the others arguing inside, hushed whispers working their way through the cracks in the walls.

I plunged my hands into the barrel of melted snow, cringing at the sting of it on my skin, and scrubbed until the water turned pink. My reflection wavered on its surface. Circles under my eyes and the glow of a bruise still healing across my cheek.

I could see Inge through the door, setting the saddlebags onto the table and packing. Her face was twisted into a knot, her lip sucked in between her teeth. She'd given in, and although it was what I wanted, some part of me trembled.

"I came to thank you."

I turned, holding the edges of the barrel, the water still dripping from my hair.

The Tala stood on the path with her hands folded in front of her clean dress. Her hair was pulled up off her shoulders and her green eyes were brighter against her reddened face. The same rope burns that encircled Halvard's neck wrapped around hers.

"Why did you help me?" She tilted her head to one side, looking me up and down. When I didn't answer, she stepped closer. "I know you saw me that night. When Thorpe left you in the forest."

I didn't know what to say because I didn't know the answer. I had no reason for helping her. I just did. And I almost wished I hadn't. No one would have ever known if I'd left her there.

Her lips parted in a grin. "Thora has her eye on you, Aska. I could see it the first time I met you."

"I don't serve Thora," I reminded her. "I don't care about her will and I don't want her favor."

She smiled wider. "Neither did Iri."

My eyes drifted back to the house. The defenses in me readied.

"Inge told me this morning."

I felt my mouth drop open and my heart soured inside me. Inge said she wouldn't tell anyone.

"When we returned from the forest, I could see it. When you came through the door. I feel foolish for not seeing it sooner, really. You look just like him, Eelyn."

I tried to pick apart the tone in her voice. I tried to line it up with the calm look on her face.

"You don't have to worry about Iri." She waved a hand at me. "We're beyond that now, I think. I'll speak to Vidr. You've earned our trust. Now maybe we can earn yours."

My eyes narrowed. "Why would you want my trust?"

"You're a warrior. And something tells me we will need every warrior from here to the fjord on our side if we are going to keep the Herja from coming back here and finishing what they started."

"The Aska?" I laughed. "On *your* side?"

"Depending on what you find in Hylli, there may not be two sides anymore."

I looked over my shoulder, to the door. "How did you know I was going to Hylli?"

"They're your people." She looked at me, and a bit of that warmth I'd seen her give to the others, she gave to me.

I could see it in her eyes. She thought the Aska were gone. Or close to it.

"In the morning, we send the Riki souls to *Friðr* and then we leave for the next village. If you want to go to Hylli, we can take you as far as Möor." She reached out to me, setting her hand on my shoulder, and I tensed, looking at it.

"Fiske and Iri are taking me." I lifted my chin.

Her eyes jumped past me, toward the house, and I wished I hadn't said it. She rolled a thought around behind her gaze before it settled into place and her look turned knowing.

"Maybe you'll find your way back up the mountain after you find what you're looking for." Her hand squeezed me gently before it dropped.

The fury reared its head inside me again. She couldn't just give me a smile and offer me kindness and expect me to give the Riki loyalty. Or trust. I wasn't Iri.

"Tell me." I held her gaze. "Tell me about the dream you had."

The sparkle ignited behind the green in her eyes again and she glanced back to the house.

"I saw you." Her eyes squinted, considering it. "With a bear in the forest." Her head tilted to the side again. She was trying to read me.

I kept myself still, trying to keep my face from giving anything away. Anything she may be looking for.

"You don't know." She reached into the neckline of her dress and pulled out a bronze pendant on a long chain. She opened her hand flat, holding it out to me. It was etched with the head of a bear, like the one on the doors of the ritual house. "The bears are sacred to Thora. Before she made her people from the melted rock of the mountain, she created them."

I waited.

"They are her messengers."

"If you believe Thora favors me, then why did you leave me in the forest that night? Why did you just walk away?"

She looked up to the sky, thinking. "It was the only way I'd know for sure if I was right about you. And I was. Thora preserved you."

"Fiske saved my life, not Thora."

She smirked. "Believe what you like, Eelyn. The bear is an omen." The words came slowly on her thin lips. "And omens often bring change."

THIRTY

THE RIKI STOOD TOGETHER IN THE EARLY MORNING, gathered against the bite of cold as the snow fell softly, floating down from the sky. The little flakes swayed back and forth as they made their way down, where they were eaten by the great fire that burned in front of the ritual house.

I listened to the Tala pray for the fallen Riki, asking Thora to accept them. To keep them until their families joined them in the afterlife. There was no emotion on her face as she spoke. The light in her eyes was dim, but there was still a surety thick in her voice. She was steady and firm. And I could feel each of the Riki holding onto her strength, eagerly looking to her to keep them from flying away on the wind of grief.

The heat of the fire pushed against us and the roaring sound of it found the bitter cries of the mourning, swallowing them up too. I'd heard that sound many times. Usually when we came home from fighting and families searched for the missing faces of loved ones.

There was no sound like that—like the soul tearing.

"Heill para," she called out, looking up to the sky.

"Heill para." The words repeated on the lips of every Riki and Fiske's deep voice sounded at my back.

Safe travels.

The Tala walked across the front of the altar, to a man who was weeping with his shoulders hunched over beneath a thick fur. She whispered into his ear and the choking sobs slowed. He quieted and she looked up into his face before letting him go again and moving to the next person.

I was glad I didn't know what he'd lost. Who he'd lost.

The bodies of the Riki burned, sending black smoke up into the air. The souls were headed for *Friðr,* on their way to see lost loved ones. I closed my eyes, trying to push down the dread that was still lingering in my mind. Wondering if I'd be weeping for my father's soul in two days' time.

People peeled off from the crowd and I looked for Iri. He stood with Runa, who stared into the flames, her cheeks red on her ashen face. His arm touched hers as her little sister wrapped her arms around Iri's leg, holding tight.

More Riki fell away, slowly walking down the path back into the village, and I made my way to them. The sharp light of the flames reflected in Runa's tired eyes.

"I'm sorry," I said, still thinking of my father.

She nodded, swallowing, before she bent down to pick

up her sister and followed her mother down the path. Iri watched them.

"You should stay." I said.

Iri shook his head. "I can't."

"I can make it to Hylli. Your place is here, with her." I nodded toward Runa. "You'll have to fight. Soon. You may not have much time left with her."

He looked down at me, his eyes scanning my face for what I wasn't saying. "What is it?"

I wrapped my arms around myself, now cold away from the fire. "I don't know what they will do to you—the Aska. I should talk to them first."

He nodded, understanding my meaning. There was no way to know how they would react to the truth about Iri. "Alright."

I WAITED FOR FISKE AND IRI OUTSIDE OF THE RITUAL house, watching the last embers of the fire smolder on the altar. The bodies were nothing but ash now, their spirits and flesh gone from this world.

The warriors had gathered to hear Vidr's plan, but when I tried to go in, two Riki shut the doors on me. I sat against the wall, my fingers hooked into each other, and listened. I could hear them, piping up to argue or calling out in agreement, but it was mostly quiet and I didn't like the feeling that had fallen over the village. The Riki had always been a capable enemy. They were strong. If they were unsure of what direction to take it meant that they were afraid.

When the doors finally opened, I stood, falling into step beside Iri as he and Fiske came through the doors. "What did he say?"

He was tired and it was beginning to show on his face. It leaked into the grinding of his voice. "They're going to meet the other village leaders to find out how many we've lost. How much help we might need."

"From the Aska," I murmured under my breath.

He stopped. "The Herja are too many, Eelyn."

I turned back to him, my throat constricting. "You know that will never happen." I shifted on my feet. "Maybe they will leave. Like last time."

"This isn't like last time," he said, almost sadly.

And I knew it was true. When the Herja came before, they only came once. And there hadn't been so many dead. There hadn't been so much destroyed. This was different.

We walked the rest of the way in silence, the weight of it sinking in. The Herja that came to Fela could only be a small group of them. There were probably many, many more than either clan knew.

Fiske opened the door, going inside, and he was talking to Inge a moment later, leaving Iri and me alone.

"What did he say?" I asked. Fiske was sitting on the table next to Halvard, checking his nose again.

"He's going to go with you."

I breathed, "Why?"

"Eelyn, does everything have to be hard with you?" He shook his head. "You need him to go. He's going."

He stepped around me and Inge touched his arm as he passed. She looked at me as I came in and then her eyes went to Fiske.

"They're gathering. We should go." He stood.

I picked up my weapons from the bench and fit them into place. Halvard jumped down from the table and ran outside, his feet slapping on the stone.

"You'll be careful, *sváss.*" Inge lifted Fiske's chin to look at her. "And then you'll come back."

He didn't answer her, instead looking into her eyes word-lessly as she held onto his shoulders, praying under her breath. When she was finished, he tried to smile at her. "What are you thinking?" he asked.

She smiled back at him, but it was slanted. Sad. "I'm think-ing that you always surprise me." Her eyes flitted to me again before she let him go and Fiske went to Iri, hugging him. Iri was talking to him, his voice low.

"*Qnd eldr.*" Iri let him go.

"*Qnd eldr.*"

They were words I'd heard before. Breathe fire. The Riki said them to each other on the battlefield.

Inge came to the door, pulling my hair out from under the strap of my axe sheath. "Can I?" she asked from behind me.

A chill ran over my skin as I nodded, sitting down onto

the stool in the corner. The one I'd eaten on, watching them at the table together. As a family.

She pulled the length of my hair down my back, working it into thick sections, and braided them down over my shoulder, tying the end. The feeling made me shake, the hazy memories of my mother bubbling up from the depths of my mind. Memories I thought I'd lost.

I stared at the floor. "Is there anything Fiske wouldn't do for Iri?"

"He loves Iri more than he loves himself, but this isn't about Iri anymore." She looked down into my face for a long moment before setting her hands softly on my head. She was praying again.

I held the breath deep inside me, because I knew what it would bring up when I let it go. A hot, stabbing pain in my chest. I wiped at my eyes as she finished and stood, walking toward the door without looking back. Halvard had the reins of the horses, holding them on the path. He didn't look up to me as I went to him.

"Are you going to come back?" he asked, kicking the snow with his boots.

I took the reins of Iri's horse, running my hand up his snout. "I don't know."

"You could. You could come back if you want."

I reached into my armor vest and took his hand. "Thank you."

"For what?" He looked at me, his face changing.

"For being kind to me."

I dropped the gift into his palm, a simple idol. I didn't know what his father looked like, and I wasn't a talented carver, but I'd used the rest of the wood Inge gave me to make it for him.

"Is this my father?" he asked, his voice small.

I nodded, pulling him by his tunic and wrapping my arms around him. He buried his face into my vest, squeezing me, and I tried to push the hair from his face, but it was too wild. The dark purple bruises under his eyes made the blue in them look brighter.

Iri, Fiske, and Inge came from inside the house and Iri stopped in front of me. I stared into his chest, the Riki armor no longer strange to me. Now, the Aska leathers wouldn't look right on him.

"*Elska ykkarr,*" he said, and the warmth of the words wound around me.

I love you.

I leaned into him, letting him hold me. I loved him, too. More than anything. But I wondered if I would ever be able to admit it to him again. I wondered if a part of me would always be angry. "What do you want me to tell our father?"

He sighed. "The truth."

I didn't want to tell him about Iri. But I could never lie to him.

He kissed the top of my head and held the reins as I lifted myself up onto the horse. Down the path, the Riki were already waiting. Again, I didn't look back as the bend of the trail took us out of sight. I kept my eyes on Fiske's back, Iri's horse following his. I'd thought more than once that I'd seen my brother for the last time. I'd been sure. I didn't want to feel that feeling again.

"How many days?" I asked, winding the reins tighter around my fists.

But before we'd even reached the ritual house, Fiske was dismounting again, dropping to the ground and taking my horse by the riggings.

"What are you doing?" I tried to pull back but the horse followed him.

He didn't answer, leading me off the main path, away from the others, until we stopped in front of the blacksmith's tent. The forge blazed in the shadow.

My brow pulled. "What are you—"

The blacksmith stopped his pounding and looked up at me, a hammer in one hand and his dark leather apron wrapped tightly around his waist.

He looked between the two of us.

"I want you to take it off," Fiske said. "The collar." He spoke to the blacksmith, saying something I couldn't hear over my thoughts.

The blacksmith shrugged. "Alright."

I held onto the saddle, my fingers white.

"Come on, then." He tossed the hammer onto the table.

I slid down off the horse as he picked up a long-handled tool with a hook on it. "Here."

I stepped into the tent and he grabbed hold of the collar,

lowering me down to hook one side of it onto an iron bar driven into the trunk of a thick tree.

"Stay still," he grunted.

He secured the tool into the other side of the collar and took a deep breath before he leaned back, pulling against it with his weight. The collar widened slowly and I stayed still, trying to keep it from touching the burns. When he stood and leaned back to pull again, I pinched my eyes closed and it scraped against me.

He slipped the ring from around my neck and dropped it to the ground in front of me, a broken black circle sunken into the snow.

My fingers ran over the skin on my neck, freed from the weight and the cold of the collar. "Why did you do that?"

"If you're going home, it won't be as a *dýr*." He uncrossed his arms, going back to the horse. The blacksmith went back to his work and the pounding of iron on the forge rang out around us.

"You don't owe me anything." I could hear the Riki down the path starting to move. "You saved my life. More than once. We're even."

He glanced down at the ground and I waited for the words building behind his lips.

"We'll never be even."

THIRTY-ONE

WE RODE IN A LONG LINE THROUGH THE FOREST, AND I finally understood what Fiske meant when he told me that I'd never find my way off the mountain alone. There was no clear path in the snow. We cut left and right down buried trails and around cliff faces in erratic patterns that made no sense. It took me half the day to realize that we were avoiding the overhanging slopes of the mountain that were packed with a threatening avalanche.

Every movement was specific. They kept their pace slow, staying quiet when we were out from under the cover of the trees. Far ahead of us, Vidr led the group, looking up around us as we moved, studying the rise of the mountain.

The Riki ignored my presence and that was better than noticing me. Many of them had been the ones to watch me pluck the eye from the Herja. I shuddered, remembering the hot, soft thing clutched in my shaking hand. Maybe they knew I'd saved the Tala. Maybe I'd earned their trust, like she said. But none of it mattered to me now. I wanted off the mountain. I just needed to get home.

We travelled well into the night and I sat up straight, trying to stretch my back and my tender shoulder. It was still sore and stinging where it was trying to heal, but I kept reinjuring it. I lifted the arm up slowly, gently stretching the muscles, and glanced back at Fiske, where he'd fallen back to ride behind me. The winter moon rose early in the sky, huge and misshapen. It hung over the forest like a buoy floating in the water and the cold hardened around us as the sun went down. With every turn in the path, the dread buried beneath every thought grew heavier, my imagination running wild with what waited for me in the fjord.

A whistle sounded ahead, long and low, and the horses slowed to a stop. Fiske's boots hit the ground and he waited for me to dismount and tie my horse beside his.

"We'll sleep a few hours and start again." He pulled the saddles from the horses and slipped the bearskins from under them.

"Sleep out here?" There was nothing but deep snow.

He pointed to the rock face behind me, where the Riki were disappearing. I hoisted my saddlebag over my good shoulder and we headed in the same direction. Slipping into a wide crack running up the rock from the ground, I recoiled, feeling the need to take my knife into my hand.

The strike of fire-steel lit the cave as someone started a fire, and then another lit behind us. They popped up one by one until I could see the inside of the cavern, aglow with the orange light. It was huge, with a ceiling reaching down in points of dripping stone, like fingers coming to snatch us up and pull us into the belly of the mountain. And it was quiet. So quiet that I could hear the scrape of every boot on the dirt below us.

Fiske moved us toward the fire at the back of the cave and I stepped around the Riki already settling down for sleep. I leaned into the wall, sliding until I was sitting on the ground, and looked around me. The Riki gathered around the other fires, leaving Fiske and me on the edge of the group. It was still strange to see them this way—tired and weak. Heartbroken. The spirit in them was sleeping somewhere deep inside, but it was there. It was like the stillness of the air before an angry storm. And I didn't like the idea of sleeping in the middle of it.

A head of bright red hair stopped my gaze and I flinched, recognizing Thorpe. He sat beside a fire across the cave, pulling a wool blanket up over his chest. His face was cut and bruised, his eye swollen.

Fiske wedged a dry log underneath the fire to build it up. His hands were still scabbed at the knuckles from where they'd inflicted Thorpe's wounds only a few days before. When he saw me staring, he looked down at his hands and then to Thorpe.

"Will he want revenge for what you did?" I asked quietly.

"He won't touch you again."

I looked back up to Thorpe. I'd seen him at the burning of the Riki bodies, too, and he hadn't even looked at me.

Fiske kicked the saddlebags closer to me and I reached inside to pull out the bread Inge had packed. I tore it in half and handed one side to Fiske, pulling my knees up into my chest. The taste of it reminded me of their home and I swallowed it down. Because thinking of Inge and Halvard made me feel strange. The gentle pull back to Fela twisted in my chest. Not like home. Something else.

"Do you believe what Inge says? About you and Iri?" I watched his face carefully, trying to read him.

His eyebrows raised, surprised by the question. "The *sál fjotra*?"

I nodded, taking another bite.

"I don't know." He leaned back into the wall, staring at the bread in his hands.

"What do you think happened?"

He thought for a long moment before he answered. "I think I saw myself in Iri."

"What do you mean?"

"We've been taught our whole lives that we're different from each other." His eyes met mine. "But we're the same. I think that scared me."

I sunk back into the shadow, away from the firelight. I didn't want him to see anything my face betrayed. Because I knew what he was saying. It was the thing that folded around my heart when I looked at Halvard. It was the thought pushing into my mind, watching the Riki raise the walls of Kerling's barn. The sound of their voices, singing.

"If you believe that, then why were you fighting in Aurvanger?"

He ran a hand through his hair. "Because whether or not we are the same, we are enemies. My people die in the fighting season. At the hands of the Aska."

I wished I hadn't asked. Because thinking we were the same made too many things possible. It made paths fork where they didn't before. It was terrifying. "Are we still enemies? You and I?"

"No," he answered, simply.

I looked up and Fiske was still watching me. His gaze trailed over my hair, back down to my face, making me tremble. I dropped my eyes back to the fire, my face burning.

The Riki quieted and silence overtook the cave. Fiske laid the bearskin out on the damp ground and I curled against the wall, facing the open space. The fire was warm, but I didn't like having my back open and exposed. I pulled a blanket up over me, tucking it under my chin as Fiske moved the logs strategically around the flames so they'd burn longer. He wasn't complaining about the pain in his ribs, but he held his arm closer to his body than usual and tried not to carry too much weight on that side. When he finished, he settled next to me.

I watched him draw in a deep breath and let it go, sinking into the ground as he pulled his blanket over him. I tried to picture Hylli. The dirt trails that wound around the village like river inlets. The way things looked crisp when the sun was overhead. The birds that flew over the fjord, swooping down with their wings spread and their talons outstretched to pull fish from the water.

My breaths stuttered over each other and I stuck my hands down between my thighs to try to pull the heat to the center of my body. I shook. It wasn't just the cold. It was the Herja. It was Hylli. It was the wondering what I'd find at the fjord.

The dirt in front of me shifted and I opened my eyes. Fiske was looking over his shoulder, his eyes running over my blanket, and he slid himself back, into the space between us.

I waited for his breaths to slow before I scooted closer to him, letting the line of my body fit to his and feeling the heat come off his skin. I pushed my face into the warm place where his back met the bearskin and stared at the woven leather of his armor vest, following its pattern with my eyes until they were so heavy I couldn't hold them open. I fell asleep to the sound of his breathing, his back rising and falling against me, like the sound of seawater kissing the fjord.

THIRTY-TWO

THE FIRST BODY ON THE TRAIL WAS LYING HALF BURIED in a fresh snowfall. Her long hair was splayed out around her head with the shining furs hardened in the cold wind. She was Herja.

Ahead, a string of frozen corpses spread through the forest and Fiske looked back to catch my eyes. We were close to Möor, the first and largest of the Riki villages.

The top of the huge ritual house rose before the slope of the mountain as we came down. A section of the roof was caved in, blackened by smoke, but it was still standing. The homes weren't as fortunate. Almost every one of them was a pile of charred wood. A few Riki were already starting to rebuild, planing lumber to repair the walls, and the sound of their tools scraping over the wood rose up to us on the ridge.

They stopped as we came down the trail and a few

minutes later, a group of them emerged from inside the ritual house. Large doors carved like the ones in Fela swung open and a white-haired man led them toward us. His face was stitched together down the line of a deep sword's gash that reached up over his eye. The other men were pieced together as well, their faces and bodies showing the echoes of the raid. They hadn't fared nearly as well as Fela.

"Vidr," the white-haired man called out, stopping to wait for us.

"Latham." Vidr dropped from his horse, taking Latham's hand and pulling him close to clap him on the back.

The others dismounted and I melted into the group, trying to blend in. If the Riki in Möor looked closely, they would know I wasn't one of them. But looking around at what remained of the village, I thought for the first time that maybe it didn't matter anymore.

Fiske untied the saddlebag Inge packed full of medicines and bandages and we followed them up the path to the ritual house. We ducked beneath the fallen beam at the door and entered the dank, smoky room. My breath caught.

The floor was covered wall to wall with Riki children, camped on blankets and stools, a few belongings gathered here and there. They sunk down together like little birds huddled in nests. Filthy, with wounds uncared for. Their healer was either dead or tending to more serious injuries.

At the altar, one body lay on the platform with the light from the broken roof casting over him. It was a man, wrapped in a blue cloak with a scrolling iron clasp fastened at the neck.

He'd been cleaned and his hands folded onto his chest neatly where strands of wooden beads hung. Their Tala.

"When did they come?" Vidr looked out over the room, probably thinking the same thing I was. Fela had been lucky.

"Five days ago. In the middle of the night." Latham's voice was hollow and hoarse. "They came through the trees like ghosts."

Silence grew thick in the smoky air. The paleness was still settled beneath their skin and the shakiness still beneath their words. It had been the same after the Herja came to Hylli when I was a child.

Vidr stared at the man's body on the altar.

Latham gave a hesitant nod. "He died of infection yesterday." He took a stool from the wall and sat, offering a seat to Vidr. I tried to move closer to listen. "We are the fifth Riki village to be raided in the last two weeks. You're the sixth. And they'll be back."

"How many did you lose?"

"One hundred and forty-eight."

The silence was abrupt. Fela had only lost fifty-four. But Möor was much bigger. If the other villages had lost those kinds of numbers, the Riki didn't have a chance against the Herja. My thoughts went back to Hylli. If they'd been able to do this on the mountain, what had they done on the fjord? The villages down there were more exposed. More accessible. I swallowed hard, the trembling starting to surface again.

Vidr sat, taking the bearskin from his shoulders and laying it across his lap. "We've learned they attacked the Aska before they came up the mountain."

"The Aska?" Latham sat up, his crooked face lifting in surprise.

"We don't know yet how they've fared. One of ours is going down to see what's become of them." He glanced at Fiske.

"They are too many, Vidr. I don't know where they all came from."

"Yes, you do." He eyed the man and a chill fell over the group of them.

There had always been whispers about the Herja. No one knew where they lived or where they retreated to. It had long been said that they weren't entirely human. That they were more spirit than flesh, and that they brought the wrath of some angry god. If it was true, maybe there was nothing we could do to beat them.

"The others who've survived are meeting us back in Fela. They should arrive in the next day or two."

"When they do, we'll decide what's to be done. Together." Vidr leaned forward to catch Latham's eyes.

"We'll have to fight." But that ferocious look of the Riki was still missing from Latham's face.

I stepped around the group as they talked, finding a path in the makeshift encampment of the ritual house. The Riki children looked up at me with dirty faces, wrapped in their blankets, some clutching bowls of cold food. The fire in the middle of the room blazed, sending the heat pushing around us, and I stopped as Fiske came to stand beside me.

The strain reaching through his whole body was carefully concealed, but I could see it in the set of his eyes. The news of losing so many Riki was a blow. And taking on the Herja would be certain death. He was thinking of Inge. And Halvard. Iri.

"When do we leave for Hylli?" I asked.

"Morning. I'll treat whoever I can until then." He looked around the room. "But I'm not my mother."

I walked past the fire to a kettle on the other side of the altar that was filled with water. I set it onto the coals and took the child nearest to me first. She looked at me warily as I sat her on a bench near the fire. When the water was warm, I cleaned her face, wiping the dirt and ash from her fair, freckled skin as she looked up at me with eyes the color of oiled Riki leather. Her long blond hair fell down her back in a tangled knot.

Fiske took her leg into his hands, looking at the gouge in her calf. It looked like the work of an axe blade and it was still open, red and inflamed at the edges. I scrubbed her skin, working at the grime as Fiske closed it up. He pulled a needle through the skin slowly, holding the thread between his teeth. She refused to cry, watching him hold the flesh together with his hands. When he was done, he moved to the next child. A blond boy with his arm in a makeshift sling. I followed, cleaning each of their faces as Fiske tended whatever wounds they carried from the raid. My entire life, I'd

ADRIENNE YOUNG

never thought of the Riki as small children. I'd only ever known the fierce faces of their warriors in battle. But now they had pasts. Names. Souls.

Njord.

Idunn.

Aila.

Frigg.

I looked into their eyes. They were young and afraid but strong, the way they'd been taught to be. They gritted their teeth and bore the bite of stitches and the sting of infected wounds. Behind the haze of tears and the pink on their noses, they were like fire-steel.

I braided their hair back out of their faces, pulling it into order. Fiske smiled without looking at me, his eyes trained on the cut across a little boy's shoulder.

"What?"

He glanced up, his chin tipping toward them. "They look like Aska."

And he was right. I almost laughed. I was never very good at it, but I knew a few Aska braids well. I'd been doing them since I was a child. They gathered around, arms crossed over their chests, watching us.

Like little warriors. Like Iri and I had been. Like we still were.

THIRTY-THREE

I waited down the path on my horse while Fiske talked with Vidr and Latham. The sun was just coming up and the village was still quiet, but I had been packed and ready since before we'd slept. I could feel the pull. Hylli reached up the mountain and wrapped its fingers around me. Calling me to the fjord. It was something I'd never felt before. The Aska had died in battle and in raids, but there was never a time I'd thought the Aska may end.

Fiske climbed onto his horse and came down the path, passing me to lead the way back to the trail, and Vidr watched us, the wind blowing his hair across his face. *"Qnd eldr!"* His voice echoed in the forest.

The horses knew the way, though I could still make no sense of it. I was used to navigating by landmarks, but with everything covered in snow, it was impossible. Fiske's eyes were on the treetops and the angle of the mountain, not on the ground. The sun rose up higher and the land grew steeper. The horses slid, their legs shaking, sending rocks rolling on the patches of ground that were bare. Fiske leaned back, compensating for the shift in weight, and I did the same as we made our way down the most treacherous parts of the trail. When we reached the bottom, the view widened to the valley far below where a distant stretch of green lay beyond the white expanse.

As the day warmed and the snow began to melt, the ground grew slicker. We walked the horses when the trail turned steep again and then stopped to let them rest. I walked to the ledge of a drop-off, looking out over the trees. The canopy of the forest looked like the churned froth on top of seawater, fluffy and thick with snowfall.

"What do you think will happen when the Riki go after the Herja?"

Fiske tightened the saddle on the horse. "I think we will be defeated." There was nothing in his voice to indicate fear.

"But you'll still fight?"

He looked up at me with disapproval. "Of course we will."

I watched an eagle glide out over the trees, tipping left then right. "But if you can't win . . ."

"If we don't fight, the Herja will kill us anyway. We die fighting or we die hiding. Which would you choose?"

He knew my answer as well as I did. I'd never wait, hunkered down in a half-burned village, for the Herja to come back for me, even if it meant death. But I didn't like the idea of Iri going into a hopeless fight. I couldn't stomach the idea of Inge and Halvard cut down by the Herja. Fiske, eyes open and empty, staring into the sky as his soul left his body. A chill ran over my skin.

"The Riki could resettle." I pointed out over the horizon, past the fjord. "Beyond the valley."

"In Aska territory?" He tilted his head to one side.

I shrugged. "The Herja change things. Either way, the Aska and the Riki won't fight each other if they're in the valley. They are the bigger enemy."

"They are the common enemy," he corrected.

I crossed my arms in front of me. I had been thinking the same thing, but I couldn't picture it. I couldn't imagine a world where the Aska and Riki were on the same side. The age-old tangle of brown and red leathers, bronze and iron on the battlefield. But fighting *together*.

"And if we won? Then what?" I asked, watching as the eagle turned, tilting its wings to the side as it made its way back toward us.

He let go of the saddle, scratching at the horse's mane. "I don't know."

We started again, taking a more level decline and slowing our progress so the horses didn't tire. My body shook from the tension of controlling the animal, my jaw sore from biting down as I focused on preventing a slide. Once we were back on the slope, I looked behind us, up the towering face of the mountain piled with heavy snow. I could feel the power of it, hovering like it was waiting for the chance to come rolling down over us. And I imagined, for just a moment, what it would be like to be buried in it. To slowly give way to the cold and close my eyes in surrender to death. Like the night Thorpe left me in the forest. Like the days Iri spent lying in the trench, dying. But now, something about the idea was almost comforting. It meant no more wondering. Wondering if the Aska had survived. If I'd get home or what would happen to Iri. Wondering about the thread that seemed to be tied between Fiske and me, slowly tightening.

The sun sunk lower in the sky, making the world blue and cold again as we headed into the trees. The forest was quiet, the horses' breaths and hooves the only sound. When we met a break in the thicket, the light was almost gone.

Fiske moved out from under the trees ahead of me and the white moonlight spilled down on him as he slid off the horse. I tried not to stare at the way his form looked against the frigid night.

I came through the trees and my horse stopped at the gravel edge of a large frozen lake. The surface stretched out in both directions like frosted black glass. "How do we go around it?" I dismounted, walking to the edge and tapping the heel of my boot on the thick ice.

"We don't." He pulled the bag from the saddle and dropped it over his head to hang across his shoulder. "We walk across."

"Across?" I stared at him.

"Across."

The mountain stood over us, watching. "There's no way to go around?"

"There is, but it will take another full day to go that way." He worked on my saddlebag, pulling at the riggings.

I stared at the lake. "What if we fall in?"

"We won't." He smiled, and I looked away when I felt heat painting across my skin again.

He tossed me the bag and I hung it over me as he turned the horses back toward the mountain and slapped them above their hind legs. They took off, their galloping steps like distant thunder in the dark forest.

"They know the way back." He stepped out onto the ice.

It groaned beneath his feet, making my heart twist up on itself. I gulped down a chest full of air, lifting my eyes to the other side, invisible in the dark. I started behind him, walking at an angle like my father had taught me to keep too much weight off of the ice. The powdery snow slid under my boots as we got farther on the surface, and then dissipated, leaving the ice smooth and polished.

The sound of the wind blowing whistled around us and I gasped when I finally looked down, stopping mid-stride. I turned in a circle, my eyes going wide. The night sky was reflecting on the ice in crisp shapes and colors, bright strings of stars swirling out around each other and a huge, round, speckled moon staring up at me.

It hung above its reflection, like the sky was folded in on itself. We were standing on it. Like the world was upside down.

I touched my lips with my fingertips, my eyes flitting over the surface. Fiske stopped, one thumb hooked into the strap across his chest, watching me. The light bouncing off the ice lit up the side of his face.

He looked up at the moon. "It only does this for a week or two. The ice starts to cloud as it thins."

I squatted down and pressed my hand to it, watching it fog around my fingers. When I lifted them, the hazy outline was still there, frozen onto the surface. "When we were little, I almost drowned in the fjord. I fell through the ice." I looked at myself in the reflection. "Iri and I were trying to see how far out we could make it and when I heard the crack, I looked up and saw his face just before it gave way beneath me."

He took a step toward me.

"It was so dark. I could hardly see. And then his hands had me, yanking me up and throwing me back onto the ice." I remembered the way it looked. The water was a darker blue than I'd ever seen. "I don't know how he didn't fall in. I was so angry with him for coming to the edge like that." My words trailed off.

Once, he'd loved me enough to jump into the frozen water for me. But then he left.

"We do things we have to do." Fiske broke the thin silence between us. "If he hadn't jumped in, you would have died." He paused. "If I hadn't taken you that night in Aurvanger, that Riki would have killed you."

I stood to face him. "I know."

"If I hadn't put the arrow into your shoulder, someone else would have put one in your heart. If I hadn't taken you as a *dýr*, you'd be in one of those other burned villages on the mountain."

"I know," I said again.

"I would do it again," he said. "All of it."

But still, those things singed. Another moment and Fiske's sword would have been the end of me. And that night, I would have killed him without thinking twice. Now, the thought made me feel like I was trapped under the ice beneath us, sinking into the dark.

I looked at him. "Why did you come with me?"

He let go of the strap on his chest and shifted on his feet.

"Why are you here?"

And when his eyes finally met mine, they were open. They let me in.

I took a step back.

My mouth opened to say something, but the words wouldn't come. They were stuck in the back of my throat, wrapped tightly around my windpipe. I was suddenly aware of the icy, opaque depths beneath us again, waiting for the smallest crack to pull us down into it. Waiting to feed on us. My heart pulsed in my veins as the fear pressed down on me, making me feel heavier. It was terrifying—that feeling—like there was something tying me to him. Because if one of us fell into the darkness, the other would too.

I stepped around him, walking faster toward the other side. Toward solid ground and safety. The lake grumbled beneath my weight. Growling. Hungry. I closed my eyes, trying not to see it. That depth within me, sealed down under the surface. I kept my eyes ahead, leaving Fiske standing in between the middle of the two night skies, the stars and the moon encircling him. The only hot, living thing on the ice. The only thing I could feel.

THIRTY-FOUR

We didn't stop. Because I couldn't.

We walked through the forest in the dead of night as the sky darkened and lightened with the clouds passing overhead. The moon disappeared beyond the valley as the sun pulled up over the mountain behind us.

I stayed ahead of Fiske, each step coming a little quicker as I felt the fjord getting nearer. The trees thinned as we reached the valley, spreading out from one another as the ground pushed up from under the snow. The shadow of tree-tops gave way to a sun-drenched sea of new green grass so bright I had to blink at the sight. It was the first push against winter that would make its way up the mountain in the coming weeks.

We kept to the forest, out of the exposure of the valley. I could smell the sea. The cool, salty taste of it ran over my tongue and it begged me to forget where I was and what I was doing. To forget about the night I saw Iri and the pain in my shoulder and the raid. To forget the Herja. I walked the trail I'd walked my whole life, through the valley and toward the fjord, and it felt like none of it had ever happened.

But memory crept in again, slithering up the back of my mind as the land lifted up in front of us and led to the bluff that overlooked my village. The grass faded into rock that warmed in the sun and when my feet touched it, they stopped. They held me there as the slice of blue sea came into view. It sat beneath a gray winter sky, calm and clear, and Fiske's footsteps stopped beside me, waiting.

I looked at my boots, taking a breath, and then I walked straight for the drop-off. I picked up my pace as I came up over the ridge, the view peeling down until I could see the beach. An alarm sounded in my mind. It was too quiet.

Another step and the village came into view. My home. And the wind was snatched from my lungs.

Below, Hylli was nothing but ash. Destruction and slaughter.

My eyes searched the broken rooftops as I ran, my feet sliding over the loose rock down the ridge. The village looked empty, and in the distance, a black halo stained the earth where the ritual house once was.

My hands flew out to steady me before I clapped them over my nose against the stench of rot. I came down the end of the trail with my feet stumbling over each other and took off, jumping over the bodies decaying in the afternoon sun.

"Aghi!" I screamed, but I could hardly hear my own voice over the thunder between my ears.

I pushed harder, flying past the burned-out, crumbling structures. When I came upon our home, I doubled over, my hands on my knees. It was barely standing, the walls jutting up from the ground in sections. My chest pushed and pulled beneath my armor vest, my eyes burning.

In the doorway, a clay bowl lay broken over the threshold.

I stepped inside as Fiske came down the path and looked around with my breath still held hostage inside of me. More broken dishes littered the floor around the fire pit and my cot was lying on its side with the blanket half burned and wet from water dripping from the hole in the roof. Flies buzzed over an iron pot spilled over with spoiled food.

"Eelyn." Fiske's voice sounded behind me.

But I ignored him, picking up the table and setting it upright and then gathering the pottery pieces from the ground. I stacked them neatly into my hand, my mind racing.

"Eelyn," he said again, louder. "The tools and weapons are gone and the bodies outside are Herja. The Aska have left."

I set the shards carefully into the pot, waving the flies away, and picked up the cot. I pulled the blanket into my arms. My mother wove it when she wasn't much older than me. Now it was an unraveling mess, the red and orange designs coming undone.

"If it was bad enough that they left, he's dead," I choked. The strangled sound pierced my throat again and I pushed my face into the wet blanket, sobbing. "They're dead," I cried. "They're all dead."

The warmth of him wrapped around me and I collapsed into it, letting his arms hold my weight. I reeled, my fists pressing into my chest, and I felt it being torn from me. The small, fragile hope I'd carried down the mountain. The faith that the Aska were strong enough.

But they were gone.

Fiske's arms pulled tighter around me and my legs gave, imagining my father's body. Burning on the altar. His beard catching flame. His flesh blackened. And if he was dead, then we all were. Because he was the strongest of us, and without him, my world lost what held it together.

Fiske's voice was soft in my ear. "The Aska bodies were burned. The house is cleaned out. There were survivors, Eelyn."

I couldn't let myself believe it. I couldn't hold the possibility in my mind. There was no room for it in the heartbreak that was consuming every part of my body. The grief of losing my home. My people.

"Think. Where would they have gone?" He let go of me, holding me back to look up at him. His hands pushed the hair from my face. "Where is a safe place? Another Aska village?"

I closed my eyes, trying to think. I knew where they would go, but I wasn't supposed to tell anyone who wasn't Aska. It was a secret. And I'd never even been there. I looked up into his eyes and they stared back at me, searching. Willing me to seize control of my frantic, desperate mind. They were like torches lit in the dark.

"Virki." I wiped my face with my sleeves. "They would go to Virki."

THIRTY-FIVE

Fɪsᴋᴇ ʙᴜɪʟᴛ ᴀ ғɪʀᴇ ɪɴ ᴛʜᴇ ᴘɪᴛ ᴀs I ᴘɪᴄᴋᴇᴅ ᴜᴘ ᴛʜᴇ ᴘɪᴇᴄᴇs of my home and put them back together. If we ever lived here again, it would have to be rebuilt. Most everything was ruined. But I needed to put things back in their places, even if I never saw this place again.

When I was finished, I took the fur up from my father's cot into my hands, smelling it. Spice and dirt and sea. The sting behind my eyes made me blink and I pressed my lips together, trying to keep the tears at bay.

I sat down on the stone in front of the fire. Fiske came to sit beside me, handing me the last of our bread, and I took it, turning it over in my hands. He leaned closer to the flames, stretching his fingers out against the heat and then curling them into his palms. He always changed in the firelight. The look of his face was harsh. Like the way I remembered him when I first saw him in Aurvanger. But that seemed so long ago. Now, the look that had once made the fight rise up in me broke me down. Peeled me back.

"What do you think would have happened if you'd killed me that night?" I picked at the crust of the bread in my hands.

He chewed, his eyes moving from the fire to me. "I don't know. I don't know if Iri would have ever known. Maybe I would never have known who you were."

"What if he knew? What if he didn't get there in time?"

"I don't think he would have ever been able to forgive me." The depth of his voice made him sound afraid.

"He's like you." I shifted on the stone to face him, suddenly desperate to hear the things he wasn't saying.

His eyes changed again, falling down to the small space of stone between us. "What do you mean?"

"Family is everything to you."

He took another bite.

"How many people have you killed?" I asked.

He turned to face me and I almost wanted to scoot back again. "I don't know." He pulled the axe sheath over his head and set it onto the table behind us. "How many people have you killed?"

I tried to think about it even though I knew the answer. I had no idea. I shook my head in answer. "Who was the first?"

The air between us changed—the space growing small.

"A man in my first fighting season." He scratched his chin. "I was fighting with my father and he knocked him down. He held him up and told me to cut his throat. So I did." He looked back at me from the top of his gaze.

"How old were you?" My voice quieted in the dark.

"Twelve. You?"

"Eleven."

He didn't ask who it was or how it happened and I was grateful. It was the only time I remember killing someone and feeling something other than survival. I'd been scared. And I'd been deeply ashamed of my fear.

I'd fallen asleep in our tent that night with hot tears falling down my face and my father didn't say anything. He prayed with me for my mother's soul and then he sat beside my cot until I fell asleep. The next day, I killed four. The day after that, three. And I didn't cry about it ever again. But I could feel them now—those same tears that had fallen down my face as a young girl. They were fresh and raw, seeping from the same place within me. Hot against cold.

"What is it?" Fiske looked at me.

One tear rolled down my cheek and I let it. "It's a strange feeling," I whispered.

"What is?"

"Being so alone. I've never felt like this." I looked around the dark home. "Even in Fela, I still had the Aska." I sniffed. "I was going through each day to get back to them. But they're just . . . gone. I feel like . . ." I caught the sob in my chest and swallowed it, suddenly embarrassed.

He leaned in closer to me. "Like what?"

My eyes ran over his face. The scruff on his jaw. The dark lashes around his blue eyes. "Like I'm a flame about to burn out." My voice was so thin it sounded like I could reach out and break it with my fingers. "Like I'm going to disappear."

The room quieted, the space between us sucking everything into it. His eyes dropped down to my mouth and the burning in my chest ran into the rest of my body. It found every dark, hidden place and lit it on fire.

I tried to breathe, but it wouldn't come. I was underwater, trapped beneath that frozen lake. And as soon as he moved, it broke loose and the sound of my breath rang in my ears so loud that every thought ran like a retreating army. The heat of him hit me just before his lips touched mine and I froze, trying to feel it. That stinging, throbbing pulse beneath my skin.

I lifted my hands slowly, opening my eyes to look at him. My fingertips touched the lines on the sides of his face and he pulled his mouth from mine, looking back at me like he wasn't sure I was still there.

His breath touched me.

Somewhere I didn't know I could feel.

Somewhere I didn't know existed.

"Fiske." I said his name in a voice that wasn't mine and it hung between us in the silence.

He pressed his lips together. "What?"

I stood at the threshold of the thought. The thought of Fiske that had been buried alive in the back of my mind. I looked over the edge of it, peering down into the darkness. It called to me. It screamed my name.

And I jumped.

I found his mouth with mine again, the breaths coming like the waves in a storm now—crashing into me and pulling me under. I grabbed hold of his armor vest and his hands pressed into me, pulling me forward. I slid across the stone, trying to get closer to him.

The writhing, bleeding hole inside of me closed up.

I let him erase it. I let him make it go away.

His lips moved down to the hollow at my neck and when he stopped, breathing there, his chest rising and falling against me, the silence came back. And it was just long enough for it to erupt again. That pain.

I fell into him, the weight so heavy that I couldn't draw another breath. His arms slid around me and I pushed my face into his shoulder. I wept. A dark, sacred cry rising up out of me. He held me together, keeping the pieces from falling down around us. And I cried until I couldn't feel. I cried until I couldn't think.

The moon rose up over my broken home and I broke with it.

THIRTY-SIX

I WOKE UP IN MY FATHER'S COT WITH THE BLANKET tucked in around me as the seabirds called out over the water and the smell of the dead found me again. It brought me rushing back. Back to Hylli.

I sat up, swinging my legs to the ground, and my head pounded inside my skull. I rubbed my swollen face, looking around the small house. It was empty.

The sun was already halfway up the sky, sending the light casting down through the house in beams hazed with ash and dust. I pulled my sheath and belt on and walked down the path to the dock with my arms wrapped tightly around me.

The dirt turned to gravel and when I reached the water, the familiar crunch of my boots over the round black stones broke the silence of the village. I pulled the clean sea air coming off the water into my lungs and crouched down, scooping it

245

up and splashing it over my face. My fingers raked back into my hair and I looked out to the horizon.

The green of the water hugging the shore melted into blue as it deepened. I closed my eyes and opened them again. It was just the same. The same sea. The same beach. But then I looked back to the village. And the truth resurfaced in my mind. Nothing would ever be the same again.

A splash sounded over the whisper of the wind and I looked up to see Fiske. He stood on the dock at the other end of the beach, pulling a net full of fish up out of the water. He had his knife between his teeth, his arms hinging against its weight, leaning back until it slid onto the dock. The fish were like crystals, glittering as they flicked back and forth in the sunlight.

When he looked up to me, I blushed, still feeling the warmth of him on my lips. Remembering him touching me. Remembering feeling like I was so small that I could vanish into him. It was an arrow in my chest.

I walked along the water's edge until I reached the dock and watched him pull four fish from the net and let the rest spill back into the water. He walked to meet me halfway, stopping in front of me with the knife clutched in one hand and a pail in the other.

The hair blew around my face and I caught it with my hand, holding it over my shoulder. "I'm sorry." I squinted against the sunlight.

His eyes searched mine. "For what?"

I looked down at the water, trying to find the words. "For last night."

He smiled and the heat came back up into my face.

"I—"

"How long will it take to get to Virki?" he interrupted, saving me the embarrassment of finishing.

"We can be there tomorrow morning if we leave now."

He nodded, looking over me, to the village. "Then let's go."

I should have told him that he didn't have to come. That he'd repaid whatever debt he thought he owed me twice over. But inside, I was weak enough that I couldn't hide from myself.

I didn't want to be alone. I didn't want him to leave.

"Thank you."

He nodded and I turned against the wind, watching his shadow move next to mine on the ground as we walked. We climbed the beach and made our way back onto the path. I led us back to the house, feeling a chill run up my spine as I ducked into the doorway, headed for our saddlebags. The scream froze in my throat as the head of an arrow lifted in front of my face. Red hair glowed in the dark and the creak of the bowstring pulled tight.

Mýra.

Aiming for Fiske.

"No!" I wheezed, throwing myself forward. I plowed into her as her fingers slipped from the bowstring.

The arrow hit and I scrambled over Mýra to look. Fiske stood in the doorway, his eyes wide, holding the pail of fish up in front of him. It swung from the handle on his fingers with the arrow plunked into its side.

I could see his mind racing, his hand going for the sword at his hip.

Mýra shoved me aside and I rolled into the stone circling the fire pit. The muscle in my shoulder ripped away from the bone and I groaned as Mýra shot up from the ground with her axe in her hand. Ash clouded the air as she grunted, swinging it to catch Fiske in the neck, but he flung himself back, falling into the wall. The house shook around us.

"Mýra!" I grabbed for her leg but I could hardly see, choking on the dust.

She ignored me, swinging again, and then Fiske was after her, pushing off the wall and catching her by the neck with his hand. She dropped the axe, clawing at his grip as he pushed her into the opposite wall. Her small body flailed against his strength.

"Stop." I pushed against him but he didn't budge. "Let her go!"

He looked at me from the corner of his eye before his fingers unwound from her neck and he replaced them with the knife clutched in his fist.

She stilled, looking from him to me.

"Fiske."

"Who else is here?" He bent over her with the blade still pressing into her skin.

Her eyes flitted back to me, her jaw clenching.

I reached up slowly and put my hand over his. "Let her go."

"Who is she?"

"She's my friend."

Mýra looked at me wide-eyed as he lowered the knife and the tears spilled over before I could reach her. She threw her arms around me and her cries muffled into my hair as I held her, looking over her shoulder to Fiske. He stood half-lit in the shadows, sliding his knife back into his belt.

"How are you here?" Her words tripped over one another. "What are you doing here?" She pushed me back, looking up at me. The faded *kol* around her eyes dragged down her wet cheeks.

I bit my lip, trying to decide how much to tell her. How much she could understand. "I was captured at Aurvanger. I came when I heard what happened."

"How did you get off the mountain before the thaw?"

I nodded to Fiske.

She dragged her palms over her face and her breaths slowed. "Why?"

But none of that mattered. I leveled my eyes at her, bracing myself as I spit the word out. "Is he dead?"

"No." She took hold of my wrist, squeezing. "He's alive. He's in Virki."

I looked back at Fiske, the smile breaking onto my face as I leaned over, putting my hands on my knees to steady myself. "How many? How many survived?"

Her face turned grave and the house went quiet with it.

"Most died. Maybe forty from our village survived. And some were captured."

I sank back on the stone, trying to stop the spinning. The world was moving around me in blurred, colorless lines. I shook my head, trying to cut her words from the truth. "Your family?"

She didn't answer, her face stone.

I stood again, going for the door, desperate for the air.

She came out behind me. "What are you doing with a Riki, Eelyn?"

"I need to get to Virki."

"What is *he* doing here?" She shoved me and I recoiled, hissing. "What is it?" She pulled me to her, pushing the neck of my tunic open to look at the wound that festered in my shoulder. "Arrow?"

I nodded.

She checked the back of my shoulder and her hands suddenly stilled on me. "Is that . . . ?" Her gaze fell to the burns circling my neck. "Did they . . . ?"

I dropped my eyes, the shame of it too overwhelming.

She pushed past me, squaring off in front of Fiske as he came out the door. Her hands pushed into him hard. "What did you *do*?"

He looked down, expressionless, his frame towering over her.

"Why is he helping you, Eelyn?" She turned back toward me.

"The Herja came into the mountains." I leaned into the

tree that stood beside my home. The one Mýra and I climbed as children. "They're everywhere."

I watched her think. She brought her hands together, pressing her thumbs into her bottom lip.

"The Riki lost many. Too many."

"Good," she muttered, shooting her eyes to Fiske.

He tensed, pressing his mouth into a line.

"They'll kill us, Mýra. *All* of us. I need to get to my father."

Her eyes were still on Fiske, who silently stood in the doorway. "What about *him*?"

"He's coming with me."

"No." She shook her head, taking a step back. "I'm not taking him to Virki. He'll come back with the rest of the Riki and finish us off!"

"No, he won't. The Riki are weak. They can't fight." I swallowed. "Not on their own."

Mýra gaped at me. "You aren't serious. The Aska will *never* fight with them. And Sigr will never allow peace with Thora."

"Even if it means surviving? The Herja will come back. Look at this!" I flung my arms out around me to the village. "The thaw is coming, Mýra. And when it does, they'll be back!"

"*Vegr yfir fjor.*" She bit down, her nostrils flaring. "We can't trust them, Eelyn. You know that."

I glanced at Fiske. Even if I did trust him, I would never trust his people. Not really. "I know."

He lifted his chin, looking down at me.

"Fine. Bring him. The Aska will kill him when we get to Virki anyway." Mýra looked at us both before she turned on her heel, slinging her bow over her head and starting down the path alone.

THIRTY-SEVEN

We walked in a single file line down the edge of the coast. The wind blew up the cliff faces in gusts, pushing us back as we moved south. I clutched my throbbing arm to my body as the blood seeped out of it and soaked into my tunic.

Hylli grew small in the distance and the trees grew thicker, turning into the coastal forest that most of the other Aska villages were nestled into. It was a trail Mýra and I had taken many times, going with my father to Utan and Lund to trade fish for things Hylli needed like timber and herbs that could only be found in the forest.

She didn't look back at me as we walked, but her shoulders were set in a hard line. She kept one hand on the handle of her knife and the other hooked into the string of her bow. She wouldn't hesitate to kill Fiske and I wasn't sure her loyalty to me outweighed her hatred of the Riki. She'd lost her father to fever when we were young and then she lost her sister the day I lost Iri. Now, she'd lost everyone else to the Herja. And I should have been there.

I didn't want to imagine her, watching the bodies burn with the ritual words on her lips. I didn't want to think of her holding the last of her family in her arms. I knew Mýra as well as I knew myself. I knew the way she held every broken piece of her heart in place, refusing to fall apart. And she was left to face it alone, because I was selfish. I'd left her in Aurvanger. Just like I'd left Iri.

Whether or not she would forgive me, I'd never forgive myself.

WE CAME UPON THE BAY CARVED INTO THE CLIFFS LIKE A half moon. The sea was still crusted with ice at its edges in the shallows. Schools of fish swam beneath it like a shifting plume of smoke.

Fiske hadn't spoken a word since we left Hylli. His attention was on the slick, rocky ground as his boots struggled to find footholds. This wasn't his terrain just like the snowy mountain wasn't mine. I pulled the hood of the cloak up when the wind turned bitter and watched the fog roll into the land, spilling over the ground as the sun went down. The water below crashed harder onto the rocks and when we could no longer see it, we stopped, making camp inland near the forest.

Mýra watched Fiske moving through the trees as he gathered wood. "How could you tell him about Virki?" she ground out in a furious whisper.

I pulled the fish from my bag, choosing my words carefully. "What were you doing in Hylli?"

"I went back for my family's things. What was left of them."

I took a deep breath. "Iri's alive, Mýra."

Her hands froze on her axe's handle and her eyes left the trees, coming to land on me hard. *"What?"*

"He's alive. He's been living with the Riki this whole time." The words sank in and as they did, I listened to the way it sounded, saying it out loud. Saying it to Mýra was one thing. Saying it to the rest of the Aska would be another. Iri had been beloved and admired in Hylli, but they would have his life for what he'd done. And I was tainted by it too. So was my father.

"How? Why?" She stood.

"He wasn't dead when we left him in Aurvanger. The Riki found him. They saved his life. *Fiske* saved his life."

"No. I saw him. We saw him." She paced before me, her eyes frantic.

"It's true."

"And what? Now he's one of them?"

"Yes." It was the first time I really believed it.

"You can't change your blood, Eelyn! You can't just erase all the Aska the Riki have killed!" Her voice was raw and I knew she was thinking about her sister.

"We can't erase any of it." And that was the most terrifying part of all.

Fiske came out of the trees with a pile of wood under his arm and started on the fire as Mýra watched. The glare in her eyes fell heavy on him but he ignored her.

She returned her axe to its place on her back. "I'll take watch."

"Sleep, I'll do it." I stood.

"So he can cut my throat?" She huffed, pulling the idols of her sister and her father from inside her vest. "You're a fool if you think I'm going to *sleep* this close to a Riki." She turned and stalked off into the dark, leaving us.

Fiske worked at the fire as if he hadn't heard her, his face lit up.

"She doesn't trust you." I handed him another piece of wood. "None of them will."

Behind us, in the darkness, I could hear the faint sound of Mýra's prayers.

He sat against the tree, taking the axe from his back so he could lean into it. "Do you trust me?" His face was hard. Unreadable, like always.

"Yes." His eyes lifted to meet mine and they looked into me. The way they had in Hylli. "But I don't know if the Aska will listen to us."

"You think this is the end?" He looked at his hands.

"The end of what?"

"The end of everything. The Riki. The Aska." The words hung in the air over us, burning in the fire.

"Is that what you think?"

"No. I think you'll convince them."

The stillness of the night turned to something fragile, threatening to break. Because I wasn't sure. "How do you know?"

He smiled at the corner of his mouth. "Because you have fire in your blood."

It was what Inge said about me the night I watched them from the loft and he told Halvard I was dangerous.

"Do you trust me, Fiske?"

"I'm here, aren't I?"

The memory of his lips on mine came flooding back. His hands finding me in the dark, pulling me across the stone. I fisted my hands, resisting the urge to touch him. "And if the Aska do join the Riki and together we defeat the Herja? What then?"

He reached into the fire with his axe, knocking a log closer to the flames. "Then things change."

"What things?"

He leaned back against the tree, his eyes running over my face, and his voice softened. "Everything."

WE CAME UP OVER THE HILL, TOO FAR FROM THE SEA now to see it through the forest. We lay against the incline on our stomachs, peering over the top, to the glade in the distance. It was still. Quiet.

"How many Aska?" I kept my eyes on the trees.

"At least ten. Hagen should be with them," Mýra answered.

I'd known Hagen since I was a child. I'd fought with him. And I knew how he'd feel about me bringing a Riki into our camp.

"Take his weapons." Mýra nodded toward Fiske.

He slid back. "No."

"If they see them, they'll put an arrow in you before we have a chance to talk." I held out my hand.

"I'm not going into an Aska camp without weapons."

"Like I did when I was tied up and dragged into Fela with an arrow in my arm?" I raised an eyebrow at him. "They won't kill you. I won't let them."

"At least not right away. They'll torture you first." Mýra laughed, but it was dark. I turned to see the wicked smile on her face. "*Then* they'll kill you."

I pushed my open hand toward him. "My father is down there. I can talk to them."

He looked at it before he unbuckled his scabbard and belt, winding the length of the leather around the sheaths in a tight bundle. He handed them to me, shaking his head.

"I'll go first." Mýra scanned the trees one more time before she stood, stepping over the top of the hill and walking into the forest slowly with her hands out to her sides.

I held Fiske's weapons to me with my good arm, waiting a few paces before we followed.

But Fiske caught my waist, stopping me. "If they . . ." He glanced over me, his fingers finding the soft skin above my hip and holding onto me. I knew what he was going to say. "I have to get back to my family. If that means killing Aska to get out of Virki and back up the mountain, I will. Do you understand?"

I followed the length of him with my eyes. He didn't need weapons to be a threat to my people. And once he went to Virki, there was no going back. He could bring every Riki down on the vulnerable Aska. They hung like the last leaves of autumn, waiting to drop. He'd do what he had to, and so would I.

"I understand."

THIRTY-EIGHT

A BALL OF FIRELIGHT GLOWED IN THE DARKNESS AHEAD. As we neared, it turned into many, stretching out to each side, and the night fog flowed toward us like a hungry breath until my feet disappeared beneath its thick cover.

Mýra called out and we stopped, waiting. I kept my eyes on the torches until one of the orbs began to move. A man jumped down from a tree, seeing Mýra standing up ahead of us. Then he looked past her, to Fiske and me. "Eelyn?" He squinted in the dark, holding up the torch between us.

"It's me," I answered.

"Who's this?" He stepped forward.

"He's a Riki, Hagen." I spoke the words as calmly as I could. "He's alone and he's here to speak with Espen."

But Hagen's sword was already drawn before I'd finished, his eyes looking into the trees around us. The other men stepped out of the brush, followed by the sound of more blades sliding from their sheaths.

"We're alone." I held up a hand to him.

"Check." He called out over his shoulder, eyeing me angrily as the others followed his order. They spread out into the forest and the glow of their torches fanned out around us.

He held his sword at the ready, checking Fiske for weapons.

"He's not armed." I lifted my hands higher as the men returned from the trees.

Fiske was wound tight beside me, eyes alert and catching every movement.

"It's clear, Hagen," one of the men shouted.

He looked at me for a long moment with his jaw working, before he finally lifted his hand and grasped my right shoulder. I did the same, meeting his eyes. "Espen won't like this. Neither will your father, Eelyn."

I nodded for Fiske to go first and followed behind him, deeper into the trees where the humming sound of moving water took over the quiet. The torches stilled and the sound of feet stopped at a wall of black.

"We're going down." Mýra came through the men to meet me.

"Down where?" I followed her to where the others stood and it wasn't until my feet were at the ledge that I realized it was a drop-off.

She handed me a rope. "Tie it around you like this."

I watched her carefully, doing as she instructed. When

the knots were tight, Hagen clipped his rope into the metal hooks of one that was lying on the ground. He gave the other men a look before crouching down and throwing himself back over the cliff without warning. My heart jumped, watching the rope pull taut and then go slack again.

Mýra followed, backing up to the cliff's edge and meeting my eyes before disappearing. I looked down, trying to see her, but there was only the movement of water catching moonlight. The men pulled the ropes back up and the clips at the end were empty. Two others were next, pushing out from the cliff without any hesitation.

Fiske tied his own ropes and I clipped a metal hook into the knots around me. He backed up, bringing his heels in line with the edge, and braced me with his hand as I did the same, trying to secure my arm against me. It would hurt no matter what I did.

"Ready?" I whispered.

He gave me a nod.

I crouched down and threw my weight back as hard as I could, sinking into the air. The length of the rope rippled out before me like a snake against the night sky above. The light of the torches disappeared over the cliff above us and the rope caught us at an angle just as the others came into view, putting their hands up, fingers splayed to catch us.

"Eelyn!"

The sound coiled around my heart as I swung toward the cliff wall and something caught my boot, sending me spinning until more hands slowed me. When I stopped, my father was shouldering his way through the crowd.

My hands shook, reaching for him as I still hung from the rope. The cry broke free from my throat and I clutched at the air until his big hands found me and pulled me to him. I wept into his shoulder and he shook against me, a cry slipping from his lips as the others unclipped the rope from around me. I squeezed him tighter. He lifted me up and a piece of the fractured world inside me settled back into place. When I came over the ridge to see Hylli burned and broken, I'd been so sure I would never see him again. But he was here, back from the dead, like Iri. Like me.

He pulled my face to look at me, his hand running over my hair. The tears in his eyes fell down into his thick, bushy beard and landed on the laugh bubbling up from inside of him. I had only seen my father cry twice. Once when my mother died and once when Iri died.

The truth seared inside me.

"I knew you were alive. I knew I'd see you again," he choked out. "The Riki took you?"

I nodded, sniffing back the rest of the tears. But it only took him seconds to see the thing I hoped he never would. His fingers dropped from my face to my neck, running along the skin beginning to scar from the burns.

His breaths came harder, his eyes going wild. It crashed over me, violent and angry. Because I'd never seen my father look at me like that.

Shouts rang against the rock and I tore my eyes from

my father, trying to find Fiske. But there were only Aska in every direction, pushing in around us. I lifted up onto my toes, letting go of my father and shoving into the bodies around us as panic rose up inside of me. When I broke through the crowd, Fiske was standing with his back against the cliff face, surrounded. His hands were down by his sides, pumping into fists. I hoped the murderous instinct beneath his hardened face was invisible to the others. His eyes shot from left to right, looking for me.

My father pushed through and I reached out for him when I saw the look on his face. But he broke from my grip, going for Fiske.

"Aghi." I ran after him, trying to stand in his path, but he was too strong. My boots slid on the sand as he pushed forward.

He took Fiske's armor vest in his clutches, slamming him back into the wall. A growl erupted between his lips as he pulled his sword from its sheath.

I wedged myself between them, my back pushing into Fiske's chest and my hands pressing against my father. "Don't!"

His breath was angry in his chest, the hatred in his eyes shining.

Espen appeared behind him with his axe in his hand. "What is he doing here?"

"Listen, please," I said, Fiske breathing against me. The tension in his body radiated out of him and bled through my armor vest. "He's not here to fight. He helped me get off the mountain."

My father took a step back. "What is he *doing* here, Eelyn?" He echoed Espen's words, but they were bloodthirsty in my father's mouth.

"The Riki . . ." I tried to get it out. But I could see in their faces they were all waiting for the chance to rip Fiske to pieces. "They've all been raided. Like Hylli."

The crowd went silent, the Aska turning toward each other. Espen lowered his axe, setting it against his leg, and looked to my father. They didn't know.

"The Herja came to Fela. The village suffered losses, but not as many as others did. I saw Möor before I came here. It's almost gone."

"They'll come back to finish us." My father turned to Espen.

His eyes were on the sand, thinking. "We've had scouts running to their camp. They're at least eight hundred."

My stomach dropped.

"They have a group raiding on the mountain. At least fifty of them after their losses." Every head snapped up at the sound of Fiske's voice.

Espen bit his lip. He turned and the crowd opened up to let him through. "Bring him."

We followed, weaving through the Aska. They snarled and spit at Fiske as we passed, curses riding under their breath. When we made it out from under the overhang, I finally looked up. The cliff came over the sandy bank sharply, like a roof, and the water ran past in a fast, white-capped current. We followed the rock wall until we reached a line of huts made of bowed branches and grassy tops. Fire pits sat beside each one, dug out of the sand, and the howling wind hit the wall with the smell of mud and wet stone.

Espen stood with my father and the village leaders in front of a large wooden table at the end of the small bank, waiting.

"How many Aska are left?" I'd been dreading the answer.

My father looked as if he didn't want to respond in front of Fiske, his eyes skipping between us. "Two hundred and ninety able to fight from all the villages. How many Riki?"

I looked at Fiske. The number was low. Too low. All those Aska. Gone.

He met my eyes. "We aren't sure. When we left, the other village leaders hadn't come together yet. I would say a little less than three hundred from Fela and Möor together. Maybe five hundred including the other villages' survivors."

My father's eyebrows lifted in surprise.

"Are you speaking for the Riki then?" Espen leaned into the table.

Fiske relaxed a little, still keeping an eye on the shadows down the bank. "I am. The Riki leaders want you to join with them to fight the Herja."

Espen and my father looked at each other.

"They are too many for you and too many for us. But together, we may be able to win."

"And then?" Espen crossed his arms over his broad chest.

"That's for you to figure out with the Riki. I'm not a leader."

"Then why did they send you?" My father's fists rested before him on the table. "How do we know we can trust you?"

"You don't." I stepped forward, meeting my father's eyes. "The same way they don't know they can trust us. But we need each other. If we don't come together, our people are finished. Our way of life is gone."

They were quiet.

"I saw Hylli," I added quietly. "We don't have a choice."

THIRTY-NINE

THE MEN QUESTIONED FISKE WELL INTO THE NIGHT AND it was a long time before they finished talking. I could see that he was uncomfortable giving them the answers they wanted, but he gave them anyway. They were things that compromised the Riki's defense against the Aska. Things that couldn't be unsaid.

"I'll go." My father was the first to agree.

But Espen looked uncertain. "We can't send others with you, Aghi."

"I'll go with them." Mýra's eyes were pinned on me, from where she stood shoulder to shoulder with my father.

Fiske still stood apart from the rest of us, keeping his back to the cliff face. He wasn't going to give anyone the chance to catch him off guard.

"You'll speak for the Aska, then," Espen agreed. "And we will meet in Aurvanger."

SKY IN THE DEEP

I ran a hand through my hair, unsettled. For generations, we'd met in Aurvanger. The Riki and the Aska. But it was to draw each other's blood. This time, it would be to save us all. I wondered if we could be warriors fighting alongside each other. If it would make us weaker or stronger.

When they dismissed us, my father led us through the sleeping camp to a place along the cliff wall that was separated by an outcropping of rock. Down the bank, the Aska leaders continued to argue in the torchlight. Their bent, exhausted whispers rose up over the sound of the water.

"You can sleep here." My father handed Fiske one of the rolled woven mats he was carrying. "We leave at daybreak."

He turned to leave and I followed him around the sharp section of rock that cut into the water. "I'm staying here." I swallowed, trying to sound sure. Calm.

He turned on his heel, facing me. "What?"

"He can't sleep alone out here. He'll be dead by morning."

His eyes moved over me slowly. Reading me. He, Iri, and Mýra were the only people who could do that.

"I've been travelling with him for days. He's not a threat to me. And if he becomes one, I can take care of myself."

He hesitated. "What is this, *sváss*?"

"We need him to get back to Fela. To meet with the Riki." I sighed. "Trust me. Please."

His hand reached out for me and I saw his eyes drop to the scars on my neck again before he pulled me into his arms. "Alright."

The angry throb in my shoulder swelled as he tightened

his hold. I leaned into his big frame, letting the familiar smell of him fill me. It made me think of the fighting season, hunkered down together in our tent every night in Aurvanger.

He handed me the other mat rolled beneath his arm. And then he walked into the dark, toward the huts, without looking back. He'd always trusted me completely. But I could feel that faith wavering, threatening to give way to suspicion. I came back around the outcropping and unrolled the mat on the sand. The silence that had fallen between Fiske and me since the night we stayed in Hylli was still there. Every glance and unspoken word echoed within it.

"You should go with him."

I reached into the back of my belt and pulled his knife from where it was tucked under my tunic. I held it out to him.

He looked at it. "Am I going to need this?"

"I hope not." If something happened and Fiske killed an Aska, it would be my responsibility. And it would be the end of any hope to join together.

He stepped toward me but instead of reaching for the knife, his hand landed on my wrist. His fingers wrapped around my arm and my pulse quickened. "You need to be careful." The fever building under my skin burned where he was touching me. "If the Aska think you're protecting me, they won't trust you." His fingers pressed deeper. "You need them to trust you, Eelyn. We both do."

I looked down at his hand on me and then up to his face. It brought that moment in Aurvanger back so vividly. The moment I first saw him, standing in the fog, his sword drawn.

"Why did you come?" I whispered, asking again.

"The same reason you just told your father that you were sleeping here." He took another step closer and every muscle in my body tightened, waiting. "You don't really want to know why." His hand slid down my arm to the knife and he took it, reaching behind him to tuck it into his belt. "And right now, it doesn't matter."

He was right. I wasn't ready to hear him say it. I wasn't even ready to let myself think it. I didn't have the room in my thoughts for trying to figure out what it meant and all that it would bring. Because we could all be dead in the next few days.

"You didn't tell them about Iri." He looked back out at the water as I settled onto my mat.

"I couldn't."

"You'll have to."

"I know," I whispered.

LITTLE FACES PEERED OVER THE ROCK AT ME AS I TURNED over, waking. When I looked up, they hopped down, running down the bank and kicking up sand around them.

Fiske crouched down, splashing water onto his face and looking up and down the shore. The water was calmer this morning and now I could see that the river was wide. Wider than any I had ever seen. On each side, tall cliff faces rose up above small sandy banks.

I sat up and leaned forward to see that the stretch of

overhang was actually longer than I'd thought it was and every inch of the sand beneath it was in use. Shelters, nets, fires, worktables. A large rectangle had been chiseled out of the wall and bows, arrows, swords, and knives hung side by side in orderly rows. Farther down, small wooden boats were suspended from the ceiling by rope systems that ran back to the wall and were staked into the ground. It was hard to find, and anyone trying to attack would either have to cross the river or come down over the cliff. It was a perfect hiding place.

And that thought was painful. The Aska were *hiding*. A strong and fierce people, now reduced to the shadows.

"It's impressive, what they've done here." Fiske wiped the water from his face, looking up at the overhang. He stood, holding a hand out to pull me to my feet.

Down the bank, a group of women walked up the shore dragging lines of fish behind them with their eyes on us.

"We should go," I said, my voice still hoarse with sleep.

My father and Mýra walked down the edge of the water toward us with Hagen and two others when we came around the outcropping. A man with long hair braided away from his face smiled, holding out a small loaf of bread. I took it when Fiske didn't, breaking it in half and giving a piece to him. He hesitated before he took it from me.

"How long?" my father said.

"Two days. Maybe three, depending on the snow," Fiske answered.

Behind us, Espen and Hagen were already pulling a boat down from the riggings on the rock ceiling.

"You'll meet us in Aurvanger." My father met my eyes before he turned toward the boats.

Fiske bristled.

I fell into step beside my father, speaking lowly. "I'm going with you."

He peered down at me, his forehead wrinkling. "Why? You just came from there. You just got home."

"This isn't home."

"Mýra will go. You will stay."

"I know the leaders. I know the village. You need me there." I held his gaze, trying not to let him see too much. But he could. He always could. And whatever he caught a glimpse of, he didn't like. "Please."

He looked out at the water, thinking. And then over his shoulder, to Espen. "Alright." He chose to trust me. I wondered if it would be the last time.

Fiske slung our saddlebags over his shoulder and followed him to the boat, where Hagen stood knee-deep in the water, holding it in place as we climbed in. Mýra watched me, biting the inside of her cheek. I knew that look. She was worried.

I gave her a small smile, but she didn't look reassured. Her eyes moved to Fiske and then back to me, in a question. One I didn't answer. Because I could never make her understand something I didn't understand myself.

My father took her hands and pulled her inside.

"You don't have to come," I said, sliding over to make room for her.

She took an oar into her hands, sitting down as the boat rocked. "The only family I have left is in this boat."

We floated out into the deep, away from Espen and Hagen standing on shore. Espen looked to my father and something silent was exchanged between them. When my father's eyes skidded over me, toward the river, my heart twisted. I could feel him pull away from me. I knew when he was hiding something.

I looked back to Hagen and Espen, but they were already gone. Fiske studied my father. He hadn't missed it either.

We watched the cliffs as we floated through the gorge, the river stretched out before and behind us. Mýra kept one paddle in the water, steering us against the current to keep us from the rocks while my father used the other to direct the front of the boat. The river went around bend after bend until we reached a shallow stretch and my father got out to guide the boat to shore. Fiske and I jumped into the water, helping him pull it up onto the sand of a little bank at the bottom of another cliff, and Mýra climbed out behind us.

Rocks skipped down the side of the cliff as a rope ladder unrolled above us. The end of it slapped against the wet ground as three men leaned over the edge above. Fiske climbed first and when his feet went up over the top, my father held the ladder. I fit my hands and my boots onto the frayed rope rungs.

His eyes still avoided mine.

"What are you planning with Espen?"

Mýra came up from the water and handed a bag to my father. She looked between us.

He looked up to the cliff's edge where Fiske had just disappeared. "Our loyalty is to the Aska, Eelyn. You know that."

"She knows, Aghi." Mýra squared her shoulders at me, standing behind my father.

I searched his face. "I do. But we *need* the Riki. You see that, don't you?"

Above, Fiske's head reappeared over the cliff.

"Let's go." My father dismissed me.

I pulled myself up, wincing at the sharp pain in my arm, and when I reached the top, Fiske took hold of my armor vest and lifted me up onto the ground.

He looked at my shoulder. "Let me look at it."

"Later." I turned back to watch my father and Mýra at the bottom.

Fiske leaned over beside me, his words low so that only I could hear. "I won't take your people to Fela if I can't trust them. You need to tell him about Iri."

I knew he was right. But I knew my father. "It might break him."

Fiske caught my eyes. "It might sway him."

FORTY

WE FOLLOWED THE SEA CLIFFS BACK IN THE DIRECTION of Fela. Mýra and my father walked together behind us, leaning into the wind coming up off the water, and Fiske led, walking ahead without looking back at us. My father and Mýra didn't say anything when I gave Fiske back his weapons, but I could tell by the way they watched him fit his scabbard around his waist that they didn't like it.

The mountain came into view as the fog burned off the land. The shadowed outline of it loomed over us, looking down as if it could see us. As if Thora was watching us. Listening. Fiske looked small before it and I imagined what we must look like from up there, four tiny figures moving against a winter sea.

Me between Fiske and the others.

Between Aska and Riki.

We made camp before we reached the valley and no one

spoke as we built the fire and laid out our cloaks onto the ground. The nights were getting warmer every day but they would grow colder again as we made our way back toward Fela. Remembering the cold made me shiver. I could still remember the blue, night-shrouded forest that had almost taken my life the night Thorpe tried to kill me.

I slid my saddlebag from my arm carefully, trying to keep the pain at bay.

"Let me." Fiske reached for my arm but my father was already stepping forward to stand between us. Fiske dropped his hand, lifting his chin toward my shoulder. "She's torn it open."

My father looked me over, his heavy hand landing on my arm, and I flinched. "What happened?"

"I took an arrow in my shoulder. It's healing." I brushed him off.

Fiske eyed me. "It's not healing. Let me look."

My father looked at Fiske warily. "Are you a healer?"

"My mother is. We've been treating it."

My father's eyes narrowed on me, not leaving my face. The corners of his mouth twitched, turning down as the thoughts flickered in his mind. That bit of trust between us was rattling in the wind. He gave a nod, and I untied the armor vest below my arm. Fiske lifted it over my head, pulling the shoulder of my tunic open. The old bruising was encircled by new bruising and the back opening of the wound was still closed up. But the front was swollen, seeping fresh blood.

"Sit down." Fiske went for his bag and when he came back, my father was standing over me.

"How did it happen?" he asked.

Fiske straightened.

"I tried to escape when they were taking me to Fela. One of them shot me."

Fiske opened the jar of salve that Inge had given to us. As soon as the smell hit my nose, I could see her, standing over the fire in their home, stirring the big iron pot.

"It needs to drain." He leaned in closer.

I nodded through a sigh, knowing what that meant. "Do it." I took the knife from my belt and handed it to him.

My father tensed beside me, taking another step closer.

Fiske held the blade in the flames for a moment, turning it over so that it reflected the light. When it was starting to glow at the edges, he lifted it up and let it cool in the night air. He held the handle of the knife in his teeth as he gently pulled at the opening of the wound with his thumbs. I pinched my eyes closed, the warmth of infection dripping down my arm. The pain spread out from my shoulder to the rest of my body, making my head pound.

"Hold this." He positioned my hand over the cloth beneath my shoulder.

He fit the tip of the blade at the opening of the wound and sliced it down quickly. I bit down hard, pushing out a long, loud breath. The blood spilled out, running over my skin and absorbing into the cloth as he squeezed my arm to get as much of the poisoned blood out as possible. I groaned, finding my father's leg where he stood beside me and pushing my face into it, breathing.

When Fiske was finished, he packed the salve back into the broken skin and bound it up tightly in a fresh bandage. He put the knife back into the fire and my blood boiled off the blade as the throbbing wracked my body.

As soon as he moved away from me, my father relaxed, going back to the fire and pulling a strip of dried meat from his bag. He handed me a piece and I took it, but I was too nauseous to eat. I sat still, trying to let the pulsating pain subside.

They ate in the heavy quiet as night fell, all looking into the fire between us. Every unspoken thought grew wild in it. Whatever my father was hiding, Mýra knew. I could tell by the way they didn't look at each other.

When he walked into the trees to gather more wood, I stood. Mýra read my movements and followed me into the trees, leaving Fiske at the fire. I caught up to him, bending low to pick up the thick branch he'd just cut in two with his axe. I hugged it against my chest, waiting for him to load up Mýra's arms.

"What is it?" He could feel the hesitation coming off me like steam in the cold.

I tried to feel the weight of my body down in my feet to steady myself. To feel stronger somehow. Like if I was planted there the words I said couldn't blow me away. "I need to tell you something."

He turned, leaning into the tree beside him and hooking his thumbs into his armor vest. Behind him, Mýra shifted the wood to her hip, waiting.

I swallowed against the burn in my throat. "Iri's alive."

The words rang in my ears like a guttural roar. They echoed in the forest and wound around us like a snake. My father's face hardened. He stopped breathing and I didn't look away from his eyes. I held his gaze, trying to give him something to hold onto as a storm erupted in his mind.

"He's alive. I did see him that day in Aurvanger." The words became smaller as each one left my mouth. "He was fighting with the Riki."

My father stood up off the tree, dropping his hands at his sides.

"He wasn't dead. When we left him in the trench, he wasn't dead. The Riki took him to Fela. Their healer took him in."

"What do you mean *took* him in?" My father finally spoke, but it was twisted and strained. Rage conjured behind his eyes.

"The other boy in the trench—it was Fiske. He saved Iri's life. They took him to Fela and made him well and . . ." I sighed. "I don't know. He joined them."

My father looked over my head, into the black of the forest.

"I found him again at the last battle and he captured me to keep the Riki from killing me. He planned to keep me with him in Fela until the thaw and then let me escape."

His hands ran over his face and he breathed into them.

"Iri's been living with Fiske's family these last five years."

He turned to the orange glow in the trees in the distance where Fiske was still sitting by the fire.

"Why didn't he come with you? Why didn't he come back to the Aska?" Mýra stepped in front of me.

"I told him to stay." I looked to my feet. "I was afraid of what may happen to him if I brought him back. I wanted to tell you first."

My father paced before me.

"Fiske's family has become his family." I didn't need to see him to know what that did to him, because I remembered it too well. But I couldn't look away. His body responded to it, going rigid from head to toe. "I don't understand it," I said. "But he's become one of them."

The sounds of the forest came up around us in the night and he looked at me for a long time before he finally looked at Mýra. And that same look passed between them, but this time Mýra's jaw clenched, her arms tightening around the wood. The question on her face transformed into anger and she gathered up the rest of the wood, starting back toward the camp and leaving my father and me alone. I stood, waiting. I couldn't guess what he might do.

But when his eyes looked up to me again, half hidden beneath his thick eyebrows, they glistened, his nose turning red.

"We left him." The whisper was smothered. Suffocated.

I nodded, the tears in my eyes reflecting his. "But he's alive."

FORTY-ONE

I DREAMED OF THE BEAR.

I stood in the path that snaked through Fela with my feet buried in the snow. The flakes came down clinging to one another in big clumps landing on the golden-brown fur that framed its face and it looked up at me, with the same wide, black eyes. They were like a starless night sky. There was no end to them.

The prickling of his stare ran over my body, making me shake as I lifted my hand and spread my fingers, reaching out to him. He looked at it, taking a small step toward me until I could feel his breath on the palm of my hand.

But then he was gone.

I turned in a circle, looking around the empty village, but the bear had vanished. His footprints were still punched into the snow before me.

I sucked in a breath, my eyes opening, and that same smell of cold that had been in my dream was all around me. I blinked, pulling my numb hands back into the furs. Fiske was lying on the other side of the fire with one arm tucked beneath his head and the tautness of his face smoothed with sleep.

The rustling of soft, slow footfalls sounded nearby and my hand reached for my knife. I stilled, opening my eyes wider so they could adjust to the dark as a shadow slid over me, onto the ground before the fire. By the time I saw it, it was too late.

Mýra was standing over Fiske's body, her axe pulled up over her head.

"No!" I screamed, throwing the furs off of me and launching forward.

The flames licked my legs as I jumped over the fire. Fiske was already rolling out of the way. Mýra's axe hit the ground where his head had been seconds earlier and my father came up onto his feet, his sword drawn. I threw myself between Mýra and Fiske, my knife in my hand.

Mýra's furious stare was pinned on him. "Get out of the way!" She lifted her axe.

"Mýra." My father's voice was a warning behind her.

But she couldn't hear it. It couldn't touch her. I stepped forward and she swung the axe at me, nearly catching my chest.

Fiske rushed past me, snatching her wrist up with his hand and taking her by the throat.

I wrapped my arms around him, yanking him back. "Let her go!"

He threw her down and she landed on her back. In the next breath, she was back on her feet, coming after him. I grabbed her by the vest, shoving her toward the tree line. "What are you doing?"

She spoke through her teeth, looking over me to my father. "I'm going to kill him, like we were supposed to!"

"What?" I looked back to my father and his face answered my question. "You were going to betray us?"

"Us?" Mýra's voice strained.

"We made a deal with him, Mýra." I pushed her back.

Mýra turned back to my father. "You heard what Espen said."

Fiske stood on the other side of the fire, listening with his sword readied in his hand.

"That was before I knew about Iri." My father slid his axe back into its sheath.

"What is wrong with the two of you?" she screamed, looking from me to my father. "They are *Riki*. They will kill us all the first chance they get!"

"No, they won't." I forced the words. I wanted desperately to believe them.

"If we stay in Virki, the Herja won't find us. We'll be safe there. We find the Riki village, kill Fiske so he can't lead them back to us, and go back for the others so we can finish them off," she sputtered between angry breaths. "*That's* what we agreed. And I don't care if Iri's alive. He's betrayed us all!"

She took another step toward Fiske, raising her axe, and I lifted my knife. "Don't," I growled. I would never hurt her. I'd die before I ever let anything happen to Mýra. But I couldn't let her kill Fiske.

Her eyes widened, boring into mine. "What is this about?" Her voice dropped lower.

"Surviving!" I answered. But it was only half true. It was about so much more.

I watched her think. I knew Mýra too well. I knew what she was going to do before she did it. She pivoted on her heel, spinning around me and going for Fiske. I dove into her and we hit the ground hard, rolling toward the trees. Her axe scraped against my leg, tearing into my pants, and she pinned me down.

Fiske stalked toward us and my father caught him, pulling him back. "Don't."

I looked up into Mýra's face, twisted with madness. It was the look she gave our enemy in battle, and now it fell on me. I rolled, coming on top of her, and slammed the butt of my knife into her wrist, trying to free her grip on the axe. She bucked me off, throwing me to the side.

I didn't give her the chance to swing it again. I threw my knife, watching it spin in the air past her face before it stuck into the trunk of a tree behind her. She froze, staring at me in shock. Her face flashed back and forth between that of the girl I knew better than anyone and that of the deadly warrior who fought by my side. The glimmer of hot tears shone in her eyes as they narrowed at me. And then she was running. She dropped the axe to the ground and when she reached me, she slammed her fist into the side of my face. My head whipped to the side and I plunged into her, knocking her back down.

I hit her. Hard. "What is wrong with you?" I screamed, hitting her again.

She kicked, fighting me, but it was no use. All the strength and rage bled out of her, giving way to something fragile and weak. It filled her eyes until tears spilled over onto her cheeks and she covered her face with her arms, trembling.

"Mýra." I pulled at her arms, trying to see her, and she kicked me off.

When she was on her feet again, she stumbled toward the trees, sobbing.

"Mýra!" I reached for her shoulder, trying to turn her around, but she wrenched free, tripping. I took hold of her vest and didn't let go.

She turned to face me, her kol-rimmed eyes red and swollen. "Are you one of them now too?" she asked, the words broken. "You want to be one of them, like Iri?"

"No!" I met her eyes. "I'm Aska, Mýra. I want our people to survive. That's all."

She fell into me, burying her face in my shoulder, and I wrapped my arms around her, squeezing. She wept, folding into me, and I held her. My father and Fiske stood as black silhouettes before the fire, watching us.

"I'm alone," she cried. "You and Aghi are all I have." Her

voice bent into a whisper. "Please don't leave. Please," she begged.

I pulled back to look at her. "You're not alone," I said, emotion thick in my throat. "And I'm not leaving. Ever."

Her weight grew heavy in my arms and when I couldn't hold her any longer, I slid to the ground and pulled her into my lap. *"Elska ykkarr,"* I whispered into her hair. *"Elska ykkarr."*

She cried like I'd never seen her cry and the sound of it echoed through the trees. She cried for her family. For Hylli. For the Aska. For everything. And I cried with her.

FORTY-TWO

Mýra trailed far behind us as Fiske led us up the mountain. She hadn't spoken a word since dawn and neither had Fiske. I walked between them, keeping an eye on her as the snow deepened under our feet.

My father was cumbersome in the snow-covered forest. His massive frame rocked from side to side in front of me as we climbed the slope. The quiet that had fallen over him was like a burden being dragged behind us. I couldn't tell where his heart was. I knew he was happy that Iri was alive, but the warrior in my father probably wanted to kill him. More than that, guilt would follow both of us for the rest of our lives. We had left Iri and there was no changing it.

The way back up the mountain was different than the way down. Fiske led us through blue icy caverns as the snow started to fall again. The ice rose up around us like waves frozen in midair, the sound of our footsteps bouncing around us as we walked.

I knew we were close when the trees opened up into a grassy clearing studded with tall, frosted stalks of yarrow. Their leaves had turned yellow against the worst of the cold and the heads of the flowers had grown brittle in the days since I was last there. I ran a hand over the tops as we cut through the thick of them, remembering the way Halvard ducked behind their height, spying on me as I worked on my hands and knees in the dirt. I caught one in my fingers, plucking it up and pulling it into my cloak.

The trail that led into the village came into view ahead as the forest turned dark. Fiske stopped us, raising a hand. "I'll signal them. They know we're coming."

Mýra looked around him down the path.

"We're keeping our weapons." My father's grip tightened on his belt.

Fiske nodded, but the unease in their faces wasn't hidden. It was the same unease bubbling up inside of me. I was leading my family into the den of the enemy.

"Iri's in there?" My father stared in the direction of the village.

"He is." I tried to soothe the voice of doubt inside of me.

"I want to see him. I want to see him first."

Fiske nodded, stepping forward, and he whistled into the trees. We waited silently, my heart pounding, until a whistle sounded back. "We'll meet them in the ritual house."

"No." My father's tone turned sharp.

I shook my head at Fiske. My father was a superstitious man. There was nothing that would convince him to step foot into a ritual house for Thora.

"My house then," Fiske agreed.

My father and Mýra both freed their axes from their sheaths, stepping heavier into their feet as we walked. I did the same, finding my axe with my fingertips at my back. When we finally broke into view, my steps faltered, my eyes going wide. It was dark, but the homes were lit like little fires in a winding trail and more Riki were camped in every open space. They covered every inch of the village.

Armed. Ready for battle.

I slowed, and Mýra and my father's swords slid free. I instinctively set my hand on the hilt of mine as the defenses woke inside me. I hadn't seen this many Riki together in one place since I was captured in Aurvanger.

We stayed at the village's edge and moved against the trees, keeping out of sight. Fiske came to the other side of my father, pulling his axe from his back. The four of us walked in a line, shoulder to shoulder with our weapons ready. Heads turned toward us, like a ripple over water, as we made our way closer. They were quiet. Eyes gleaming.

Cold stares and angry whispers surrounded us, closing us in as we headed up the incline, and the buzz of battle ignited in my bones, ready to turn and swing my axe. I met their eyes as I passed, telling them what I wasn't saying out loud.

That we weren't afraid.

That I would kill them.

That everything I had left to lose was right here in this village.

Fiske led us toward the familiar wood-planked house standing on the fringes of the village and whistled again. Smoke trailed up from the roof and the door opened.

Inge stood with her hands pressed, palms together, in front of her chest. Long, unbraided black hair fell over her shoulders like a raven's wings.

"Fiske!" The high-pitched tone of Halvard's voice broke the silence.

He appeared in the doorway and barreled into Fiske, wrapping his arms around his waist. Fiske put one hand on him, still watching around us. When Halvard opened his eyes, he let go of Fiske, running until he slammed into me. I held my axe up in the air and squeezed him against me with my other hand, unable to help the smile on my face. I pulled the yarrow bloom from my cloak and handed it to him. His grin widened before he took it, running back into the house toward Inge.

Mýra and my father watched me, shock written across their faces in deep, hard lines. And then my father's face fell, looking beyond me into the house, where Iri stood in the shadows against the back wall. His shoulders were hunched, his frame bent low to see through the doorway.

My father didn't think. In the next breath, he was moving, one pounding footstep over the other through the snow, and Inge stepped aside, moving out of his way. I followed, trying to keep up, but he was past the gate before I could catch him. And then he was through the door, moving past Inge. I came into the house and stopped short, my heart jumping into my throat.

My father had his arms wound around Iri like ropes, hunched over and weeping into his shoulder, his body wracked with sobs. The sound of it filled the house and spilled out into the village. And Iri was the same, his face broken into pieces as my father held onto him. I closed the door as soon as Fiske and Mýra came through, leaving the rest of the Riki outside. Runa stood beside the fire, watching them with her hands tucked into her elbows. Inge, too, stood at the wall, staring.

I gulped down the cry forcing its way up from my chest. My father was a proud man and I'd wondered which would have a stronger hold on him—his Aska blood or his love for Iri. Relief flooded through me, unwinding every tense muscle and calming my heart. I already knew that Iri's betrayal was nothing compared to the truth that he was ours, but seeing my father know it, too, made it more real.

He was saying something into Iri's ear, but the sound of it muffled against his hair. Iri nodded, wiping at his face and trying to catch his breath. He had outgrown my father only in width, their tall statures matching. Behind me, Mýra watched with the eyes of a warrior, her weapons still clasped in each hand.

"Eelyn." Inge's soft voice lifted beside me and she touched my back, smiling. "I'm glad you're back," she whispered.

I breathed in the smell I'd come to associate with this place. Toasted grains and drying herbs. "This is my father, Aghi," I said. "And this is Mýra. My friend."

Inge nodded to both of them in greeting and Halvard came around me to look up at Mýra inquisitively. My father wiped his face on his sleeve, coming back into himself, and I instantly felt safer. Seeing him lose control was something that scared me. He looked across the small house, taking it in, until his eyes landed on Inge. They looked at each other in silence.

A knock pounded on the door and Inge stepped forward, lifting the latch. Vidr stood on the other side of the threshold with the Tala behind him, her eyes landing on me first. They stepped into the house and we fanned out against the back wall as more Riki I didn't recognize filed in. My father looked to me and I watched his hand tighten on his axe. Mýra watched them from the top of her gaze in the corner. Their faces, too, were shrouded in suspicion.

Vidr stood at the front, sizing up my father from head to toe. "We're glad you've come."

My father looked them over carefully, left to right. He stood beside me, his sword still hanging at his side. The glisten of tears still shone on his cheeks, but my father was a dangerous man. Anyone could see that.

Beside me, Halvard was still inspecting Mýra. He reached up to touch her hair and she recoiled, moving closer to the wall to get away from him.

"Welcome to Fela." The Tala stepped forward, breaking the silence. Her fingers tangled into her necklaces. "We understand the Aska have been raided by the Herja. As you can see, we've suffered great losses as well."

My father didn't answer.

Vidr watched him with flinty eyes. "These are our other village leaders—Freydis, Latham, Torin, and Hildi." He motioned to each of the faces in the crowded room.

"There are *seven* Riki villages," my father corrected.

"The other village leaders are dead," Freydis answered. Her cloak was pulled over one shoulder, an injured arm hanging out.

"What is it you want from us?" My father took command of the conversation the way I'd seen him do many times before. He was always in control.

"We have a common enemy. One that will likely be the end to both our clans." Vidr took a step forward. "We want the Aska to join with us against the Herja."

"And after?" My father unveiled his real concern. They would find out soon enough that the Aska were weaker than they were. "What's to keep the Riki from turning on the Aska after we've defeated the Herja?"

The other village leaders looked to Vidr, as if they wanted the answer as much as we did. "A truce. Neither of us will be able to fight after we take on the Herja. And even if we are, we won't fight each other."

"And generations of war will end just like that?" I asked, my eyes narrowed on the Tala.

She let the silence widen before she answered. "Perhaps the gods have a new path for us."

"A new path?" The skepticism in my father's voice mirrored the look on Mýra's face. She was stone beside me.

"We don't always understand the gods' ways, do we? What we do know is that the Herja have emerged again from whatever hell they come from. I don't know how the Aska have fared, but they have wiped out more than half our clan in a matter of weeks. Another month and we may all be gone. They'll go back down the mountain and do the same to the Aska." She looked to each of us. "Or we could join together."

My father wasn't convinced. I could see doubt in every shift of his eyes. He didn't trust them to keep the truce. Niether did I. Not really.

"The Aska live and die by their word," he said.

Vidr's voice rose in defense. "So do the Riki."

"The Riki who killed my sister are probably out there, right now," Mýra muttered.

"Two sons," Freydis snarled. "Two sons I've lost in Aurvanger in the last ten years. I don't want to stand around the same fire as the Aska. I don't want to trust one at my back in a fight. But I have two more sons." She raised a hand, pointing to the door. "Out there."

Inge pulled Halvard to her. "You can abandon your blood feud, Freydis?"

"To save them? Yes."

"But can the others?" I looked to the Tala before my eyes drifted back to Mýra. "Can *we*?"

The Tala reached to Vidr's belt and pulled his knife free. In one quick motion, she slid the blade across her palm. Her hand filled with blood.

"Tala?" Vidr reached for her.

She stepped forward, looking to my father before she held her hand out to me.

I pressed myself to the wall. "What are you doing?"

"I'm offering a blood oath." Her hand hung in the space between us, blood dripping to the floor.

They all stared at her, but her eyes were on me. It was the most precious thing she could offer and she knew it. She couldn't break a blood oath without sacrificing the afterlife. And if anyone wanted to go against the Tala, they'd have to kill her. Slaying a Tala would bring the same bleak fate.

I pulled out my knife before anyone could object, cutting into my flesh and taking her hand. She smiled, pressing her palm to mine.

Vidr watched us, clearly worried. She'd put herself in a vulnerable position, binding herself to me. If he'd harbored any secret plans against the Aska, they were undone.

The Tala turned to my father. "Do this and we will owe each other a debt—a debt that can never be repaid."

Fiske was quiet, standing with Iri and Runa behind the table piled high with fresh bundles of sage. He looked at me.

I didn't want to think about what it all meant. What a future like that *could* mean. The same weight that had been with me since the day I looked into the bear's eyes at the river pressed me further into the ground. I pulled my sore shoulder back to stretch it. To feel something else, even if it was pain.

The room suddenly felt small. The air was too hot. I couldn't breathe.

I stepped to the side, finding a path to the door, and quietly slipped out into the air, gulping it in as I paced toward the garden, where Inge had plowed rows for planting. I pulled my axe free from its sheath and opened the neck of my tunic trying to cool my skin. The tree at the edge of the forest was marked up with the slashes of axe throws. I threw my arm back over my head and swung it down hard, flinging my axe forward and sending it through the air. It landed with a loud crack in the trunk of the tree.

The door latch rattled and I didn't turn around to look at him. Feeling him was enough. It was something I recognized now. I stared at my axe, lodged in the wood.

"They're leaving at first light to go back to Virki." Fiske spoke behind me.

I walked toward the tree and pried the blade free, pressing against its edge with my thumb. "And then what?"

"And then they return with the Aska. We'll meet them in Aurvanger in two days."

297

I pressed my thumb harder to the metal. "And then we all die?"

"Maybe." He kept his distance from me. "Will you go with them? Back to Virki?"

I looked at the house, where my father was still talking with the Riki. How did we get here? How could we ever go back? I wanted to push my face into the snow. I wanted to scream.

He stepped toward me, taking my cut hand into his. He turned it over before wrapping a strip of cloth around it, knotting it on my palm. I breathed through the feeling flowing through me, like candle wax melting. "Don't." The word hit me in the chest as he said it.

I bit down on my lip until my eyes watered. To keep myself from speaking. I was afraid of what I would say if I did.

"Stay with me and come with us to the valley. We'll meet the Aska there."

I closed my eyes as a tear rolled down my flushed face. Trying to escape. Trying to leave this moment and pretend like I hadn't chosen a path to get here. It wasn't a command. It was a request. One that I didn't think I could deny. He'd left his family and come with me down the mountain as his people reeled in the aftermath of a raid. He'd taken me home. Helped me find my father. Now it was my turn to make a choice.

To choose him the way he'd chosen me.

I turned back toward the tree as he left, boots crunching all the way to the door, and the latch clicked again. I crouched

down and put my face into my hands, feeling the village spinning around me. I tried to remember who I was.

Strong. Brave. Fierce. Sure.

I tried to summon her to me—*that* Eelyn who would
choose her people over anything else. I searched for her
within myself, but she was different now. *I* was different. And
it was something that was already done. Something I couldn't
change.

FORTY-THREE

THEY WERE TALKING ABOUT NUMBERS.

The number of Aska.

The number of Riki.

The number of Herja.

After hours of discussion, the Riki village leaders left the house quiet. The fire crackled in the pit between Iri's old family and his new one. I swallowed hard, wondering which one I was part of now.

My father asked questions, but not too many. He didn't want too many answers. He just wanted to be happy that Iri's heart was still beating. But Iri would have to answer for what he'd done eventually, and we all knew it.

Inge came down the ladder with two mats for my father and Mýra. "Your cot is still in the loft."

I knew it wouldn't take long for them to put it together. The understanding sunk into Mýra's face, followed by my father's. And the confusion written there quickly turned to disgust. "You were *their dýr*?" Mýra spat, standing.

I sighed, running a hand through my hair. I was exhausted. I didn't have the will to explain. And there was no explanation that could satisfy them. Not ever. If I were Mýra, I'd feel the same way.

My father looked down at Inge with a hard, cold stare before he wrenched the mats from her arms and went outside. Mýra followed him, slamming the door behind her, and Inge flinched.

"I'm sorry." Her face fell.

I didn't answer. I didn't say it was alright, because it wasn't. Instead, I took the newly bound bundles of sage from the table and pulled a torch from the wall. I leaned over the fire, lighting it, and then headed for the door. I needed the sky stretching out over me and drowning out the swirl of everyone and everything in this village.

I walked out into the dark and could sense the bodies behind the closed doors and in the trees. Fela had become a sanctuary, seething with the anger of the Riki. The houses glowed with night fires burning to keep mourning families warm.

I swallowed it down.

The dead Aska. The dead Riki. All of it.

The path curved toward the incline until I reached the cellar. I kicked the snow from before the door so I could open it and put the torch into the mount on the wall. The scent of the sweet sage made my head swim with the memory of the first time I'd walked into Fiske's home. And I couldn't understand the feeling that followed it. I wanted it all to fit into a place inside me that made sense. I wanted to hate them all for everything that had happened.

But when I followed the trail back, it had started with me.

I was the one who watched Iri get cut down in battle. I left him. And I was the one who followed him into the forest the night they captured me.

It began with me. I'd made a choice.

Like Fiske had made a choice when he saved Iri's life.

The hinges on the door creaked and I went for my knife.

Fiske stood at its opening. He pushed the door closed behind him and the moonlight was cut out, leaving only the light of the torch on the wall. My hands clenched tighter around the sage, the scent still fragrant in my lungs. He looked at me and the hardness that always hid his face fell away. I could see him again. The way I had at the river. The way I had in Hylli. The open, tender part of him that was reaching out. It moved across the floor of the cellar and touched me. It lit the inside of me on fire.

Tears stung behind my eyes and I tried to blink them back, but I wanted to see him. I wanted to feel him. And as if he could hear me think it, he crossed the space between us slowly. The toes of his boots almost touched mine as he took the bundles of sage from my arms and he reached up, leaning over me to hang them from the line.

"What are you doing?" I whispered.

But he didn't answer. He looked down at me before his

hands lifted, finding my face, and he stepped closer. His fingers wound into my hair until I tipped my head back and I sucked in a breath.

"I'm sorry." His voice was deep.

I searched his face. "For what?"

He dropped his head down, his lips hovering over mine. "For everything."

His fingers curled tighter into my braids and he kissed me. He dove down deep inside of me, filling me up with the warmth the winter had stolen away. Melting the frosted, frozen pieces.

His hands were hot on my skin, trailing down my neck, over my collarbones to slide around my waist and pull me up, into him. I lifted up onto my toes, trying to get closer. Trying to wade through the thick, murky stream of thoughts in my head. To flush them out. He pushed the top of my tunic open and when his lips moved to the top of my shoulder, I groaned. Because it hurt. More than the arrow wound. More than the day I lost Iri. This was a different kind of pain.

His hands slid from around me, hovering over the scar encircling my neck that was still healing from the collar. He leaned away from me and the hardness carved its way back onto his face.

I took hold of his armor vest, pulling him back to me. But the guard was going back up over him, one thought at a time. "I don't belong to you." I repeated the words I said to him the night he pulled the stitches from my arm. This time, to lift the weight that pressed down onto him and silence whatever words were whispering in his mind.

And because a small part of me still wanted them to be true.

"Yes, you do." He pulled the hair back out of my face so he could look at me. "Like I belong to you."

I couldn't feel the tears falling anymore. I couldn't feel anything except for the parts of me that were touching him. I reached up to the clasps of his armor vest, keeping my eyes on his. I pulled them free, working it loose until I could fit my hands up under his tunic and press my palms against his skin. I slid my fingers over his ribs and he shook against me, his breaths coming harder.

I pushed the uncertainty and doubt down to the very deepest part of me. I buried them there, along with the beliefs and traditions that had made up who I was. I pulled the tunic up over Fiske's head and dropped it on the ground with the armor vest and touched the scars perforating his skin in raised, chaotic lines. The deep blue stains of the bruises on his side. The shape of him. He wiped the tears from my face, spreading his thumbs over my cheeks, and I smiled.

He unbuckled my vest and I lifted my arms so that he could pull it off with my tunic. And when he kissed me again, the seconds slowed. They stretched out and made more time. I felt his body against mine, unraveling everything else that was between us, and my soul unwound, threading itself to his.

And I let it. I gave myself to him. Because I was already his.

FORTY-FOUR

Iri held Inge in his arms, looking over her shoulder at me. He didn't need to ask because I knew what he was thinking. We'd see Runa safely to Aurvanger while he went with my father to the Aska.

He let her go, and he didn't reach for me. He didn't have to say it. That he was sorry. And I was too. I let my father hold me, saying good-bye as Mýra stood back against the house, talking to Fiske. He towered over her, but she stood squarely, meeting his gaze with a fierce look in her eye that I recognized. That was Mýra. Small but ferocious. I'd seen her take down men twice his size. She could have killed him that night on the way to Fela just as he could have killed her.

She walked to me with her eyes down, her thumbs hooked into her belt. I reached up to grasp her right shoulder and she did the same.

"I'm sorry," she said, reaching up to touch the bruise on my face where she'd hit me.

I didn't forgive her because I didn't need to. I understood Mýra. I knew that fear of everything being ripped away and the last of what you love being threatened. We were warriors. And she was willing to fight for me the way I was willing to fight for her. Nothing would ever change that.

It wasn't until they were scaling down the snowy ridge that I knew what I'd done. I'd spent every waking moment trying to get back to them and now I was sending them off without me. If there was a last chance, this was it. But my feet stayed planted where they were.

"Two days." Fiske tried to calm the unease he could see coming to life in me.

"What did she say to you?" I asked, watching Mýra disappear over the hill.

"That she would kill me if anything happens to you." He laughed. "I believe her."

A soon as they were out of sight, we got to work. I listened to Fiske and Inge talk. About plans. Supplies. Traveling to Aurvanger. I ignored the feeling of my heart being pulled down the mountain and let the sound of his voice brush up against me and touch that place in the center of me that was still soft. It made me tremble, thinking of his hands on me. Remembering the way his mouth tasted on mine. I couldn't undo the tether between us. And I didn't want to.

We prepared everything Inge and Runa needed to treat the wounded. We checked weapons, riggings on the horses, we filled saddlebags and wrapped bread. When we were packed, we went to Runa's and helped her family. Her mother was going to fight for the first time in twenty years. She pulled her scabbard from a dust-covered trunk in the shadows of their house and I sat outside, mending the hole in her armor vest. I watched the others load up their horses, feeling truly invisible among them for the first time. As if they'd forgotten me.

We headed down the mountain the next morning in one long line, trailing the path, and I walked beside Inge's horse with Halvard. Fiske looked back to keep his eye on us from where he rode ahead with Vidr and Freydis. Inge looked at them from the corner of her eye. I'd noticed her doing it after the attack, when Vidr and the Tala seemed to keep noticing Fiske. How they kept singling him out. I didn't like it either. And I didn't like what it may mean in battle.

We camped in the forest, huddling together around small fires to keep warm, and Fiske took a turn scouting with a group that went out with Latham. The Herja still lingered below, at the foot of the mountain in the northern valley. The light of their fires showed how big their camp was and I was glad we couldn't see their numbers. I didn't want to know how many there were when I stepped onto the battlefield. I wanted to fight the way I always had. Without thinking about odds.

Inge, Halvard, and I slept side by side on the forest floor and I woke in the middle of the night to Fiske sliding beneath my blanket in the dark. His face went into my hair, his arms winding tightly around me. I dreamed until he was pulling free again to meet with Vidr and the others in the very first light of morning. He kissed me between the eyes and I listened to his footsteps fall quiet as he moved back into the trees.

I rolled over to see Inge buried in a bearskin, facing me. Her tired eyes were half opened, looking at me over Halvard's sleeping body, and my heart twisted in my chest. I waited for fear or disapproval to find its way onto her face, but it didn't come. Instead, her hand reached for me. When I took it, she lifted up the bearskin and pulled me closer to Halvard's side, tucking its edge around me. She smiled before she slipped back into sleep and I watched them breathing in and out peacefully, until the camp broke up to move again. Halvard stretched, his feet finding mine beneath the blankets.

We took the long way around the lake because there were so many of us. I kept my eye on Runa, staying close to her as we walked through the second night. When we came around the last bend of the mountain, the Aska were visible in the eastern valley, gathered behind the switchbacks. They looked so small compared to the Herja camp.

They were the last of us. The last of my people.

Fiske stopped beside me at the edge of the drop-off, looking down at them. We stood there in silence for a long time as the line of Riki passed, the wind rushing over us in big gusts. The sound of it roared in my ears.

"What are you thinking?" He took my hand.

"I'm thinking I don't want to fight anymore."

His fingers tightened around mine. It seemed so foolish now, all the fighting. All the death and loss and mourning. The feud between our clans was nothing in the shadow of the heartbreak that had befallen us.

"What will you do?" he asked, his voice low. "After."

I looked at him, but his eyes stayed on the camp, not meeting mine. "My father and Mýra are in Hylli." It was the only answer I could give him. I tried to imagine going home and leaving him in Fela. But there was no point in trying to imagine what may never come. We could both die fighting the Herja.

His lips parted, as if he might speak, but he didn't. His arm came around my shoulders to pull me close.

The sun was setting by the time we reached the valley, and the Riki made camp across the river. The leaders agreed that keeping the clans separate would give us the best chance at avoiding complications. The Aska stood in a line at the edge of the water, looking out to us. But this time, not for battle.

I made my way across the river and walked the path through the white tents, searching for my father and Iri. Hagen pointed in the direction of the meeting tent and I found them sitting around a fire with Espen. Iri stood, coming to meet me. The sight of him standing among them, still wearing Riki armor, was strange and unfamiliar. But that's what it would look like in battle. Aska and Riki together.

"Runa?"

"She's with Inge." I nodded. "Where's Mýra?"

"Helping Kalda prepare for the wounded." He nodded toward the healer's tent, where shadows moved against the canvas in the firelight.

"Vidr wants to meet in the morning. Tonight, they'll make camp and watch the edge of the valley to make sure the Herja don't know we're here."

"We won't have much time. Maybe a day before we have to attack." Espen spoke behind him.

My father nodded. "I agree."

The sun finished sinking as I walked with Iri back to the river. We found the shallows and when I stopped, he turned to wait for me.

"I'm staying here tonight."

The Riki camp across the water in the distance was beginning to glow with night fire. We stood shoulder to shoulder, looking out at it.

"I'll tell Fiske." His deep voice was delicate. Careful.

I tried to read the look on his face, but he was doing the same to me. "I don't know what to do." I'd already made a choice, but I didn't know if it was one my clan could live with.

"Yes, you do." He looked at me again.

"I can't leave the Aska," I whispered. "Not now."

"Maybe you won't have to."

But Fiske living among the Aska the way Iri lived among the Riki was something I'd never ask of him.

I stood, watching Iri cross the river as night fell. When I scanned the water's edge, I spotted Fiske. A silhouetted outline standing on the bank of the river. He looked out over the water toward our camp and I wondered if he could see me in the darkness. If he could feel me watching him.

"Eelyn." My father's voice found me and I took one last look over my shoulder to where Fiske stood before I went to him. I ducked into the tent where he and Mýra were waiting for me. Her hair fell over her shoulders, reaching down to her hips. She looked just like she did when we were young. I sat on a stool and she tilted my face to the side, dragging her blade carefully over the shorn part of my scalp, beneath the length of hair on the right side of my head. When she finished, I reached up, running my fingers over it.

"What happened in Fela?" She wiped her blade against her pants. "Before you came to Hylli?"

My eyes drifted to my father, but he was bent over his sword, sharpening the blade. "What do you mean?"

"You've given your heart to that Riki." There was nothing in her tone that revealed her thoughts.

I wasn't going to deny it. Mýra knew me as well as my father did. But he'd had the sense not to ask what he didn't want to know. "You won't understand," I whispered. And I pinched my eyes closed, remembering Iri speaking the same words to me.

She slid the knife back into its sheath and looked down at me. "I don't need to understand." She offered me her hand and I took it. "You're alive and you're with us. That's all I care about."

They settled down onto their knees and I found my place beside them, pulling the idol of my mother from my armor vest. Beside me, Mýra held the idols of her entire family in both her hands. Her mother, her father, her sister, and her brother. I could still see their faces in my mind and guilt, hard and solid in my throat, made it difficult to breathe.

I let out a long exhale, warmed in the familiar sound of the prayers. Their whispered words lifted in the tent and I stayed quiet, listening to their voices. I closed my eyes, pressing the idol to my heart, but I didn't cry. The unsteadiness was gone, being near them and knowing that Iri and Fiske were on the other side of the river, safe. Inge, Halvard, and Runa too.

I touched the face of my mother's idol. I pressed my lips to it and prayed. The same prayers I'd prayed to Sigr since the day she died.

And then I did something I'd never done in my life.

I prayed to Thora.

FORTY-FIVE

THOSE WHO WEREN'T FIGHTING SET OUT FOR VIRKI IN two separate groups, mostly the elderly and the children. Halvard was given to Gyda, who had her baby strapped to her back. He walked behind Kerling's horse, looking back at us as they crossed the valley. He didn't argue, but he didn't like it, and neither did Kerling. They wanted to fight. It blazed like an inferno on their faces.

I helped Inge prepare bandages and waited for Fiske to come, but he didn't. And when the Riki settled down into their tents, I stood outside, waiting. The smell of the altar fire was in the air, riding on the wind across the river from the Aska camp. They were making sacrifices and asking Sigr to bless our battle.

Fiske didn't come down the path until after dark. He stood in the tent's opening, his face drawn and tired, watching me.

I braided my hair for war, letting it fall down my back in long woven strands. I checked all my armor and weapons one last time, and looked up from the top of my gaze to watch Fiske do the same. How many times had we both done this before, preparing to fight one another?

I pulled his hair back into a tight knot and took the *kol* from my saddlebag so I could rim his eyes with my thumbs. Then I sat on the cot and looked up at him so he could paint it onto me. I tilted my head back and closed my eyes as his calloused fingers dragged over my skin.

"Will it work?" I asked.

His hands stilled on me and I opened my eyes. "Yes," he answered.

But I wasn't as sure. I'd come close to death too many times. Whatever favor Sigr had given me was probably running out. "If I die tomorrow"—I swallowed—"you'll take care of Iri."

He nodded. He wasn't going to say it wouldn't happen because we'd both seen enough clansmen fall to know it could. "And if you don't?"

"What do you mean?"

He looked down into my face, putting the words together in his mind before he said them. "If you go back to Hylli, I want to come with you."

I twisted the corner of the blanket in my hands. "What about your family?"

"I'll go where you go." This time, the words were unyielding.

I nodded, trying to suck in a breath past the tears coming up in my throat. I didn't want to cry. I reached for him and he came down onto his knees in front of me, between my legs, and he let out a long breath as he leaned into me. I held his weight, holding him tightly. "I didn't want to ask you," I said in a cracked whisper.

He set his head onto my shoulder. "You didn't have to ask me."

I smiled, my lips pressed to his ear. Because Fiske lived in lockstep with his heart. He did what he believed in. It was the reason he hadn't left Iri in the trench and the reason he'd taken me home.

He climbed up onto the cot beside me and tangled his legs into mine. I pulled the blanket over us and watched him fall deep into a dream, his face relaxing and the lines that creased his forehead smoothing. I kissed him there and looked at him until my eyes were too heavy to stay open.

And then I followed him into sleep.

A DISTANT WHISTLE SOUNDED AND MY EYES POPPED open. Fiske was already rolling onto his feet, rubbing his face with both of his hands and pulling his boots on. I sat up slowly, finding mine in the dark and standing so I could fit my scabbard to me. I crossed my arms over my chest, hooking my fingers over my shoulders, and let Fiske tighten the clasps. He tucked the idol of my mother inside, against my chest. I'd hoped the ache in my shoulder would be better.

The rest of the camp readied outside as I worked at his armor, checking everything twice. When my hands went back a third time, he caught them with his and waited for me to look up at him.

"Left side, near the dock." His voice was still waking. "I'll be there with Iri."

I nodded. I'd been right about Vidr's plans. He'd made Fiske head of one of the groups.

He pulled my hand up and opened my fist, pressing his lips to my palm, and the feel of him ran through me, grounding me. Then his lips found mine in the dark, soft and warm, molding against mine.

"*Qnd eldr.*" I whispered his people's battle cry against his lips. Breathe fire.

He smiled, taking the back of my head with his hand and kissing my cheek. "*Qnd eldr.*"

We ducked out of the tent, into the predawn darkness. He squeezed my hand one last time before he took off down the path, falling in line with the other Riki headed to their places. I didn't look back as I ran in the opposite direction, toward the Aska. Each clan had their job and if we succeeded, we'd see the Riki in Hylli.

Those of us who made it.

I came up on the line, looking for Mýra. I saw my father first and his eyes caught mine as I came to him. He leaned low to kiss me before he pushed me to my place without a word.

Mýra was already waiting for me and we checked each other's armor again.

Her eyes dropped down to my shoulder. "How is it?"

I rolled it back on itself and it hurt. "I can use it. But it's weak," I admitted.

She nodded, pressing her lips together. "Then stay on my right."

She would have to lead with her left and her left wasn't her strong side. But I'd done as much for her in the past. It's what we did for each other. It's how we survived. And being back on the front line with her was like going home. A home that could never be burned or broken.

I turned toward the blackened eastern valley. We couldn't see the forest that separated us from the Herja, but it was there. And we knew that forest. We'd been fighting in it all our lives.

I reached into my vest for the idol of my mother and my fingers hit something else. I fished it from where it was tucked against my heart and I held it out before me. A smile pulled wide at my lips, threatening tears. It was a *taufr*, the talismans the Riki used to protect the ones they loved. Fiske must have slipped it into my vest with the idol. The stone was smooth and black, the words etched into its surface.

Ala sál. Soul bearer.

I returned the *taufr* to my vest.

Mýra lifted her shield in front of her and I pulled my sword and axe free, feeling their weight at my sides. My clansmen's prayers began and I joined them, pinning my eyes on the darkness as my heart picked up speed. Each muscle awakened around every bone, calling my body to life.

I prayed to Sigr for my father and Mýra. I prayed to Thora for Iri and Fiske.

The whistle sounded and we started at an even run. Our feet hit the ground almost in unison and we melted into the forest before us, keeping our lines as we wove in and out of the trees. As we came up on scouts, the Aska to our right cut them down, dropping them on the forest floor one at a time. We reached the other side of the forest and the stars still hung over the camp in a clear, crisp sky. The Herja who were keeping watch were right where we needed them to be.

We sunk low to the ground and came down the hill, spreading out around the eastern side of the camp. And we didn't stop. We moved together like a flock of birds and I signaled to Mýra when I picked a tent. She tipped her chin in answer and followed me as I cut left. We stopped at both sides of the opening and I caught her eyes in the moonlight before I slipped inside, my feet silent on the damp ground.

There were two cots, one man and one woman. We didn't hesitate. We each stood over a sleeping body, knives in the air, and I swallowed a breath as I pressed one hand to the Herja woman's mouth and dragged the blade over her throat. She kicked back and I leaned into her, trapping the shriek as she writhed beneath me. I waited for her to go still.

Behind me, Mýra was already waiting at the opening.

We ran to the next tent and the other Aska darted in the dark around us. We killed seven more sleeping Herja before the first loud scream rang out in the silence. I froze, standing over the still-warm body on the cot, listening over the sounds of my breath coming fast.

Mumbling.

Something being knocked over.

The whistle. They knew we were here.

I pivoted on my heel as the camp erupted in shouting and a man sprung from the opening of the tent beside us, wielding his axe. I swung my arm over my head and let mine fly. It struck him in the shoulder and he fell to his knees before landing on his face, burying my axe.

I ran and slid in the dirt, rolling him over to retrieve it as another man came from behind us. Mýra ran him through with her sword and clicked her tongue at me. Time to go. I hopped up, digging a heel into the ground to propel me forward, back toward the forest with the Aska. My sword and axe slid into place and I ran.

The panic in the camp spread quickly behind us and the sound of shouts and clanging metal filled the air as the Herja called out orders. I jumped over a body on the ground, looking around us. Our numbers were still good. We could make it.

We disappeared behind the tree line and didn't stop. We pushed toward Hylli, running with light feet over the tree roots and rocks that tangled in a maze on the forest floor. The familiar sound of Mýra's footfalls stayed close beside me as we ran faster.

The rumble of Herja came when we reached the eastern valley. As the first morning light shined through the trees, we could see them in the distance. Coming after us.

FORTY-SIX

I PUSHED HARDER INTO EACH STEP AND PICKED UP MY pace, pumping my arms at my sides as we flew across the valley on foot. Behind us, the Herja followed in a chaotic mass. Ahead, the Riki waited in Hylli.

Fiske and Iri waited.

I measured my breaths carefully, my eyes toward the sea. I could smell it on the wind. The smell of home. It found its way around me, driving me forward. It carried me.

The sound of the Herja grew behind us and the sword swinging from my hip was beginning to bruise my leg. But I ran faster. I pushed harder. I dug down deep and found her again. The Eelyn who had fought and survived more times than she could count.

I rooted out every memory of battle and replayed them in my mind. Iri, by my side, an axe in each hand. Mýra, running before me, a roar in her throat. I reminded myself of who I was—an Aska warrior who'd lost everything. A girl with fire in her blood. I told her to keep running.

They moved in fast, gaining on us. The scorched rooftops of Hylli came into view and a whistle echoed over the hills. The Aska cut sharply right toward the cliffs where seabirds hovered, gliding on the wind. I let my head fall back, trying to find the last of my strength to take me a little farther.

We didn't slow. We flew toward the drop-off, where the blue sky met the rock in a hard line and the water churned white foam below. The momentum of the hour's run carried us toward it. My clansmen disappeared over the edge in front of me as I spotted heads popping up from their places in the village. Archers. The first arrows hissed through the air, soaring over us in an arc as Mýra and I reached the cliff.

We counted our steps, throwing our weight forward as the ground slanted down in front of us, and I landed on my side, sliding down feet first with my hand dragging out behind me. My body glided over the loose rock until the cliff cut out from under us and then we were falling. The wind whipped around me and I straightened my body, my hand clamped down over my sword at my side, and I sucked in a breath, filling my lungs as the jeweled blue of the sea came closer.

I hit the water, the surface slamming into me hard. Bubbles raced up around me in wavering trails as more bodies fell into the water and I broke the surface, looking for Mýra. She drifted toward the shore, struggling to carve through the water with one arm. I kicked toward her, my lungs burning and the cold water seizing my fatigued muscles.

I broke back through to the air, pulled in every direction by the current. Mýra dragged herself onto the rocks, slumped over as more Aska slid over the cliff above and dropped into the water. In a few moments, it would be Herja coming down around us. Near the village, the dock reached out over the water and I scanned the faces, looking for Fiske and Iri. When I found them, their eyes were already on me. They stood, waiting to pick off the Herja in the water one by one. I let out a long breath at the sight of them before I ordered my thoughts back into line. The sharp corner of a rock scraped across my back as I clawed my way onto shore to where Mýra was trying to get to her feet.

"Mýra!" I called to her and she dropped to her knees, clutching her arm.

She looked up at me with a pale face. "It's out. My arm."

I knelt beside her, pulling the shield off and reaching beneath the armor vest to feel the bones in her shoulder. My fingers pressed until they found the soft indentation at the top of the arm and she cringed, moaning. She was right. It was dislocated. I pulled my knife free and cut the fasteners of the armor vest beneath her arm. There was no time. I yanked it over her head and she arched her back, crying out.

The Aska climbed up out of the water around us, headed toward the village. I sat back, fitting the heel of my boot into the ribs under her arm as the waves crashed around us.

I took her wrist into both hands, meeting her eyes, and waited for her nod. She sucked in a breath. "Go!"

I slowly leaned my weight back, carefully pulling the arm as she growled deep in her chest. I waited for the joint to slide back into place, keeping my grip on her tight and even. It popped and Mýra's eyes shot open as she gasped. She looked over me, her eyes going wider.

"Eelyn!"

I let go of her, finding my knife in the sand. A Herja woman was coming toward us, her legs kicking up the water as she ran. I sprang up from the ground and threw my body into hers, taking her down under the water. She struggled against me until I shoved the knife blade into her stomach and the water turned red around us as her blood spilled out. Her body was picked up by the next wave and I looked up to see more Herja falling over the cliff, some with arrows sticking out of them. They fell into the water like boulders, arms flailing and legs kicking.

Mýra was already on her feet when I made it back to the beach. I worked fast, picking her scabbard up from the rocks before I slung it over her head and tightened it diagonally across her chest so that it held her arm in place. I shoved the sword into her other hand and we ran toward Hylli as more Herja plunged into the sea.

Another swarm of arrows soared overhead, hitting their marks behind us, and we found the smooth part of the beach that led up to the ritual house. My eyes went back to the dock. It was still covered with Riki, but I couldn't see Fiske and Iri anymore. We moved toward the main path that led through the village and the Herja that didn't follow us over the cliff came down the hill, just like my father had planned.

Another whistle sounded and the first line of Riki pushed toward them. They met on the slope in a loud crash and Mýra and I darted through the abandoned houses, headed for the bare ground where the ritual house once stood. The Herja would push in. And we would be there to meet them.

The sky grayed with clouds rolling in over us and I kept my eyes on Mýra. She ran with her arm pinned to her side, carrying her sword in her left hand, and when we reached our mark among the other Aska, she sunk down onto her heels, breathing through the pain.

I pushed through the bodies and came down beside her. "Alright?"

She nodded with gritted teeth. "I'm fine."

I looked behind us, down the beach to the cove I knew lay tucked behind the rock.

When I turned back to her, she glared at me, her eyes hot as coals. "Don't you dare say it," she barked.

She would never forgive me for telling her to hide. I knew because I'd feel the same way. She would never retreat. Especially if I was still fighting. I pulled her up by her left arm and helped her stand beside me. She straightened, pulling in a steadying breath and steeling herself.

The Riki were tangled with the Herja on the beach. A swarm of fighting warriors covered almost every inch of ground, blades flying over heads and screams roaring up over the sound of the waves. As bodies parted, I could see the Tala, spinning around with an axe overhead. She swung, years of battle evident in the way she moved. She came over a fallen Herja and held his head up by his hair so she could slit his throat. As she stood, she flicked the blood from the blade, looking for the next one.

I held my place, waiting, and when another group of Herja came over the slope above the village, we leaned into the wind and ran for them.

I matched Mýra's pace and found my first mark. A fair-haired Herja with the deep grooves of a sword blade etched into the silver armor on his chest. When he saw me, he locked his eyes on mine, adjusting his course to collide with me. I ran straight for him, grunting as my feet hit the ground and then I pivoted, letting my axe swing over my head to propel me to the side. My feet lifted off the ground and I curled my arms in, the blade finding his hip, and then I hit the ground and rolled.

A boot caught me in the shoulder and I cried out. When I spotted him, he was lying on his back with his arms out to his sides, looking at the sky as feet ran past. I came over him, pulling my axe from his flesh, and the blood ran freely, pulling the light from his eyes.

Mýra freed her sword from a body nearby, hobbling with her right side sinking. Two more warriors were headed for us. I took the shield off a body on the ground and sank into my heels, lifting my axe. I waited for the first woman to come close and crouched, toppling her. She flew over the shield and I swung my arm, my axe driving into her back.

Mýra was on the ground below the other Herja. He was about to bring his sword down on her.

"No!" The panic ignited in me like the earth breaking open under us.

I jumped over the woman bleeding out on the ground and dropped the shield on top of Mýra. She curled up under it and I turned to face the Herja. His sword came down between us and I lifted my axe to stop it. It caught the blade with a force that made my axe slip through my fingers, falling to the ground beside me.

The knife in his other hand swiped toward me and I tried to slide back, but the blade cut into my side, below my ribs. I looked up from the blood pouring out from beneath my vest and took my arms out wide, tackling him at the waist. We rolled until the sword left his hand. When I fell onto my back, Mýra was standing over us with the shield. She lifted it up and brought it down on the man's head with a guttural scream. His bones crunched beneath the weight of it and his body went limp next to me before I crawled to my axe.

The warriors left standing were headed to the beach, where the last group of the Herja were pinned on the rocks between the village and the water. We headed toward them. I ignored the sting at my side, the blood pumping through my body so hard that I could barely feel it. Mýra took the first Herja in our way and I took the second, my eyes landing on the water, where bodies were floating, knocking into each other in an ocean of red.

Aska. Herja. A tall, broad Riki with dark hair pulled back into an unraveling knot.

The howling wind of a hole opened up inside of me and I ran into the water, grasping hold of the body and turning it over. But it wasn't him.

I reached for another.

And another.

My heart stopped beating in my chest and I forgot the sound of the fighting around me. I forgot the smell of blood soaked into my armor. I searched frantically, turning bodies over in the water around me until a sob broke from my chest.

Mýra pushed her way toward me.

"I can't find him," I stammered. A Herja came into view behind her and I wiped at my face to clear my vision. "Down!"

She obeyed and I pulled the knife from my belt and threw it. The blade sank into his neck. I pushed through the water and left him clutching at his throat.

"Eelyn!"

I heard his voice and everything stopped. The water. The fighting. The wind. I looked to the beach, trying to find him, but saw Iri first. He brought his axe down in an arc, landing on a Herja on the beach.

"Eelyn!"

And then I found him. Fiske stood at the water's edge, looking at me, his chest heaving up and down. His sword hung at his side heavily, the glittering red of wet Herja blood dripping from its edge. His eyes met mine and my sword sank to my side in the water. My body suddenly felt weak. Heavy. The relief unwound every straining, aching muscle. And then his eyes changed. His lips parted, his face twisting. And I knew that look. I remembered it. From the day we saw Halvard tied to the horse, blood running from his nose.

The weight of a body crashed into me, knocking me off my feet, and my sword sank to the sea floor. I was underwater, sunlight breaking through the clouds and lighting the red water like a pink veil around me. Legs appeared beside me and hands plunged down, taking hold of my throat and squeezing. The bubbles erupted around me as I screamed. The man was a blurry outline above the surface, his face gnarled up, teeth bared. I thrashed beneath his weight, kicking, trying to find a foothold. But there was none. The sand and rocks shifted beneath me, giving way as my fingers clawed at his arms. I could feel myself growing weaker.

I writhed, trying to slip free, but the Herja was too strong. His hold was too tight. And when I stopped moving, I watched my hands float up in front of my face, my hair lifting in golden streaks before my eyes. The thoughts slowly left my mind, my face relaxing, and I set my gaze on the sky, past the man's face, as the cold seawater poured into my lungs.

The sunlight gleamed on his silver armor and the bright light widened and grew until it was everything. It swallowed me.

Something rocked me in the water, and the hands unclenched, leaving me. I blinked slowly, and the man was gone. There was nothing but wavering sky. I came up out of the water and I could see his face. Fiske. The square line of his jaw widened as he shouted, looking into my face. I couldn't hear him.

And then the water rushed up out of me, the salt burning in my chest and throat. He pulled me to him, and the sound came back. The water, the village, the warriors. He lifted me up, with both arms around the middle of me as I coughed, choking. I wrapped my arms around his neck, holding on so tightly that the wound at my side seared with pain.

He let go of me, his hands coming to my face, turning it from side to side. They moved down my arms, checking my skin. He looked over me carefully until he found the gash below my ribs. I hissed as he spread the skin to see how deep it was.

"I'm alright," I panted, pulling him back to me.

He pushed his palm into it firmly, and my blood spilled out between his fingers. "You're alright." He repeated the words, almost to himself.

I pressed my cheek to his, trying to catch my breath, and his other arm lifted me up. We pushed through the water toward the beach. Mýra was making her way toward us from the side, a gash on her forehead bleeding freely. Behind her, Iri stood on the rocks and the final whistle sounded. The one that signaled it was over.

I looked at the village. My village.

It sat crippled on the shore. Lifeless bodies littered the paths and floated in the sea around us. But Hylli still stood, filled with the Aska and Riki left standing.

FORTY-SEVEN

I took Runa's dark, shining hair into my hands, combing through it with my fingers. She sat, looking into the fire in Inge's home, and when a single tear fell slowly down her cheek, she wiped it with the hem of her skirt.

It had only been five weeks since her mother died in the battle in Hylli. I knew what it was to lose a mother. And I knew what it was to find one again. I looked up to where Inge sat across from us, weaving a crown of early spring wild-flowers for Runa's head.

The journey back from Hylli had been a long one. When the fighting was over, we went back to the Herja camp where the captured Aska and Riki were waiting. We brought the wounded Riki back up the mountain and those that couldn't be moved stayed in Hylli under the care of the only two Aska healers left. But the thaw had come a week early, and as soon as the snow began to melt, Runa said she didn't want to wait to have the wedding.

I wound the intricate braids up on top of her head and Inge fit the crown over them, yellow and white blooms floating up above her like butterflies. She wore the dress her mother was married in, a pale blue wool with golden trim. She looked like a goddess, standing against the snow-covered mountain in the meadow.

The pain settled deeply into her eyes was matched by the love that also lived there. She looked up at Iri as they stood together before the Tala and recited the sacred words, with the Riki watching. Fiske stood beside me smiling and when he caught me staring at him, he leaned into me, his hip against mine making my long skirt sway around my ankles. The black dress I'd worn to *Adalgildi* covered almost all my healing wounds and scars, but it didn't erase them.

We followed the procession back to the ritual house and feasted, but this time my father and I sat with Inge's family. Iri's hand found mine under the table as he leaned over to kiss me softly behind my ear.

I remembered the way he looked, lying with eyes staring into the sky that day I'd left him in the trench in Aurvanger. The broken boy bleeding in the snow beside my brother. I wondered if the gods had a plan then. I'd thought about it almost every moment since it first struck me, standing in the sea after the battle in Hylli. That if Iri and Fiske hadn't found each other on the battlefield that day five years ago, he would never have been left. He would never have been found or loved by the Riki. He would never have joined them and I would never have seen him that night. I would never have been taken prisoner or been there when the Herja came. The Aska never would have joined with their enemies. We would all be dead or surviving on the fringes of what was once our lives.

And it wasn't because of me. I wasn't special. But Iri was.

My throat tightened, watching him hold Runa's little brother in the ritual house. Her siblings would now be Iri and Runa's responsibility. And just like Inge had become a mother to Iri, Iri would become a father to them. It was all too much for my heart to hold. It was still finding a home within me, replacing what had once held only hate for the Riki.

And now my heart belonged to them. In so many ways.

THE WATER IN THE FJORD TRANSFORMED INTO A BRIL-liant blue, like it knew we were coming home. But the image of the gleaming red water in battle was still seared into my mind.

Inge and I each held a side of the door while Fiske set it on its hinges.

When we told her that Fiske was coming with me to Hylli, she laughed and said she'd known long before we did. But the smile on her face was heartbroken and lonely. It was months before she agreed to come with Halvard and live on the fjord with us. The Aska from other villages went back home, leaving Hylli bare and without a healer. Before the next winter fell over Thora's mountain, one Riki in Hylli became three.

Inge had watched the house grow smaller behind us as we set out on the trail. We traveled down the mountain and I could feel everything still undone between Iri and me. It would take maybe the rest of our lives to understand what had happened. But maybe we had time now.

We built our home on the far south side of the village, overlooking the water on a plot of land where a home once stood. The black outline still stained the earth where it had burned to the ground. I remembered them. An old man named Evander and his son. But they were gone now, their souls in *Sólbjǫrg* with Evander's wife who'd died years ago.

Mýra took my place at home with my father. In a way, she'd always belonged there. He stood back, watching us work. The wound on his leg from battle was slowly healing, but he leaned his weight into a cane that he would likely have for the rest of his days. It didn't scare me like it would have before the winter because there was no fighting season coming. Not ever again.

Almost every Herja that had come to the valley was slaughtered in Hylli. The few that weren't were hunted down. We hung their bones from the trees up on the cliffs, but I still dreamed of them in the forest. I dreamed of them in the sea. If there were any left, whatever god they served had pulled them back into the shadows.

I sat out on the bluff that night as the sun went down, my

bare feet swinging against the wind that pulled the scent of salt and fish up from the water. The image of bodies floating flashed in my mind, but I pushed it away. I closed my eyes to remember the old Hylli. A small Aska village nestled on the fjord that was home to Sigr's people and sent them out when the fighting season came.

And that was the way of it. Things belonging where they didn't. Like two night skies on a frozen lake. One looking down from above and one looking up from the deep. I turned my hand over, tracing the scar that ran down the center of my palm. It was the promise the Tala had made to me and it was a promise she kept.

The door opened and I felt Fiske's warmth against my back as he sat down behind me, his legs falling to either side of mine and his arms winding around my middle. He pulled me to him in the dimming light and tucked his face into my neck, breathing me in.

We watched Halvard running on the beach below, shouting and throwing stones with the other children.

Aska children.

"It will be different," Fiske said. "It will be different for him."

Halvard wouldn't grow up training for the fighting season. He wouldn't grow up hating the Aska. Now, he lived among them. He would be strong for different reasons than we were.

I could still see a young Eelyn standing on the beach turned into the wind, a sword in one hand and an axe in the other. I hadn't lost her. I hadn't buried her. I'd only let her change into something new. I'd envied Iri my whole life for his open heart, and now mine had been pried open too.

I was the same. But I was different.

I closed my eyes again, laying my head back to rest on Fiske's shoulder, and wove my fingers into his. Where the people we had once been and the people we were fit together.

Where we were both.

ACKNOWLEDGMENTS

THANK YOU WILL NEVER BE ENOUGH. THEY ARE FEEBLE, ILL-equipped words to hold what's in my heart.

To Joel, my constant—my North Star and seer of my truest self. Never once have you brought water to my flames. Thank you for refusing to let me give up and never letting my dreams take the back seat. Thank you for telling me again and again that I am good enough. If anyone else is responsible for what's in these pages, it's you. I love you.

To my children, the little flames of imagination that burn beneath my watch and inspire me every day.

To my family, made of iron and stone. My father, who gave me the tenacity and stubbornness to fight for what I wanted with every drop of blood in my veins. I wish so badly I could see your face as you look down at my book in your hands. But I know you're watching. My mother, who taught me what strength and steadiness are. My sister, who got every kind and gentle bone missing from my body. My brothers, two of the best characters ever written, and Rhiannon, who chose us.

To Barbara Poelle, who plucked me from the cold queries and slayed dragons for me. All words fall to the ground when I think of what you have done for me. Thank you, thank you, thank you. From the depths of my soul, thank you.

To Eileen Rothschild, my editor, who fought like a warrior for this book. Thank you for breathing fire. You and everyone at Wednesday Books have made my dream come true. You've cast a window for the world to see my heart.

To Meghan Dickerson, Kristin Watson, and Lizzie Provost, who have always accepted me as I am. You taught me what it was to be true to myself and you let me grow. I've always wanted to be like you when I grow up. I still do.

To Amy Sandvos, Angela Porras, and Andrea Torres, the refuge I run to again and again. Thank you for loving me.

To the ever-expanding Sandvos clan and my dear friends Bill and Ida Settlage, Rich and Melissa Lester, and Clay and Emily Butler. Your support means the world to me.

To Stephanie VanTassel, the first friend who ever looked me straight in the eye without blinking and told me my stories would be published. Stephanie Brubaker and Lyndsay Wilkin, flotation devices on the brutal sea of creation. And Candy Chand, who accepted an invitation to lunch from a girl who knew nothing about this industry. Natalie Faria, thank you for reading the first version of this adventure and letting these characters break your heart.

To the author community who opened their arms to a stranger, especially Renée Ahdieh. Many cliffs I could have leapt from, without your guidance and advice.

To my local author gang, who welcomed me as an equal when my uncertainty was at its absolute highest—Stephanie Garber, Shannon Dittemore, Rose Cooper, Kim Culbertson, Jenny Lundquist, and Joanna Rowland. Most of all, Jessica Taylor, who saved me in more ways than I can count. Thank you for generously giving me your time and energy and, most of all, for telling me to email Barbara.

To Stephanie and Tiffany Nordberg, who kept faithful watch over my little ones while I built a world and characters to lay them brick by brick onto these pages.

To the teachers who saw what was inside me before I ever did. The ones who weren't afraid of my rough edges, cutting through to the heart of me. You changed my life. You held a torch on a dark path for me to follow. Mrs. Zweig, my third grade teacher and the very first person to ever tell me I was a writer. Abbie Jacobson, who taught me that there are no rules in storytelling. Jay Garrett, who treated me as an intellectual and drew out my mind.

There are so many more friends and family who have cheered me on, and I'm forever grateful to you.

To Kristin Dwyer: here's your line break. You believed in that bright, twinkling dream I had hanging in the sky.

ACKNOWLEDGMENTS

With a head shake and a sigh, you granted me twenty-four hours for Eelyn and Fiske, and in those twenty-four hours, the sparks that lit their wildfire were struck. I can't wait for my line break in the back of your book. I hope it includes an apology for leaving me behind in Harry Potter World.